A POISONED FORTUNE

Jane Austen Investigations
Book Three

Laura Martin

SAPERE
BOOKS

A POISONED FORTUNE

Published by Sapere Books.

24 Trafalgar Road, Ilkley, LS29 8HH

saperebooks.com

ISBN: 978-0-85495-111-6

CHAPTER ONE

Bath, May 1797

A fat drop of rain fell from the sky and landed on the end of Jane Austen's nose, followed by another and then another. She turned her face up and frowned. It had taken her two hours this morning to persuade Cassandra to leave the house, and Jane was aware her sister would take any excuse to retreat to the sanctuary of their aunt and uncle's house at number one, The Paragon.

They were walking slowly, arm in arm, supposedly taking in the great architecture of England's finest city, but both Jane and her sister were distracted today.

"I think if we take this street we will come out onto The Crescent," Jane said, trying to summon some enthusiasm for the tour she was giving. They had arrived in Bath two days earlier, but the weather had stopped them from exploring properly until now. Jane had read much about this ancient spa town and was keen to see all the sights, but a part of her was missing the countryside. The sheer number of people bustling through the streets was a little overwhelming for a young woman who had spent her whole life living in a small village, yet Jane was keen not to show how much it unsettled her.

"This is the most exclusive street in Bath," Jane said as they rounded the corner to see the terrace of houses curving to their right. "Aunt Jane told me the rent on one of these houses is nothing less than extortionate."

Cassandra nodded, her mind clearly elsewhere. She wore the muted colours of half-mourning, a lilac dress with a black shawl over her shoulders. It had been almost two months since the news of Cassandra's fiancé's death had reached them, two dreadful months during which Jane had questioned whether her sister would survive the broken heart she nursed.

A trip to Bath had been Jane's idea. She could not bear to sit in the drawing room at the rectory in Steventon watching Cassandra fade away as she stared out of the window. She was barely speaking or eating. Jane had reasoned a change of scenery might do her older sister the world of good, which was all she could ask for at the moment. Grief was a terrible thing, and if Cassandra needed to mourn for a year or two or even five, then Jane would be there holding her hand. She just needed her sister to eat a little and take the air on occasion.

There was a grassy area positioned in front of and a little below the houses of The Crescent, and after walking the length of the road on the pavement, Jane led her sister to this. Children ran back and forth under the watchful eyes of their nannies and nursemaids, chasing one another or trying to fly little kites. One family had set out a chequered blanket on the grass and were enjoying a picnic, lifting delicacy after delicacy from a wicker hamper. There were couples as well, dressed in the latest fashions, strolling arm in arm across the grass.

"Perhaps we could ask our aunt and uncle if we can bring a picnic here one day," Jane said, glancing at her sister.

"Perhaps."

"Or I understand Parade Gardens down by the river is a lovely spot too. I do like somewhere you can hear flowing water."

Cassandra inclined her head, but Jane could see her attention was elsewhere. With a sigh, Jane fell silent, deciding that a companionable walk through the streets of Bath was enough of an achievement for today. Tomorrow she could work on trying to distract her sister with conversation.

They had crossed half the length of the grassy area when there was a high-pitched shout from in front of them. Heads turned from all directions to stare at the young woman who had uttered it. She was struggling with an energetic dog, clinging onto the lead as her pet pulled with all its might against her. The woman was petite and it was clear she was unlikely to win this battle. She let out another cry as the lead slipped from her hands and the dog streaked across the grass, tongue hanging out and looking as though it was having a wonderful time.

The young woman hurried after it, hampered by the full skirt of her dress and the parasol she held in one hand.

"Bertie!" she called, seeming not to care that everyone was staring. "Bad boy! Get back here right now."

To Jane's surprise, the dog veered in their direction. It was only when she heard an excited yapping that she realised the excitable Bertie must have spotted another dog somewhere behind them.

"Bertram Fortescue, come back here this instance!" the young woman commanded.

Jane suppressed a smile at the ridiculous name for a dog, looking over her shoulder to see if there was any way she could aid this woman in distress. She was surprised no one else had stepped in to help. In Steventon catching an escaped animal was a community affair, with neighbours volunteering their time to assist anyone in need. It would seem things were a little different in the city.

The dog was only a few feet away now, ready to pounce on the little terrier behind them and smother it with affection.

Jane didn't have much experience with dogs, but she prided herself on never shying away from challenging situations, so as the lolloping spaniel came closer she called out in a clear, firm voice. "Bertie, sit!"

The dog came to an abrupt stop, almost falling over his own paws, then looked expectantly up at Jane.

"Good boy, Bertie," she said, astounded her attempt at control had worked. Cautiously she bent down and retrieved the lead that had been flying behind him on his run across the grass, gripping it firmly. "Stay," she commanded, allowing herself a satisfied smile as the dog looked up at her, tongue hanging out of his mouth.

"Good Lord, how did you do that? He never listens to a word I say," the young woman said as she hurried over. "I thought he might eat that poor little terrier, then all of Bath would truly despise me." She had blonde hair and the most dazzling blue eyes Jane had ever seen, her face lighting up when she smiled. Her clothes were made of the finest fabric, the pale blue dress edged with delicate lace as were the silk gloves that buttoned at her wrist. "I can't thank you enough. I am Lady Arabella Waters."

"Miss Jane Austen, and this is my sister Miss Cassandra Austen."

"You are newly arrived in Bath?"

"Yes, two days ago. We are staying with my aunt, Mrs Leigh-Perrot, for a short visit only."

Lady Waters took hold of the dog's lead, gripping it tightly. "You've picked the most perfect time of year. Not today, of course, but normally the weather here in May is glorious. It is a beautiful city to walk around, and at this time of year people are still living in the city before they retire to their country estates to sit out the summer's heat."

"It sounds like you know the city well, Lady Waters. Are you from Bath?"

"No," Lady Waters laughed. "I've lived everywhere, Miss Austen. London, Brighton, Edinburgh — I even spent a little time in Paris with my second husband. I moved to Bath with my third husband, Lord Waters, after we married a little over a year ago, but it is a small place and I find society is the same everywhere. It is merely the backdrop that changes."

Jane thought she saw a little sadness in the young woman's eyes. Her face was smooth and unlined, her skin unblemished. At a guess, Jane would have placed Lady Waters at no more than twenty-five, which seemed odd given that she was talking about a third husband.

"Arabella," said raspy voice, which came from behind Lady Waters. An elderly man hobbled over to her, pausing by her side and gazing down at her with rheumy eyes. He was a tall man with a commanding presence, but he leaned heavily on his cane. "The dog got loose again."

"I know. Miss Austen and her sister were kind enough to catch him for me."

The man gave them an assessing look, nodding in satisfaction after a few moments. His chest was heaving from the exertion of moving across the park, and there was a sheen of sweat on his brow.

"This is Miss Jane Austen and Miss Cassandra Austen," Lady Waters said, completing the introductions. "And this is my dear husband, Lord Waters." She frowned and then took her husband by the arm. "You don't look well. Let us find you somewhere to sit."

Lord Waters smiled at her indulgently and waved his cane. "Don't fuss, my dear. You take a stroll with your new friends and I will rest for a moment on a bench."

Lady Waters did not argue, allowing her husband to head off at a sedate pace before turning back to Jane and Cassandra. "You may have noticed that Lord Waters is a few years older than I," Lady Waters said with a mischievous smile. "He may not be in the first bloom of youth, but he looks after me like no one else ever has."

Jane's eyes widened. She couldn't help but warm to the young woman who spoke so openly — on first acquaintance as well. "Have you been married long, Lady Waters?"

"Thirteen months. We met in Brighton. Lord Waters had been advised by his doctor to take the sea air, and I was just coming out of mourning for my second husband. Neither of us thought we would ever marry again, but fate had other plans for us."

They strolled slowly around the edge of the small park, Bertie the dog setting the pace as he sniffed at and inspected every curiosity they came across. There were plenty of people making the most of the morning before the rain arrived in earnest, but no one approached and Jane got the impression everyone was giving Lady Waters a wide berth. It was curious. Lady Waters was the wife of a lord, amongst the upper echelons of society. In any other circumstance people would be clamouring for her attention and the elevation in social status an association with her could bring.

"We planned to spend half the year in Bath and half in London, but my poor husband's health deteriorated when we first arrived here and so we decided to stay on. Where are you from, Miss Austen?"

"A little village in Hampshire called Steventon. Our father is the vicar, and we have a lovely home in the rectory."

"An idyllic country life," Lady Waters said, smiling with enthusiasm.

Jane was conscious that Cassandra hadn't uttered a word other than in initial greeting and subtly looped her arm through her sister's. She hoped these sorts of exchanges, the thrill of meeting new people, might allow her to forget her woes for a time, but she could see instead Cassandra had retreated into herself, not following the conversation.

"I am determined to show you and your sister all that Bath has to offer, Miss Austen, even if your time here is short. It is a vibrant city with much to do. There are dances at the Upper Rooms at least once a week, and there are balls to rival the Season in London."

"Thank you, Lady Waters, you are most kind. I confess it will be a thrill to have someone who is familiar with the city as our guide."

"Now I must take Lord Waters back home; he looks a little unwell. The doctor visits this afternoon, and I think he should have a rest before then. Will you call on me tomorrow? I live at number seven here in The Crescent."

"We would be delighted, Lady Waters."

Jane watched as the young woman hurried off, tugging on her dog's lead as they made their way across the grass.

"What a fascinating woman," Jane murmured.

"I think we should return home, Jane. My head is swimming, and I would like to lie down."

Biting back words of protest, Jane smiled and began leading Cassandra across the grass in the opposite direction to Lady Waters.

CHAPTER TWO

It felt cosy in the drawing room of number one, The Paragon and Jane relaxed back into her chair with a sigh of contentment. The room was warm without being stifling, and it was designed to be comfortable rather than stylish. There was a mishmash of styles, the walls covered in striped green wallpaper and the chairs upholstered in blue fabric. It was a room some might find embarrassing to entertain in, but her aunt, Mrs Leigh-Perrot, never seemed bothered by the décor.

Cassandra sat at the piano in the corner, occasionally touching the keys and letting her fingers trail over a few notes, never enough to make a tune. Jane was in a comfortable chair beside the window, with views of the street below. There was a book in her lap but she had not read more than a few pages, her thoughts distracted this morning.

Mrs Leigh-Perrot bustled in, a basket of needlework in one hand, and took the seat next to Jane's where the light was good for her sewing.

"Our walk yesterday took us up to The Crescent," Jane said as her aunt settled back and took out a needle.

"Isn't it a beautiful street? Some say it is an architectural wonder. Of course, those in The Circus think theirs is the most sought-after address in Bath, but everyone knows it is The Crescent."

"We met someone who lives in one of the houses there."

"Oh?"

"Lady Waters."

Mrs Leigh-Perrot sucked in her breath noisily and gave Jane a sharp look. "You spoke to her?"

"Yes, and her husband briefly. They were out walking their dog."

"That dog is a menace."

"You know them?"

There was a long pause as Mrs Leigh-Perrot considered her answer. "By reputation only. You would be hard pressed to find someone in Bath who is not aware of Lady Waters."

"She seemed a pleasant young woman, did she not, Cassandra?"

"Indeed. She was very friendly."

"I am sure she was," Mrs Leigh-Perrot said haughtily, and then some of the zeal left her eyes. "I am being uncharitable."

"Why is Lady Waters so infamous in Bath?"

Mrs Leigh-Perrot set down her sewing and let out a sigh. "The usual reasons, I suppose. People see her as a social climber, who has no place to be elevated to the status she has been. Society does not like it when people do not know their place."

Jane leaned forward, intrigued, and out of the corner of her eye she saw Cassandra shift on the piano stool as well. Even a flicker of interest from her sister was an improvement on the numb apathy she had shown these last two months.

"You have to tell us more now, Aunt," Jane prompted.

"I do not like to gossip…"

"Jane has arranged to call on Lady Waters later today," Cassandra said quietly. "I think it best we know what we are letting ourselves in for."

"Oh, Jane, you always did like the more colourful members of society. Do you remember when you befriended that little girl from the travelling fayre? Your mother was convinced they would kidnap you and press you into life as a performer."

Jane smiled at the memory. "Her name was Anna, and she'd had such an interesting life. She'd visited twelve countries by the age of eight. I was so jealous that I hoped they *would* kidnap me and take me on an adventure." She paused, shaking her head. "I cannot lie and pretend Lady Waters does not intrigue me."

"I do not know who her family were, or the circumstances of her first marriage. Her second marriage was to a man named Bertram Williams. He was a lawyer."

"Bertram." Jane frowned, remembering the name of the dog. It was a strange way to commemorate a dead husband.

"Barely a year after they married, Mr Williams died suddenly and left Lady Waters a widow for the second time. She had a short mourning period, and then there was the announcement of her engagement to Lord Waters."

"A man three times her age."

"Precisely. There can be no pretence it was a love match."

"Lady Waters has made a success of her marriages, but I hardly see why she should be vilified for it. Everyone tries to improve their social standing through marriage, either that or their financial situation. Surely she should be lauded as a success story rather than treated as if she is a criminal."

Mrs Leigh-Perrot shifted in her seat, but Jane could see her earlier reluctance to gossip had disappeared. This was too interesting a subject to hold back.

"Lord Waters is a very wealthy man and he has been married before. The first Lady Waters passed away ten years ago from a wasting sickness. They shared two children, Mr Henry Fortescue and Mrs Penelope Upton. Of course, they are both grown with families of their own, but there has always been the expectation that Mr Henry Fortescue will inherit his father's fortune alongside the title."

"But now the pretty young wife has come along and the inheritance is uncertain," Jane said, nodding thoughtfully.

"Yes. Some of the land and property will be entailed, but he can settle a large amount of his fortune on his new wife if he so wishes."

"Lord Waters' children are worried?"

"They're furious, and they are influential in Bath society. It means Lady Waters has not been given the warmest welcome."

"It cannot be easy for Lord Waters' children to have their father marry someone much younger than him."

"Indeed. It is a bit of a mess, but Lord Waters is besotted with his beautiful young wife and outwardly at least she is devoted to him. Everyone tolerates her when Lord Waters is present, but if she is out on her own she is snubbed."

"No wonder she was so keen for our company."

"I have to confess I have only ever seen her from a distance. What is she like?" Mrs Leigh-Perrot asked.

"Vibrant and energetic and full of life."

"If Lord Waters does settle a good income on her after he dies, then she will have made a set of very shrewd decisions these last few years. From the wife of a lawyer to a wealthy widow in no time at all."

"You do not object to us visiting her later today, Aunt Jane?"

Mrs Leigh-Perrot hesitated and then shook her head. "How can I call myself a Christian if I say yes? Although I promised your mother I would safeguard your reputations whilst you are here, as well as see to your welfare, I cannot see the harm in going to tea with a baroness, especially when her only crime is to strive to better her circumstance."

"Thank you."

"You will accompany Jane?" Mrs Leigh-Perrot directed the question to Cassandra.

"Yes."

"Good."

Jane suppressed the urge to roll her eyes. Everyone in the family thought of her as the reckless sister, even though she had never done anything more scandalous than lift her skirts to her knees to climb over a stile.

"Be careful, though, Jane. Do not entangle yourself too much into her world. Remember your uncle and I have to live here once you are gone."

With her aunt's warning fresh in her mind, it was with a spark of anticipation that Jane approached the front door of number seven, The Crescent. Cassandra was a step behind her, but came to stand at her side once Jane had rapped smartly on the door.

There was a loud barking from deep in the house before the door was opened by a flustered footman. Behind him, a maid was trying desperately to wrestle with the excitable spaniel.

"Miss Jane Austen and Miss Cassandra Austen to see Lady Waters," Jane said.

"Please come in." The footman stepped aside, allowing them past, but before they could make their way into the drawing room a portly man descended the stairs, almost barrelling into them.

"Thank you for coming, Dr Taylor," Lady Waters said as she followed him at a more sedate pace. "Good afternoon." She flashed a smile at Jane and Cassandra before turning her attention back to the doctor. "Is there anything more you can do to make him comfortable? He complains of the pains in his legs at night."

"I have left a little opium, but in the past he has declined to take it. There is a bottle by his bed if he does consent to a dose." He gave Lady Waters an indulgent smile. "Do not fret, Lady Waters. Your husband may be elderly, but he has a strong constitution and has overcome worse than this. He may be fit enough to travel to London after the summer if he rallies."

"Thank you, Dr Taylor."

"I will call again tomorrow and see how Lord Waters fares then."

The footman handed the doctor his hat and opened the door again as Lady Waters turned to Jane and Cassandra.

"Forgive me, I am sure you did not want to hear of my husband's health woes."

"Do not trouble yourself, Lady Waters. How is Lord Waters today?" asked Jane.

Lady Waters sniffed and gave a sad smile. "In truth he grows weaker each day. He is a shadow of the man I married, and that was little more than a year ago."

"I am sorry to hear that."

"Please, come into the drawing room and we will talk of happier things. My husband has to rest most of the afternoon nowadays, but I am sure he will join us if he feels able."

The room was in stark contrast to the drawing room at number one, The Paragon, with every colour and fabric complementing the next. The walls were a calming shade of pale blue, the ceiling a pristine white. Subtle pieces of gilded furniture were strategically placed around the room, but there was a sense of space and light, thanks in part to the two huge windows set in one wall and also the lack of overcrowding. Too many people succumbed to the temptation to cram in every painting, every vase, every ornament they owned, even if the result was unpleasing to the eye.

"This is my oasis of calm," Lady Waters said, watching as Jane admired the room. "If ever I feel stressed, I spend a few moments in here and all my troubles melt away."

"It is a beautiful room, Lady Waters. Did you oversee the design?"

"I did."

"The result is wonderful."

Jane saw Lady Waters flush and was reminded that the baroness might have had much more life experience than Jane and her sister, but she was still only a young woman, likely desperate for friendship and acceptance.

"When we arrived in Bath, Lord Waters gave me permission to redecorate. I think he could see everything needed to be refreshed, but he had not had the energy to do it himself before."

"Was the style very different?"

"Oh yes. All heavy wood and dark curtains, as was the style thirty years ago. It was all very oppressive. I don't think much had been changed in the intervening years."

"I cannot imagine Lord Waters' children were happy with the alterations you made." The words were out before Jane could censor them, and she reddened as Cassandra let out a little gasp beside her. Sometimes she really did speak without thinking, and it did not often enamour her to acquaintances. "I'm sorry…" she began, but Lady Waters waved a dismissive hand and laughed.

"It is refreshing, Miss Austen, to have someone say what they are thinking. All these women of society whisper behind their hands and dart cruel looks at me, but I would much rather hear what they have to say." She leaned in, as if about to share a confidence. "I see you have heard about my ongoing conflict with Mr Fortescue and Mrs Upton."

"Our aunt did mention they were less than welcoming of your marriage to Lord Waters, and as a consequence the whole of Bath society has not been kind to you."

"Your aunt is right. I understand it might be a shock for them, for their father to remarry in his eighth decade, but their mother has been dead for ten years and a man as affectionate as Lord Waters needs companionship. They could never understand that."

"Lord Waters has not tried to persuade them of his happiness?"

Lady Waters sighed and shook her head. "I was adamant when we married that I would not come between my husband and his children. I asked him not to put himself in a position where he has to choose between us, and he respected my wishes."

A smart move on Lady Waters' part, Jane realised. Never could she be blamed for inciting conflict between her husband and his children.

"I begged Lord Waters to take me to London, to get away from this city where everyone knows everyone else and the gossip circulates within hours. He agreed, but then his health prevented us from travelling." She smiled and gave a small shrug. "Bath has grown on me. It is beautiful and full of culture. If only the people would forget their snobbery."

"Perhaps with a little time, things will get better," Jane said. There was real sadness in Lady Waters' eyes, and Jane could see that despite her bravado she was lonely in a city full of people.

"Perhaps, but enough about me. I want to hear everything about you two. I am certain we will become firm friends, no matter how brief your visit to the city."

Jane was about to give a little flavour of their life in Steventon when there was a loud knocking on the front door. It sounded urgent and a little threatening, as did the voices that followed when the footman rushed to open the door.

Lady Waters rose as a man burst through the door of the drawing room, towering over her petite form. Jane and Cassandra stood too, Cassandra gripping Jane's arm as they saw the look of pure hatred on the man's face. He was in his forties, tall and broad-shouldered with brown hair slicked back and curled around the nape of his neck. His features were pinched and angry, the moustache above his lips quivering and the muscles around his eyes twitching.

Jane found herself wanting to take a step back, but her legs were already pressed up against the chair. A thin, mousy woman hurried in behind the man, travelling as if in the wake of a great warship, her face a mask of worry.

"Thief," the man said, pointing an accusing finger at Lady Waters.

"Henry…?" Lady Waters said in a placating tone, though Jane could see she was shaken by the abrupt entrance.

"Mr Fortescue," he corrected her. "You will call me Mr Fortescue."

Lady Waters inclined her head and Jane marvelled as she collected herself, smiling serenely.

"What can I do for you, Mr Fortescue?"

"You are a conniving little thief."

"I am always happy to accommodate you, Mr Fortescue, but do not think you can come into my home and insult me."

"It is not your home."

Lady Waters sighed as if she had been drawn into this argument too many times before. "I am not going to argue with you, Mr Fortescue, not in front of my guests and certainly not with your father unwell upstairs. The commotion is hardly going to be good for his health."

"Do not pretend you care one iota for his health."

"What is it you think I have stolen?" Lady Waters said, her voice calm. Many people would not have been able to ignore the multitude of insults her stepson was throwing her way, but Lady Waters seemed adept at letting them wash over her, with a mere flicker to show some were hitting their mark.

"My mother's emerald necklace," Mr Fortescue said, pointing an accusing finger at her again. "I am told you were flaunting it at the Williamson ball last week."

"I did wear an emerald necklace to the Williamson ball last week." Lady Waters turned to Jane and Cassandra and continued conversationally, as if she were not in the middle of a heated argument. "I had the most gorgeous green silk dress delivered from my modiste, and the emeralds complemented it perfectly. It was a beautiful ensemble."

Mr Fortescue's face turned an unhealthy shade of purple, the flush extending down his neck and disappearing into his short collar. "Do not jest, Lady Waters." He spat out the title as if he could not bear to have it in his mouth. "Those emeralds were my mother's, and you have stolen them."

Lady Waters levelled him with a firm stare. "My husband presented me with those emeralds and suggested I wear them. They may have once been your mother's, and if they were bequeathed to you after her death then I will speak to the family solicitor and find out why they were never passed over."

"You know very well they were not bequeathed to me."

"Then I do not see the issue. After your mother's death they returned to your father, and a few days ago he decided to make a gift of them to me." She held up a hand, halting the fresh onslaught. "I will not have Lord Waters disturbed now, but I will bring up your grievance later, when he is better able to deal with the matter. We shall ask him to arbitrate."

Mr Fortescue snorted. "No doubt with you dripping poison in his ear, Lady Waters."

The mousy woman who had so far stood silently behind Mr Fortescue placed a hand on his arm, looking nervous. "If Lord Waters is unwell, perhaps we should come back another time."

Mr Fortescue shrugged her off dismissively, his eyes still locked on his stepmother.

"Thank you for your visit," Lady Waters said, taking a step forward to signify the encounter was over. "I will speak to Lord Waters later, but for now I think it best you listen to your wife and leave."

The tension mounted in the room as the seconds ticked by. Finally Mr Fortescue stepped away, sweeping back through the house and out the front door. His wife didn't make eye contact with anyone, instead scuttling after her husband with her head bowed and her gaze fixed on the floor.

Lady Waters let out a sigh and flopped back down into her chair. "I cannot apologise enough," she said, clutching her hands together in her lap. Jane noticed how they shook. Lady Waters was trying her hardest to maintain her composure, but it was close to cracking.

Cassandra stood and walked to the door, calling out quietly to the footman in the hall. "I have asked your man to bring tea," she said, smiling kindly at their hostess.

"Thank you." Lady Waters burst into tears at Cassandra's words and stood, hurrying to the window and dabbing her eyes with a handkerchief. Jane glanced at her sister and was surprised to see her more animated than she had been for a long time. Cassandra leaned across and briefly squeezed Jane's hand, and then they waited for Lady Waters to return to them.

"I am so sorry. It is mortifying to let you see me thus."

"I marvel at how calmly you dealt with that brute," Jane said as Lady Waters took her seat again. "I am not surprised it put a strain on your emotions."

"That was Mr Fortescue, my husband's son from his first marriage." Lady Waters sighed and shook her head. "I knew there would be tensions in the family, but never did I expect them to hate me to this extent."

"Lord Waters' daughter feels the same?"

"Oh yes, Mrs Upton is much less vocal than her brother, but she is cold. The contempt in her eyes when she looks at me is chilling."

"You have much to contend with, Lady Waters," Cassandra said.

They fell silent as a maid appeared with a tray of tea, setting it on the table and laying everything out with a smooth efficiency.

"Thank you, Sarah," Lady Waters said, lifting the pot to pour herself.

The tea was restorative, calming everyone's frayed nerves and allowing them a little time to consider what had just happened.

"I do understand it must be difficult for him," Lady Waters said after a few moments of silence. "I am twenty years younger than Mr Fortescue and now mistress of his father's household. I sleep in his mother's bed, walk about his mother's rooms and now I am wearing his mother's jewellery." She sighed. "I understand the pain they feel, but I do not think it is fair all of that is directed towards me."

"It is the fate of stepmothers everywhere. Even in our fairy tales they are portrayed as evil," said Jane.

"I am far from that. I am just a woman who fell for a kindly older man and the protection he was offering."

"What will you do about Mr Fortescue?" Cassandra asked quietly.

"My husband will have heard the exchange. How could he not? I expect half of Bath heard it. He will be livid and I will play peacemaker as I always do, asking him to be lenient with his son."

"Is that the wisest course?" Jane asked, unable to stop herself. "If Mr Fortescue thinks he can burst into your home and shout at you with no consequences, will he not do so again?"

Lady Waters stared into her teacup and then nodded sadly. "I know you are right, Miss Austen, yet I do not want to be the reason there is a rift in the family."

"Lord Waters would take your side on this, you are certain?"

She gave a half-smile. "I am certain. His main goal in life is to protect me."

There was a gentle knock on the door and the young maid entered again, bobbing a neat little curtsey. "Lord Waters is asking for you, my lady."

Lady Waters sprung to her feet, with a concerned look at the door. "Please excuse me. I should see to my husband."

"We will take our leave," Cassandra said, taking Jane's arm firmly, as if warning her not to protest. "We do not wish to impose any longer."

"I am sorry for what happened. I am sure it is not what you were expecting when you agreed to call on me. I thank you for your kindness."

"Perhaps we might meet again soon," Jane ventured and was rewarded by Lady Waters' face lighting up at the prospect. No doubt the young woman thought the Austen sisters would not want to be associated with her after the events of the afternoon.

"I would love that more than you could know," she said, reaching out and grasping Jane's hand. "I will send you a note. Thank you."

Jane and Cassandra stepped out onto the street, turning back to look at the house as the door started to close behind them. They caught of a glimpse Lady Waters, face drawn, turning and hurrying up the stairs.

CHAPTER THREE

"It feels wrong, Jane. Perhaps I should return to our aunt and uncle's house. I do not mind spending the evening alone," Cassandra said as their carriage pulled up in front of the imposing townhouse. Her voice was low, and she spoke in Jane's ear even though their aunt and uncle were engrossed in their conversation on the seat opposite.

"One hour," Jane said quietly. "Give me one hour and then I will accompany you home. You do not have to dance or make merry, but I cannot leave you for another day to wallow in your grief."

"How can I go out and socialise, listen to music and dance when my Tom is gone?" Cassandra murmured, the words coming out half choked.

"I know it is difficult, Cassandra. I do not want to dismiss the pain you must feel. If you truly wish to go back to our aunt and uncle's house, then I will accompany you, but I wonder if a short period out and about, away from your bedroom, might be healthy."

Cassandra was quiet for a moment and then finally nodded her head. "If you think it is for the best, I bow to your wisdom, Jane. I know I am not thinking clearly at the moment."

"It is our turn, girls," Mrs Leigh-Perrot said as a footman stepped forward to open the carriage door.

As they alighted, it was impossible not to stare up at the imposing façade with wonder. Candles burned in every window and the steps leading to the open front door were lined with lanterns. They illuminated the whole house, making it twinkle in the darkness.

There was a crush of people already inside, all arriving at the same time, and for a moment Jane felt as though she could not breathe. She longed for the green fields and open spaces that surrounded the rectory in Steventon, where one could walk for miles without encountering a single soul.

After greeting Mr and Mrs Temple, their hosts for the evening, Mrs Leigh-Perrot began guiding them round the drawing room, introducing them to some of her friends and neighbours. All the furniture had been pushed back to the walls to make space for dancing later in the evening, so most people stood in little clusters, gossiping and watching the other guests with interest.

They had stopped to talk to an old friend of Mrs Leigh-Perrot, a middle-aged woman who had known their mother when she was young, when a tall, regal-looking woman sailed over, trailed by two young ladies.

The conversation around them died as people strained forwards to get a better view of what was occurring.

"Mrs Leigh-Perrot, these must be your darling nieces," the tall woman said, smiling down at them with an expression that exuded no warmth.

"Good evening, Mrs Upton. Yes, it is my pleasure to introduce Miss Cassandra Austen and Miss Jane Austen."

"Delighted to meet you," Mrs Upton said. Jane and Cassandra inclined their heads. "I was most anxious to make your acquaintance." She held out a hand and gave a quick dismissive gesture to the two young ladies, who had not been introduced. By their looks Jane assumed they were Mrs Upton's daughters, both tall with long, straight noses and curly brown hair like their mother. "Walk with me," she added, turning abruptly before Jane or Cassandra had time to reply.

Exchanging a bemused look with Cassandra, Jane fell into step behind the older woman, her sister coming a few paces behind.

"I hoped you might be here tonight," Mrs Upton said as they found a secluded spot half hidden from view of the ballroom by a potted plant. "I understand you met my brother earlier today in most unfortunate circumstances."

"We did, although we were not introduced."

Mrs Upton gave a long-suffering sigh. "I must apologise for my brother's behaviour. He is hot-headed and charges in before he has time to think through his actions. I am sure he is mortified that you were there to witness his outburst today."

Jane noticed she was apologising for the unpleasantness at Lord and Lady Waters' house, but not for her brother's words. "I understand tempers can be high when it comes to family," she said diplomatically.

"You are right of course, Miss Austen, although our family was perfectly content before Lady Waters came and violated the memory of our mother."

"You do not approve of your father's choice of new wife either?"

Over the past year, Jane had spent much time with Lord Hinchbrooke, the magistrate for their part of Hampshire. He was a wise and knowledgeable man, and Jane had enjoyed assisting him with legal quarrels and investigating crimes. Over the year she had learned much, but most of all she had observed how Lord Hinchbrooke asked his questions calmly and without apology. Often, if you acted reasonably, people would tell you more than was necessarily wise.

Mrs Upton gave a little snort and then laughed, covering her mouth with her hand. "My father is seventy-five and a very wealthy man. There is only one thing a woman like Lady

28

Waters can be interested in when she sets her sights on a man such as my father."

"The age gap is large," Jane said slowly, "but that is the case for many marriages."

"It is close to fifty years' difference. She is barely older than my daughters." Mrs Upton caught herself before she could say any more and smiled blandly. "But you do not want to hear of our private family matters. I merely wanted to apologise for my brother's conduct and beg you to think charitably of him. He is a man who feels everything very acutely, and he had tremendous love for our mother. Seeing another woman in her precious jewels pulled at something inside him that shouldn't have been disturbed." Mrs Upton looked from Jane to Cassandra and back again. "A word of warning to you both: think carefully whom you choose as friends. Lady Waters might seem sweet and innocent but a viper lives within her, and I would hate for you to get hurt." Without another word, Mrs Upton turned and made her way back through the crowd of people, no doubt to find the daughters she had so quickly dismissed a few minutes earlier.

Jane let out a long exhalation and turned to her sister, who was frowning.

"That is a dangerous woman," Cassandra said quietly.

It was a damning character assessment from someone who normally saw the good in everyone.

"She is more controlled than her brother," Jane commented.

"Undoubtedly, but that makes her much more dangerous."

"I pity Lady Waters having such a pair as stepchildren."

"I agree," Cassandra said, her lips puckered as she considered the matter. "Although we do not know any of these people well. Perhaps Lady Waters is not as innocent in all this as she would seem."

Jane inclined her head. Despite wanting to jump staunchly to Lady Waters' defence, she knew Cassandra was right. There was undoubtedly a lot they did not know about her.

There was a lull in the chatter about the ballroom as their hostess called for the first dance. Smiling young ladies and gentlemen paired up for a quadrille. Just as the music started, a murmur ran through the assembled guests closest to the door. Jane stood on her toes, trying to catch a glimpse of who had caused such a stir, only to see that it was Lady Waters accompanied by her husband.

Lady Waters looked resplendent in a green and gold dress. The skirt was full and made of thick panels of green velvet interspersed with thinner gold sections. Her hair was pinned high on her head and about her neck hung a heavy set of emeralds. Everything about her ensemble was designed to draw the eye to the gems at her throat.

"Less conciliatory than she would have us believe earlier," Cassandra murmured in Jane's ear.

"Unless it was Lord Waters who insisted she wear them."

"Perhaps. He might be tired of his children disparaging his new wife in such a way, invalidating his choice and treating him like a child."

Jane watched as Lady Waters fussed around her husband for a moment, fetching him a glass of sparkling wine from a tray one of the maids carried through the room.

Mrs Upton had caught sight of her father, but stood stiffly on the other side of the room. As Jane watched, she seemed to force herself to relax and pasted a smile on her face before approaching Lord and Lady Waters.

The exchange between father and daughter was short and formal, but there was no animosity, at least not to casual scrutiny. Instead, after the briefest of interactions, Mrs Upton removed herself to the other side of the drawing room, ostensibly to watch her daughters dance with their suitors.

Despite likely being the highest ranking guests in the room, no one else approached Lord and Lady Waters. Normally at events such as these, certainly at the balls in Steventon, everyone clamoured for an introduction to the local nobility. It seemed strange that people were not rushing to flatter Lord and Lady Waters and seek some connection.

"We should go and speak to them," Jane said, taking a step forward.

Cassandra lay a warning hand on her arm. "Have a care, Jane. We are here for a week or two only. I know you dislike any social injustice, but our aunt and uncle have to live with these people as their neighbours. We do not want to do anything that will taint them by association."

Jane paused, considering Cassandra's words and then walking on anyway. "Lord Waters, Lady Waters, it is lovely to see you this evening."

"Miss Austen," Lady Waters gushed, seeming relieved someone had broken the invisible barrier that separated them from the other guests. "I am delighted to see you here."

"How do you fare this evening, Lord Waters? I know your wife was concerned for your health when we visited earlier today."

"I am as fit as an ox," he said, beaming down at his wife. Jane could see the resemblance between Lord Waters and his two offspring. All three were statuesque in their build and bearing, with long, straight noses and high brows. Lord Waters still sported a full head of thick grey hair and Jane reasoned that in his youth he would have been an attractive man. "My dear wife worries about me, but I tell her she has nothing to fear. I do not plan on departing this earth for a good few years yet."

Lady Waters gave a tight smile and reached out for her husband's hand. "Please let us not talk of such serious matters tonight."

In the middle of the room the dancing continued, but Jane's eyes were fixed on the door where Mr Fortescue, Lord Waters' angry son, had just entered. She was quickly realising how small Bath society was, and how awkward any animosity would be between Lady Waters and her stepchildren.

Mr Fortescue frowned as he saw his father, hesitating for a moment before approaching.

"Father, Lady Waters," he said, with a small bow. His mousy wife trailed behind him as she had earlier, barely noticeable in the muted grey dress she wore.

"Henry, good to see you." Lord Waters beamed at his son, clapping him on the back with his free hand.

Mr Fortescue's eyes widened as he caught sight of the emeralds around his stepmother's neck, but it seemed even he was above making a scene in public.

"This is Miss Jane Austen and Miss Cassandra Austen," Lord Waters continued. "They are staying in Bath with their aunt, Mrs Leigh-Perrot."

Mr Fortescue coughed awkwardly and then gave an apologetic smile. "I fear we have met already, Father. These ladies were witness to an unfortunate outburst I had earlier. Please accept my heartfelt apology that you witnessed that. It was a private matter between family, and I should have controlled myself better."

There was no apology to Lady Waters forthcoming, and a moment later Mr Fortescue quickly took his leave.

"At least he deigned to apologise to you," Lady Waters said, linking her arm through Jane's.

"Will he apologise to you?"

"Only if his father makes him, and where is the sincerity in that?"

"Go and enjoy yourself, my dear," Lord Waters said, patting his wife on the arm. "I am going to find a quiet spot and observe proceedings."

"I can stay with you," Lady Waters said.

"No, I insist. Take a walk around the room, dance, have fun."

"I will be back to check on you in a few minutes."

With a backwards glance Lady Waters stepped away, her arm still through Jane's with Cassandra on the other side.

They had only taken three steps when there was a great crash behind them, followed by the tinkling of smashed glass. The whole ballroom fell silent as everyone craned to see what had happened.

Beside her Jane felt Lady Waters stiffen as she turned, her fingers digging into Jane's arm.

Lord Waters lay on the floor, limbs spread wide, his cane rolling away from his body. His eyes were shut, his body completely still. For one awful moment Jane was convinced he was dead, perhaps felled by a brain convulsion as he stood watching the dancers. Then she noticed the subtle rise and fall of his chest and a little flicker of movement around his mouth.

With a quick look at Cassandra, who gave a subtle nod, Jane hurried forwards, the first to move in the crowded ballroom. She crouched down beside the elderly man and took his hand. His fingers were warm and as she picked them up, she felt an involuntary flicker.

"Is he dead?" Lady Waters' voice was barely more than a whisper, but it rang out clearly in the silent drawing room.

"No," Jane said quickly. "See how his chest moves as he breathes." She leaned in closer and gently shook the old man's shoulder. "Lord Waters, can you hear me?"

His eyes flickered as she spoke.

"Give him space," Mr Fortescue demanded as he pushed his way through the crowd. "Mr Temple, can you get the guests out of here, to a different room perhaps?"

Their host sprang into action, moving quickly to usher the concerned guests out of the drawing room.

"Move aside, Miss Austen. I will see to my father," Mr Fortescue said.

Jane did not move. Instead, she focussed on the elderly man on the floor in front of her.

"He's coming round," she said, and then motioned to Mr Fortescue. "He needs something soft under his head. Your jacket, perhaps?"

For a long moment Mr Fortescue eyed Jane with distaste, but as Lord Waters groaned he reluctantly shrugged off his evening jacket and rolled it up to place under his father's head.

"Bella, where is my Bella?" Lord Waters mumbled, his eyes half open but unfocussed.

"I'm here, Father," Mr Fortescue said firmly.

"Bella…"

"He's asking for you," Jane said to Lady Waters. She hesitated for a second, as if afraid to approach her half-conscious husband, but then she rallied.

"I'm here, my dear," she said, kneeling down.

Jane made space for her, standing now that Lord Waters was surrounded by family and seemed to be recovering a little. She turned to Mr Temple, their host for the evening, who had just finished ushering the rest of the guests out of the drawing room and into another area of the house. "I wonder if you know of a doctor who lives nearby?"

"Do not trouble yourself, Mr Temple," Mrs Upton said, coming and placing herself between him and Jane. "We will call for the family doctor just as soon as we get him home."

Jane opened her mouth to protest but caught the subtle movement from her sister as she shook her head. This was not her family, not her matter to become embroiled in. If the family wished to take Lord Waters home first, then it was not her place to tell them how unwise they were being.

She watched in horror as Mr Fortescue, along with another tall, middle-aged gentleman, hauled Lord Waters to his feet, supporting him under the arms. The old man's eyes were still glazed, and he looked as though he could not focus. They had to support his weight entirely, for his legs were uncoordinated and their movements jerky.

"Make sure the carriage is at the door," Mr Fortescue commanded his wife. She scuttled off ahead of the two men as they half-carried, half-dragged Lord Waters from the room. Lady Waters was left staring after them, dazed and uncertain.

"Go," Jane said quietly, placing a hand on Lady Waters' arm. "Be with your husband and ensure he gets the care he needs."

Silence fell over the ballroom as the sound of Lady Waters' footsteps receded, leaving only Jane, Cassandra and Mr Temple present.

"Sit down for a moment, Jane. You have gone awfully pale," Cassandra said, guiding Jane to a chair.

"For a moment I thought…" Jane began.

"I know what you thought," Cassandra said quietly.

It had been over a year since Jane had found her friend Miss Emma Roscoe murdered at a ball they had been attending, but every night when she was drifting off to sleep, Jane saw Miss Roscoe's face and the bloom of blood on her dress. It was a sight that she would carry with her all her life.

"Let me get you a drink, Miss Austen," Mr Temple said with a concerned expression. "Then I will find your aunt and uncle."

"What happened? Did you see?" Jane asked Cassandra when they were left alone for a moment.

"No, I just heard the commotion and when I looked round, Lord Waters had collapsed to the floor. He looked terrible. I do hope it was not a case of apoplexy."

"What an awful situation," Jane murmured.

"Cassandra, Jane," Mrs Leigh-Perrot said as she hurried into the room. Mr Temple was with her, carrying two glasses of lemonade which he handed to Jane and Cassandra. "Jane, you are as white as a lily. Come, girls, I think we should take you home."

A sea of curious faces watched as Jane and Cassandra followed their aunt and uncle through the grand hallway to the front door. Some people were ready to leave, deciding to walk home rather than wait for their carriage in the press outside.

"Perhaps we could walk," Jane said, her head swimming.

Mrs Leigh-Perrot regarded her for a moment and then nodded. "Yes, it is not far, and the fresh air will do us all some good."

Jane slipped her arm through Cassandra's and they set off at a sedate pace, Jane desperately trying to calm her pounding heart. For a few seconds she had thought Lord Waters was dead, and with all the animosity surrounding him, all the fighting within his family, she wouldn't have been surprised if it was murder. Shaking her head, she told herself not to be so morbid. No one was dead and no was going to be murdered.

CHAPTER FOUR

Jane slipped out of bed as the first rays of sunshine began to filter through the heavy curtains. It was a little past dawn, the house quiet and the city streets not yet bustling with activity.

Cassandra groaned. "Jane, must you rise so early?"

"Go back to sleep," Jane murmured, leaning in and stroking her sister's hair.

At home in Steventon she often woke early, unable to sleep whenever her mind was fixated on something, more often than not the plot of her latest work. There she would take a walk about the garden or find a cosy spot to sit in and read her book. Other mornings she would pull on her dressing gown and sit at her desk, using the hour or so she had until the house started to stir to write. Normally Cassandra would sleep soundly through Jane's early morning risings, but recently her sister had lost her ability to sleep deeply. The loss of her fiancé had leeched into every area of her life, affecting her slumber as well as every waking moment.

There was nowhere to go here in Bath. It was not safe for her to wander the streets alone and the townhouse only had a tiny garden, so there was nowhere to take refuge. Instead, Jane pulled on her dressing gown and took out the bundle of papers that made up her current manuscript.

Taking a seat at the little writing desk in the corner of the room, Jane took a moment to run her hands over the front page of the thick pile. She had been writing this book, tentatively titled 'First Impressions', for the last few months, and it was starting to come together in her mind. Some days she scribbled furiously, her ideas tumbling out faster than she could commit them to paper. Other days she worked through the pages she had written, crossing out phrases she didn't like, sometimes even throwing away whole sections and re-writing them. Her favourite part was when she gathered her family and read a short passage to them. She liked watching their faces as she read, gleaning their reactions. Her father would often comment on the minutiae, the grammar or the structure. Cassandra would smile at her proudly, but she liked it more when one of her brothers visited and didn't hesitate to critique her style.

There hadn't been any evening readings for a while. Cassandra would often plead a headache and disappear soon after dinner, retiring to the room she and Jane shared. On the few occasions Jane had tried to follow her, her sister had asked for some privacy. As Jane had lingered outside the bedroom door, she'd heard muffled tears as Cassandra had let go of her tightly held emotions and cried into her pillow.

Here at number one, The Paragon, the little writing desk was set by the window and there was a good view of the street below. Not wanting to disturb Cassandra any more than she had already, Jane opened the curtains a few inches only. Through the gap she could see the happenings on The Paragon, but she was too high up here to be observed.

Quietly Jane tapped her pen against her chin, reading back through the last few paragraphs she had written. Sometimes she felt like a fraud, writing about true love when she had not herself experienced it. Her thoughts immediately went to Mr Tom Lefroy, the young man she had briefly known and harboured secret hopes of marrying. It had been a ridiculous notion, their acquaintance fleeting, their knowledge of one another not adequate to even be certain they would be well matched, yet there had been a spark, which meant even a year and a half later she could not put him from her mind entirely.

Cassandra's had been a very different sort of relationship with her fiancé, Thomas Fowle. Mr Fowle had been a pupil of her father's, a studious, hardworking young man whose face lit up when Cassandra entered the room. As suited Cassandra, he was quietly reliable, eager to make enough money to allow them to set up a home together before they set a date for the wedding. Jane wondered if Cassandra regretted that decision now, whether she wished she had seized the opportunity to be Mrs Fowle, even if only for a short time.

This morning her thoughts were all over the place and not on the manuscript in front of her. Sometimes it was like that. Some days Jane would sit down and write for hours on end, barely aware of time ticking by. Other days she would fiddle with her pen and stare out of the window, hardly writing more than a dozen words.

With a sigh she rose from the chair and slipped from the bedroom, thinking she might find a book to read to distract her mind.

Breakfast was a grand affair at number one, The Paragon. Mr Leigh-Perrot extolled the virtues of a hearty breakfast every morning, lecturing anyone who would listen on the need to provide the body with sustenance to allow it to work properly over the course of the day ahead. It meant the cook worked tirelessly to provide endless supplies of toast and three different sorts of eggs. Alongside that were kippers and cold slices of ham for anyone who wanted them.

"You will waste away, Cassandra," Mr Leigh-Perrot said, shaking his head admonishingly. "You need more than a single slice of toast to get you through the day."

Cassandra looked down at her plate as if surprised to find the toast there. She had not yet buttered it or added jam, and it looked quite unappetising in the middle of the delicate plate.

"Leave her alone, dear," Mrs Leigh-Perrot said, reaching across and squeezing Cassandra's hand. "She'll eat when she is ready."

"Will you pass the butter, Jane?" Cassandra asked quietly.

Jane leaned over and picked up the butter, handing it across to her sister. Mr Leigh-Perrot wasn't wrong, although he had been blunt in his choice of words. Cassandra had done nothing more than pick at her food since the news of Thomas Fowle's death, and her clothes were starting to hang a little loose on her body. Even her face had lost some of its pleasant plumpness.

"What would you like to do today, girls?" Mrs Leigh-Perrot asked. "After the excitement of the ball last night, I expect you wish to have a quiet day today, but I did wonder if you would like to accompany me to the draper's. Your mother mentioned you each having a new dress made, and it would be a good opportunity to look at material."

"What do you think, Cassandra?" Jane asked, looking to her sister.

"That sounds pleasant, Aunt. Maybe later this morning?"

As Mrs Leigh-Perrot leaned in to start discussing details, there was a knock on the door in the hall, and the murmur of voices followed as the maid answered it. She entered a minute later, carrying a tray with a letter on it, beautifully tied with a red ribbon. "A letter for Miss Austen," she said, holding the tray out to Jane.

The paper was thick and luxurious, the sort of paper Jane coveted every time she visited the stationer's shop in

Winchester. She took it and pulled at one end of the ribbon, running the satin through her fingers before opening the note.

Dear Miss Austen,

Thank you for your swift action last night when Lord Waters was taken ill. I thought you would like to know he has been seen by the doctor and has recovered now. I am planning on taking a gentle stroll through Parade Gardens later this afternoon. There will be music and drinks, quite the celebration, I am told. I wondered if you and your sister would care to join me for a stroll about the park?

With thanks again,
Lady Arabella Waters

Mrs Leigh-Perrot frowned as Jane read the note out but didn't say anything. Jane was glad of her restraint. Even though Jane knew it might not be the best idea to associate with Lady Waters, she was intrigued by the young woman who had been vilified by Bath society. "What do you think, Cassandra? Shall we join Lady Waters this afternoon in Parade Gardens?"

"Does it fit with your plans, Aunt?"

"We can visit the draper's in the early afternoon and walk to the park after."

"Is the messenger still there, Mary?" Jane asked the young maid.

"Yes, Miss, he's waiting in the hall for your reply."

Jane rose and hurried upstairs to write a reply, feeling a frisson of excitement at the thought of getting to know Lady Waters a little better. There were questions she wished to ask her that would only be appropriate on closer acquaintance.

Quickly she penned a note confirming they would meet Lady Waters in Parade Gardens at three o'clock. She handed it over to the footman waiting in the hall downstairs before returning to the breakfast table.

The morning passed slowly for Jane, who was eager to get out and explore Bath further, but Mrs Leigh-Perrot was busy going over the household accounts and Cassandra sat quietly writing letters to various members of the family. Jane found a place to sit in the drawing room, close to the window, and spent most of the morning watching the world go by outside.

After lunch they set off to the draper's, a smart-looking shop in the centre of town. The shop front and sign looked freshly painted, and there were rolls of fabric spilling out of draws in an artistic fashion in the window. It made for an enticing display, and Jane saw Cassandra's face light up for a moment.

Inside, the shop was a little oppressive. Every nook was filled with rolls and rolls of fabric, silks and satins in one corner, cottons and lace in another. There was a whole section dedicated to brightly coloured ribbons and another to hooks and fastenings.

"Good afternoon, Mrs Leigh-Perrot," the draper said as they entered. The shop was quiet, apart from one other well-dressed woman being helped by an assistant at one of the counters.

"Good afternoon, Mr Finsbury. I trust you are well?"

"I am well indeed, Mrs Leigh Perrot. I hope you and your husband are in good health?"

"We are. You are kind to enquire. I have brought my nieces with me today, Miss Cassandra Austen and Miss Jane Austen. We are looking for some material for new dresses for them."

"Of course, I am sure we can help. What sort of occasion are we thinking of?"

"Nothing fancy," Jane said quickly as she saw a roll of pink, flowery fabric out of the corner of her eye. "Something practical, for day-to-day wear."

"Practical but pretty," Mrs Leigh-Perrot countered.

"Mainly practical," Jane said firmly. It wasn't that she didn't like to wear beautiful dresses, but for most activities they were highly impractical. She liked to put on her boots and stroll through the muddy fields around Steventon, even if it was raining. A delicate satin would be ruined within minutes, and anything with lace trimming drooped at the slightest provocation. It was much better to have a simpler material, made into a practical dress that she could feel comfortable in, than to be forever chasing the latest fashions.

"I am in mourning," Cassandra said. "I would like something in a muted colour."

Mrs Leigh-Perrot looked uncomfortable and shifted a little. "I think your mother was thinking of something a little more … cheerful."

It had been decided that six weeks was the proper length of time for Cassandra to wear black before she came out into the muted grey and pastel tones of half-mourning. It was a difficult path to tread with much clearer rules if she and Thomas Fowle had been married, but even though their betrothal was a lengthy one, society had differing opinions on how long Cassandra should show outwardly that she was still hurting. Much of this was because many women would be keen to start the hunt for a new husband, ever aware of the ticking clock counting down to spinsterhood. Jane was sure that thought had never crossed Cassandra's mind, but still she was subject to the rules of society.

"We could look at some half-mourning colours, perhaps," Mr Finsbury suggested, smoothing out any disagreement between Cassandra and her aunt. "I can see you're wearing grey today, Miss Austen, but many people find a muted lilac an appropriate colour for when they have been in mourning for a little longer. I like to think of these things as a spectrum from black, when the tragedy has recently occurred, to the bright colours for when you are fully restored to society. There are many stops along the way, and you can choose which shade you feel most comfortable in."

Cassandra nodded, not looking completely convinced, but she allowed herself to be led away by the draper to look at some rolls of fabric. Mrs Leigh-Perrot followed, leaving Jane to wander through the shop, fingering the different textures as she tried to choose something for herself.

She settled on a dark blue cotton, rich in colour but practical in that it would hide a few splashes of mud on the hem. It was different enough from her other dresses to make her feel sure her mother would be pleased with her selection, and Jane could imagine it made up into a simple yet timeless dress.

Cassandra was still looking at various shades of lilac and grey, gently disagreeing with their aunt as to which colour was most appropriate for a young woman in her position. Jane took a seat in one of the chairs positioned close to the window. It was thoughtfully provided, mainly used by weary husbands or fathers of the women who came to browse for material to take to the dressmakers. The chair was comfortable and Jane found herself sinking into it whilst looking out of the window to the street beyond. Mr Finsbury's draper shop was situated on Monmouth Street, one of the main throughfares through the city. Outside was busy with people going about their business. This part of Bath was mainly filled with the well-dressed and wealthy, although as with any city there was a mix of rich and poor.

Jane let her gaze drift over the view, watching maids hurrying along with heavy baskets full of fresh food for the evening's dinner and happy couples walking arm in arm. As she watched, a couple caught her eye. It was Mr and Mrs Fortescue, Lord Waters' son and daughter-in-law. Mr Fortescue was striding along the pavement, walking so fast that his wife struggled to keep up. The timid Mrs Fortescue hurried along behind, her head bent as if battling against huge crowds. They were almost directly outside the draper's window when Mrs Fortescue reached out to her husband and caught his arm.

He spun, his expression irritated, shrugging his wife's hand from his arm so hard that she stumbled back a step or two.

"What do you want, woman?" Mr Fortescue said. His voice was deep and loud, and Jane had no trouble hearing it through the single pane of glass that separated them.

Mrs Fortescue's reply was harder to hear, and Jane had to lean forward to catch the words.

"Please, Henry, do not do this."

"Go home."

"Please, I can't bear it any longer."

Mr Fortescue gave his wife such a look of contempt that Jane could feel the animosity emanating from him even through the window.

"I do not care what you can or cannot bear. Go home and stay there." He spun and strode off without a backwards glance, leaving his wife openly sobbing in the street.

Jane hesitated only a second and then rose to go outside and comfort the woman, but by the time she had left the shop Mrs Fortescue was already hurrying off, in the opposite direction to her husband.

"Is something amiss?" Cassandra asked as Jane re-entered the shop.

"No, I just thought I saw someone I recognised."

CHAPTER FIVE

The afternoon was hot even for late May, and when Jane and Cassandra emerged from the draper's Jane was glad of the parasol her aunt had insisted she bring. It was only a short walk to the entrance of Parade Gardens, and they arrived at the domed ticket office a few minutes before three o'clock.

"Are you sure you know the way home?" Mrs Leigh-Perrot said, concern etched on her face.

"Yes, Aunt, and if we get turned around we can ask for directions," Jane said quickly. She loved her aunt dearly and was grateful of her hospitality, but she was looking forward to spending a few hours away from her watchful, concerned eyes.

"You look pale, Cassandra dear. Do you wish to accompany me home?"

"No, thank you, Aunt. I will stay with Jane. If I become tired, I can always take some rest on a bench."

"Very well, girls. I will see you back at home in an hour or two."

Arm in arm, the Austen sisters watched their aunt walk away before approaching the ticket office. There was an air of celebration about the gardens, with everyone dressed in bright colours and jaunty music drifting up from the bandstand below.

"Where are we meeting Lady Waters?" Cassandra asked as they descended the stairs into the gardens.

"I suggested just inside the entrance. Shall we find a spot in the shade?"

There was a bench within view of the steps that was in the dappled shade of an enormous apple tree, and Jane sank down onto it gratefully. Cassandra took a fan from her reticule, handing it over to Jane before snapping the little bag shut. With gratitude Jane began fanning herself, thankful for the slight breeze from the fan. Usually she coped well with the heat. In the countryside there was always a cool stream to dip her toes in or a giant oak to seek shade under. It felt hotter here in the city, the temperatures more oppressive and the crush of people making it sometimes feel as though she could not breathe.

"There is Lady Waters," Cassandra said, motioning to the brightly dressed young woman descending the stairs slowly. "Lord Waters is with her — I was not expecting him to come out today."

"Nor I," Jane said, frowning as the old man struggled down the steps. "I assumed he would be resting after the events of last night."

"Look who else is here," Cassandra murmured as Mrs Upton passed them by, arm in arm with another woman of a similar age. Mrs Upton gave them a tight smile and a nod of greeting but did not stop to talk.

"Bath society is truly hardly bigger than Steventon," Jane said, enjoying the smile on her sister's face. Perhaps coming to Bath would be good for Cassandra once she had settled into their new surroundings.

"I hope you have not been waiting for us long," Lady Waters said as she hurried over.

"Not at all, you are right on time. Cassandra and I were a few minutes early and thought we would rest a moment in the shade."

"Excellent idea," Lord Waters said, sinking onto the bench beside them. He was smiling brightly, but his chest heaved from the exertion of the walk from the street to the gardens and his face had an unhealthy purple tinge to it.

"Have you recovered from last night, Lord Waters?" Cassandra enquired, her face a picture of concern. She had always been the nurturing one in the family, the one who would volunteer to stay behind if someone was unwell, and who noticed if one of her siblings seemed withdrawn or sad. Now she looked ready to escort Lord Waters back home at the first sign of illness.

"I have, thank you. My doctor tells me I must not overdo things, but he is not overly concerned."

"I know it is a matter between you and your doctor, but should you be at home resting?"

"You are a considerate young lady, Miss Austen," Lord Waters said with an indulgent smile. His colour looked a little better now he was sitting and he allowed himself to relax against the bench, making himself comfortable.

"Lord Waters knows how much I enjoy an event such as this," Lady Waters said, beaming at her husband. "He insisted he accompany me. I think, though, it is perhaps better you watch from afar. Shall we leave you here to rest whilst we take a stroll?"

"That sounds a splendid idea," Lord Waters said, stretching his legs out in front of him. He didn't seem bothered by the fact they were in a public place, and Jane could imagine him closing his eyes and having a nap whilst they took a walk around the gardens. As they turned to go, Jane saw the old man pat his jacket pocket a few times and then look around the gardens with a frown.

"We will be back for when the music starts in earnest," Lady Waters said and leaned in to kiss her husband on the cheek. It was an audacious show of affection but it made the old man grin, and Jane realised she admired them for not caring what other people thought of their relationship.

The gardens were busy with well-dressed ladies and gentlemen strolling in couples or small groups. Many of the ladies had parasols to protect them from the sun or were fanning themselves vigorously.

"Lord Waters has truly recovered?" Cassandra said as they made their way around the perimeter of the park. It was only small, with criss-crossing paths that weaved through the neat flowerbeds.

"Oh yes, he is quite well," Lady Waters said nonchalantly. "He insisted he come this afternoon, and he scolded me for fussing." She lowered her voice a little, meaning Jane and Cassandra had to tilt their heads to hear properly. "He doesn't like people making a fuss. I think it reminds him of his age, and he does not like to be reminded of his age." She sighed and shook her head. "When we met, he said he fell in love with my energy and thirst for life."

"I am sure you keep him young at heart," Cassandra said.

"Yes, I think I do. I just worry it gets too much for him, but all I can do is express concern. It is his choice whether he rests or pushes through any exhaustion he feels."

Lady Waters stiffened as they rounded the corner to pass onto one of the diagonal paths through the gardens. Mrs Upton was heading in their direction.

"Bath is a very small town," Jane observed quietly.

Lady Waters laughed, but there was a bitter edge to it. "Too small. Every event I attend, every time I step out of my door, I am assailed by one of Lord Waters' children. This is why I am keen to visit London, to lose myself in the swathes of people. It would be pleasant to be largely anonymous, even for a few weeks."

Mrs Upton passed them, inclining her head in greeting but not deigning to stop. As she continued walking, she made no effort to lower her voice as she spoke to the woman beside her. "Did you see her dress? It is another new one. She is bleeding him dry."

Lady Waters flushed and glanced down at the beautiful gown she was wearing. "It is none of her concern what I wear," she murmured, turning to Jane and speaking with sudden vehemence. "Lord Waters has been incredibly indulgent with both of his children, despite their terrible attitudes and their squandering ways. Just last week…" She trailed off, as if realising the indiscretion she was about to commit. She coughed and shook her head. "I'm sorry, I speak out of turn. I should not let jealous words hurt me."

Before Jane could enquire any further, there was an announcement from the bandstand that the music would begin shortly.

"Come, we should return to my husband. I promised him we would listen to the music together."

It only took a couple of minutes to walk back through the park to the bench they had left Lord Waters resting on, and Jane was pleased to see he looked a better colour. He rose to his feet when he saw them, greeting his wife with a loving smile.

"Shall we find a spot in front of the bandstand?" Lady Waters suggested.

"Excellent idea, my dear. You do that and I will fetch some drinks for everyone." There was a table in the shade on which there were glasses of sparkling wine. Many people were strolling past now, sipping their drinks.

"Let me help you," Jane said, aware that Lord Waters wouldn't be able to carry four glasses filled with wine through the crowds without spilling any.

"Thank you, Miss Austen."

Lord Waters led the way through the crowds to the stall and collected four glasses, handing two to Jane. As they turned, Jane was surprised to see Mr and Mrs Fortescue close behind them.

"Good afternoon, Father," Mr Fortescue said stiffly.

"Good afternoon, Henry, Mary."

There was an awkward silence, during which Mrs Fortescue looked nervously between her husband and her father-in-law.

"It is such a beautiful day," she said eventually, the words bursting from her mouth. "We are so lucky to have a park like this, and all the talented musicians who are performing for us today. I do love Bath. I think it is the most beautiful and cultured city."

Neither man looked at her, their eyes locked on one another.

"Come, Henry," Lord Waters said eventually. "Enough of this sulking. Watch the performance with us. Then later there is a serious matter I need to discuss with you and Penelope."

As Lord Waters spoke, the band began playing the first piece and for a moment the musicians drew everyone's attention. It meant Jane did not hear Mr Fortescue's reply and by the time she had turned back, Lord Waters' son and daughter-in-law had walked past and were disappearing into the crowd behind them.

Lord Waters and Jane joined Lady Waters and Cassandra, listening to the band and watching as the musicians artfully spread an air of joviality across the park. It was billed as a summer celebration, and within a few minutes most people were swaying along to the music, caught up in the moment.

"This is really quite good," Cassandra said, leaning in and speaking into Jane's ear so she could be heard over the music. Despite her reservations, Cassandra seemed to be having a good time and Jane felt a swell of pleasure. She hated seeing her beloved sister so distressed and whilst she knew she couldn't rush Cassandra's grief, she was relieved to see her enjoying something.

Out of the corner of her eye, Jane saw Mrs Upton and her husband squeeze through the crowd to stand with Lord Waters. He certainly seemed to have a better relationship with his daughter than his son, but Jane was not sure if that was because she made more of an effort or if she merely hid her animosity towards Lady Waters better than her brother.

The sparkling wine was sweet but cool, refreshing in the heat of the afternoon. Jane drank hers far too quickly, knowing she would regret it later, but unable to stop herself once she had begun. In the crowd the temperature was oppressive, and for a few minutes she borrowed Cassandra's fan.

She was about to suggest they move to the perimeter to find a little more space when she saw Lord Waters sway a little and then stumble. For one desperate minute he turned to look at her, his eyes dark and a frantic expression on his face. Perspiration covered his brow, and Jane could see his shirt was soaked through and sticking to his body.

Lord Waters tried to say something, reaching out and grasping her arm, but no words came out. Jane stepped back in dismay, watching as his legs buckled and he collapsed to the ground.

"Get back!" she shouted, worried he would be trampled by the unsuspecting crowd. "Everyone make room."

At first it seemed like no one had heard, but after a few moments heads began to turn and a ripple of concern travelled through the crowd. It was enough for those closest to Lord Waters to step away, glancing over their shoulders at the man on the ground.

"Oliver!" Lady Waters cried, crouching down beside her husband, her eyes searching his. "What is wrong?"

For a moment it looked as though Lord Waters were about to speak but, as they watched, his eyes glazed over and his body went limp, his head falling back onto the ground with a thump.

The strangled cry that came from Lady Waters' mouth sounded like a wounded animal, and as she sobbed Jane crouched down beside her. Gently she laid a hand on the old man's chest, willing there to be the slightest of movements, but already his stare was fixed and his body unresponsive.

"He's dead," Jane said as she sat back on her heels, unable to tear her eyes away from the lifeless body of Lord Waters as his wife sobbed beside him.

CHAPTER SIX

"Get back, let me through," Mr Fortescue demanded as he pushed his way through the crowd. Some people had moved away, eager to do their bit to preserve the dignity of the deceased and his distraught widow, but many more stayed where they were, even pressing in closer to get a better view. Mr Fortescue barrelled through all of them, using his elbows when people were not quick enough to move. "What happened?"

Jane did not answer immediately and Lady Waters was still sobbing uncontrollably. Therefore, Mr Fortescue's eyes had roamed over the body of his father before anyone could break the news to him more gently.

"I am so sorry, Mr Fortescue," Jane said, rising from the ground. He might be a boorish oaf of a man, but that did not mean he deserved to see his father in this way. She touched his arm, meaning to lead him a little distance away, but he shrugged her off.

"What did you do?" His words were directed at Lady Waters, who was still crying.

"We need a doctor," Lady Waters said, calling out to the crowd. "Is there a doctor here? My husband needs help."

Mr Fortescue barged past Jane and gripped Lady Waters by the arm, hauling her to her feet none too gently. "What did you do?" he repeated.

Lady Waters turned to her stepson, confusion in her eyes. "Do?" she asked, bewildered. "I didn't do anything. He collapsed. We have to help him."

"You always were a simple-minded fool. He is dead. No one can help him now." Mr Fortescue's voice was low, but the words carried over the hushed crowd.

Still in shock, Jane began to move amongst the crowd, speaking quietly to people and urging them to leave. The band had stopped playing amidst the commotion, and the tragedy of Lord Waters' death meant the air of celebration had turned to one of shock. To her left, Jane saw with relief that Cassandra was mirroring her actions, reminding people of basic decency and asking them to leave the Fortescue family in peace.

"Might I be of assistance?" asked a smartly dressed young man, making his way through the thinning crowd. He had a frown on his face, and his eyes moved quickly, taking in everything around him. For a moment his gaze rested on the body of Lord Waters, assessing the scene before crouching down.

"He collapsed a few minutes ago," Jane said.

By the way the man reached out and checked for a pulse, it was clear he was a doctor. After half a minute of tense silence, he shook his head and gently lowered Lord Waters' eyelids over his lifeless eyes. "I am sorry," the young man said, rising to his feet. "There is nothing I can do. My condolences."

"Thank you for coming over," Jane said quietly, her head reeling from the sudden turn of events. It felt unreal that she had been talking to Lord Waters only a few minutes earlier and now he lay dead on the floor.

The crowds had dispersed, finally allowing the dead man and his family some privacy. Some people were lingering a little way off, but most were making their way through the park to the steps that led to the street above. Pushing in the opposite direction was Mrs Upton and her husband. Her expression was frantic.

"People are saying Father is…" she began, trailing off as she saw the unmoving body of her father on the floor. "No."

"She did this," Mr Fortescue said, pointing at Lady Waters, and he began to advance on her.

"No," Lady Waters said. "I haven't done anything. He just collapsed."

Jane recalled the look of petrified confusion on Lord Waters' face. He hadn't stumbled around clutching at his chest as she knew people with heart trouble sometimes did. Instead, he had looked as though he were pursued by all the demons of hell. The thought made her shudder, and she was pleased to feel Cassandra's reassuring presence by her side.

"We need to get her out of here," Cassandra murmured in Jane's ear. "Mr Fortescue is becoming more and more agitated, and Lady Waters is in shock."

Jane glanced at her new friend, and saw she did indeed look pale. Her chest was rising and falling rapidly as her breathing rate increased.

"I can't believe he is dead," Lady Waters said, then started to repeat the phrase again and again.

Mr Fortescue watched her with disgust for a moment and then strode over, raising his hand as if he were about to slap her.

Mr Upton, who so far had not uttered a word, sprang forwards, catching Mr Fortescue's arm before he could deliver the slap. For a moment it seemed as if the two men might come to blows, but after a tense few seconds Mr Fortescue lowered his arm and stepped away, shaking his head and muttering under his breath.

"Might I suggest we contact the coroner?" the doctor said, looking around the group as if unsure who to direct his words to.

"Yes," Mr Fortescue said. "That is exactly what we need to do. You —" he pointed at his stepmother — "stay here. I will go for Mr Gillingham."

As Mr Fortescue hurried off one of the park attendants stopped him, looking uneasily at the dead body. Mr Fortescue seemed to be issuing instructions, for the park attendant nodded a few times and then set about trying to clear anyone not directly involved in the unfortunate death from the park.

"Come, Lady Waters," Jane said, approaching quietly. The new widow had sunk down to her knees again beside her husband and was holding his hand. "Let us take you to a bench where you can rest a little."

"Good idea," the doctor said. "She's in shock."

Jane led her over to a bench, grateful for Cassandra and the young doctor's calm presence beside her.

"I am Dr Black, Lady Waters. I am sorry for your loss."

Lady Waters nodded absently, her eyes still fixed upon her husband.

"Doctor, might I have a word?" Jane said, ignoring the warning look from Cassandra. Her sister was understandably protective of her and always expressed her unease when Jane accompanied their local magistrate, Lord Hinchbrooke, to scenes of crimes or to apprehend a suspect. This was different, though. Here Jane had not chosen to be involved, but it was her duty to highlight any concerns she had over Lord Waters' death.

"Of course, Miss…?"

"Austen. Miss Jane Austen. This is my sister, Miss Cassandra Austen."

"What can I help you with, Miss Austen?"

"Lord Waters was an old man with a multitude of health problems, I believe," Jane spoke quietly, turning away from everyone else so they could not hear her words. "It would be tragic but not entirely unexpected for him to collapse and pass away because of one of those health problems."

Dr Black nodded but didn't speak, so Jane pressed on.

"I wonder, though…" She paused, taking a deep breath. "I saw Lord Waters' expression moments before he died, and I am concerned something else could have happened."

"Something else?"

Jane nodded, biting her lip. "I may be wrong, but it crossed my mind that his death might not have been natural."

"You think someone did this to him?"

Jane nodded, trying to read the young doctor's expression. He puffed out his cheeks.

"There are no obvious injuries," he said slowly. "You are thinking about poison?"

It was what Jane meant, but there could also be a dozen other explanations. As yet, no one had inspected Lord Waters' body. It was unlikely, but he could have a knife sticking out of his back.

"Perhaps," she said quietly.

Dr Black hesitated, looking from where Mr and Mrs Upton stood, to Lady Waters and then to Mrs Fortescue standing on her own, wringing her hands. "I know the coroner; he is a sensible man. He will not object to me taking a brief look at the body if you have concerns."

"Thank you."

Quietly they stepped over to the supine form of Lord Waters, but Dr Black hesitated before crouching down beside him.

"What was it you noticed that has given you cause for concern?"

Jane thought for a moment, forcing herself to remember those last terrible moments when Lord Waters spun and stumbled a little through the crowd. "He seemed unfocussed, his eyes fixed on something that was not there. There was a look of terror in his eyes and he lurched a few steps before thrashing his head from side to side."

"No clutching at his chest?"

"No."

"It is sometimes difficult to tell, but did it look like he had lost control of one side of his body?"

Jane shook her head. She opened her mouth to speak but then stopped herself, unsure whether it was wise to say any more or if Dr Black would judge her as hysterical.

"Go on, Miss Austen. Sometimes the things that do not quite make sense are the ones that give us that vital clue."

"His eyes seemed dark, unnaturally so. I noticed because normally he has very pale blue eyes, but when he looked at me they were like two pieces of coal."

"That is interesting." Dr Black crouched down next to Lord Waters' body and Jane sensed movement beside her.

"What are you doing?" Mrs Upton asked sharply.

"Ah, Mrs Upton," Dr Black said, standing again and reaching out to place a consoling hand on the older woman's arm. "I am sorry for your loss. Such a tragedy and a shock, I am sure."

"Thank you, Doctor," Mrs Upton said, still frowning. "What were you doing down there?"

Jane cleared her throat, knowing she needed to take responsibility for asking Dr Black to examine Lord Waters' body. It was unfair on the doctor otherwise.

"I asked him to take a quick look," Jane said, feeling the animosity emanating from Mrs Upton. "In Hampshire I assist our local magistrate in dealing with unexpected deaths, and I know how vital it is to gather any information as early as possible. I pressed Dr Black to make a few initial observations so nothing would fade by the time the coroner arrives." She chose her words carefully, deliberately, making sure she did not insinuate any wrongdoing.

"Is this truly an unexpected death, though? My father was seventy-five years old. He has outlived the vast majority of his peers," said Mrs Upton, but to Jane's relief she shrugged and motioned for the doctor to continue. "I suppose it cannot hurt to be thorough."

Dr Black crouched again, examining the body methodically. He was silent while he worked, taking his time to inspect everything from fingertips to lips. It would have been inappropriate for him to undress Lord Waters here in the middle of Parade Gardens; that would have to be arranged by the coroner once he arrived to take charge.

He paused as he opened Lord Fortescue's jacket, seeming to weigh something that was in the pocket in the palm of his hand. With a frown, he reached into the pocket and pulled out a handkerchief that was wrapped around something. Carefully he unwound the fabric, and Jane was surprised to see the glint of green in his hand. It was the emerald necklace — the one Lady Waters had been wearing at the ball the night before. The one so bitterly coveted by Mr Fortescue.

Dr Black frowned at the precious gems for a moment and then slipped them back into Lord Waters' pocket. "I will inform the coroner the emeralds are in the pocket, but he should see everything as it was for himself."

He continued with his inspection, taking his time and checking everything methodically before standing up.

"There are no external signs of injury," he said, his tone reflecting the sombre mood. "Yet there are one or two little inconsistencies I will have to mention to the coroner."

"Inconsistencies?" Mrs Upton said.

"It may be nothing, but I think they warrant a doctor taking a closer look at your father's body."

"You cannot mean he needs a post-mortem," Mrs Upton said with horror.

"Hopefully not," Dr Black said, smiling reassuringly. Jane could see he would be a popular doctor; even when delivering bad news, he had a reassuring way about him. He was attractive too, with a shock of dark hair and green eyes that were full of life. No doubt the ladies of Bath would enjoy his attention.

"What did you see, Doctor?" Jane asked, moving closer so he could tell her quietly.

"Yes, what did you see?" Mrs Upton repeated.

"His pupils are dilated. That is why his eyes looked black, Miss Austen."

"What does that mean?" Jane glanced at the dead man's face, but the doctor had closed his eyes again so the enlarged pupils were not visible.

Dr Black shrugged. "I do not wish to come to a conclusion before a full and proper examination of the body has taken place."

Jane suppressed her impatience. It was typical of a doctor not to want to commit to something that may at a later date be proved wrong. Still, he had voiced a suspicion of wrongdoing — that was enough for her to ensure the death was not dismissed as merely an elderly man collapsing because his heart had given out.

There was a commotion at the entrance to the park as Mr Fortescue returned with a large man, hurrying down the steps with an air of importance. The man was in his fifties, with a rounded belly and a ruddy complexion. As he drew closer, Jane could see he had a bulbous nose and the flushed cheeks that often identified a man as a heavy drinker. Today he seemed flustered, having been dragged away from whatever afternoon pursuit he'd been enjoying to view a dead body in Parade Gardens.

He paused a few steps away from the body, spending a few seconds looking at Lord Waters before allowing his eyes to drift around the assembled onlookers.

"I am sorry for your loss," he said, his words directed at Mrs Upton and Mr Fortescue. Lady Waters was still sitting on the bench a few feet away, but the coroner did not even acknowledge her presence. "Tell me what happened and we can then arrange for your father's body to be moved."

"He was enjoying the festivities," Mr Fortescue said solemnly, "even though he should have been at home resting after he collapsed last night. I expect Lady Waters pressed him to escort her here. One minute he was listening to the music, the next he fell to the floor."

"He collapsed last night as well, you say?"

"Yes. Dr Taylor visited when he returned home and then again this morning, I understand."

The coroner nodded, as if already coming to the conclusion he wanted.

"Mr Gillingham, might I interrupt?" Dr Black said, stepping up. To Jane's relief, the coroner did not dismiss him. He instead motioned for the doctor to move to one side with him so they could talk in private. There was a murmur of voices, too low to hear the words, the doctor doing most of the talking with the coroner occasionally interjecting.

After a few minutes the coroner turned back to the group. "I understand there is a concern the death might not have been a natural one," he said, loudly enough for everyone to hear. "With the question raised, there is no choice but to proceed to inquest after we have gathered more information."

"Whatever you think best," Mr Fortescue said, sounding the most reasonable Jane had ever heard him.

"I will ask my assistant to collect your father's body for examination. Given this is a public place, we cannot leave things untouched for the inquest, but I will make a written account of what I have seen here today."

"Thank you for being so thorough, Mr Gillingham."

"Now, who are all these people?" The coroner's eyes swept across the small crowd and came to rest on Jane and Cassandra.

"I am Miss Jane Austen and this is my sister, Miss Cassandra Austen. We had arranged to meet Lady Waters this afternoon for the entertainment."

The coroner scrutinised them both in turn. "Austen, I do not think I know that name."

"We are staying with my aunt, Mrs Leigh-Perrot, for a few weeks. Normally we reside in Hampshire."

The coroner seemed to soften a little at the mention of Mrs Leigh-Perrot, and Jane felt some of the tension ebb from her as well. "I suggest you return to your aunt's house. I will know where to contact you if a statement is needed."

"Of course Mr Gillingham." Jane hesitated, looking from the dead man to Lady Waters. "I do not know what Dr Black said, but I am concerned this was not a natural death."

The coroner stared at her hard, assessing, before he nodded for her to continue.

"The way he stumbled around, the darkness in his eyes…"

"I take my role very seriously, Miss Austen," the coroner said. "Do not doubt that. Now, I suggest that you return home and I will call on you later today, or perhaps first thing tomorrow morning. I am sure you do not want to impose on this family's tragedy any longer." The last was said with an edge to his voice. Jane could imagine the coroner was only a reasonable man up to a point; if pushed past this, then his temper would be revealed.

"Come, Jane," Cassandra said firmly. "Let us return to our aunt and uncle's house."

"But…"

Cassandra's grip tightened on her arm and Jane looked at the serious faces of Mr Gillingham and Mr Fortescue.

"We are sorry for your loss," Cassandra said as she guided Jane away. "If there is anything we can do, please do not hesitate to ask."

CHAPTER SEVEN

A terrible tension infiltrated every corner of the townhouse. Mrs Leigh-Perrot flitted from room to room like a distressed little bird whilst her husband sat brooding in his study, barking orders at the servants if they dared to venture in. Jane watched the street, desperate to be forewarned about any visitors and even Cassandra, who was normally calm, had thrown her embroidery down in frustration at least half a dozen times in the past hour.

"This is torture," Jane moaned quietly as another minute ticked by painfully slowly.

"They may not call for us at all," Cassandra said.

"Surely they have to call. There has been a suspicious death and we are witnesses."

"A sudden but not wholly unexpected death," Cassandra corrected her. "And we were two amongst a crowd of hundreds."

"Two people well acquainted with the deceased."

"Hardly well acquainted, Jane. We had met him on three occasions and spoken to him for at most five minutes."

"He was poisoned," Jane said, declaring her thoughts firmly but quietly, not wanting to distress their aunt any further.

"I am sure the coroner will do everything to ascertain whether it was a natural or unnatural death."

Jane scoffed. "Mr Gillingham seemed awfully friendly with Mr Fortescue. If he wishes the death to be hushed up…" Jane didn't get to finish the sentence, for Cassandra interrupted.

"Not every death is suspicious, Jane. Sometimes I wonder if you wish for some intrigue to relieve the boredom."

"You cannot think I would ever wish anyone ill?"

"No, of course not," Cassandra said quickly. "But I do think you enjoy looking into the unexplained."

There was no use denying it. Following her visits with Lord Hinchbrooke, Jane always came home filled with excitement at the prospect of solving puzzles and piecing together evidence.

"We should call on Lady Waters."

"No, not yet. Our aunt would be horrified."

"There is nothing wrong with going to pay our respects to a grieving widow." Jane turned away from the window, wondering if Cassandra might be persuaded.

"No," her sister said firmly. "We need to give Lady Waters time to organise her affairs and mourn with her family."

"The family all despise her. I am certain she would welcome a friendly face."

"We should not get involved, Jane."

Jane did not answer. Her attention had been caught by two figures walking down the street towards the house. They were dressed smartly and walked quickly, as if going about important business. A few seconds later, there was a knock at the door followed by the murmur of low voices.

Jane expected the men to be shown into the drawing room, but instead they entered her uncle's study, closing the door firmly behind them so there was no hope of overhearing what they were saying.

"Who is calling on Uncle?" Jane asked as their aunt hurried into the room.

"Mr Gillingham, the coroner, I believe." Mrs Leigh-Perrot fussed about the room for a moment before pressing Jane and Cassandra to sit down and assume a pose of genteel respectability.

A few minutes later they heard the door to the study open and their uncle entered the room, followed by Mr Gillingham and another man they did not know.

As one, Jane and Cassandra rose and bowed their heads in greeting.

"Cassandra, Jane, these gentlemen would like to ask you a few questions about the terrible events of yesterday afternoon."

"Of course," Cassandra said, reaching out to take Jane's hand.

"We want to help however we can," Jane said.

Mr Gillingham stepped forward, smiling in greeting. He seemed less agitated than the day before, as if he had overcome his initial shock at being summoned to the death of one of Bath's wealthiest residents and was now in his element, asking questions where they needed to be asked. His face was less flushed too, and Jane wondered if he had forgone his normal round of evening drinks the night before so as to be fresh for his role today.

"We are holding the coroner's inquest later this afternoon," he said with no preamble.

Jane knew that after a suspicious death the inquest was often held quickly. Lord Hinchbrooke had told her of coroners who liked the scene of a crime to remain untouched until it had been viewed by the jurors, meaning that sometimes a body would lie at the bottom of a flight of stairs or on a tavern floor for a day or two. Still, this meant it would be at most twenty-four hours between the death and the inquest, and Jane wondered if this was enough time to gather the evidence needed to prove Lord Waters' death wasn't simply that of an old man whose heart had failed.

"I am Mr Winters, the local magistrate," the other man introduced himself. He was softly spoken and had a kindly face. "Given the gravity of this case and the influence and importance of those involved, Mr Gillingham has asked me to assist him in his investigation into this matter."

"We will help however we can," Jane repeated quickly.

"I have spent the morning with young Dr Black," Mr Gillingham said, motioning for Jane and Cassandra to sit. "He tells me he examined the body in the park because you were worried there was something suspicious about the way Lord Waters died."

Jane nodded.

"What gave you that impression, Miss Austen?"

Over the last year Lord Hinchbrooke had taught her to formulate her thoughts before speaking, to put everything in a clear order and consider her words so her meaning was easy to fathom. He often told her to assume she was talking to someone of lesser intelligence; that way, nothing could get lost in the assumption the listener understood more than they did.

"Lord Waters was in good spirits when we met him and his wife, although a little worn out from the walk from the carriage into the park," Jane said slowly. "He sat down for a few minutes, but by the time the music started he seemed fully recovered. I accompanied him to fetch some wine and we returned to Lady Waters and Cassandra." Jane paused, recalling the sequence of events. "Shortly afterwards he turned around, and it was as if he was not aware of his surroundings. He stumbled a little and looked around, as if he could not see what was going on, and then he collapsed."

"What you describe could be a result of any number of natural ways to die in old age, Miss Austen," Mr Winters said kindly.

"No." The word came out sharper than Jane had intended. "Forgive me, but no," she said, a little more quietly. "There was something in his eyes that was unnatural, and he stumbled about as if he were trying to escape from something the rest of us could not see."

"You would swear to this in court?" Mr Gillingham said.

"I would."

"Good. It may come to that, Miss Austen. You will need to make yourself available this afternoon for the inquest. Depending on the other evidence presented, we may not need your statement, but I think it prudent you are there in case the jurors need to hear what you have to say."

Jane was surprised at the request. She had expected to be dismissed, for the coroner to argue that the death was, on balance, likely due to the baron's advanced years and known health conditions. Never had she thought it would be so easy to convince the coroner and magistrate that the death was unnatural.

"I assume Dr Black told you about the emerald necklace Lord Waters had in his pocket," Jane said.

"Yes, we have given them to Mr Fortescue for safekeeping, until Lord Waters' will is read."

"It is strange to carry such valuable gems in a pocket out in public, is it not?"

Mr Winters shrugged. "To you or me, yes indeed it is, but Lord Waters was extraordinarily wealthy and the rich often have strange views as to what is important. Do not fear, Miss Austen; we have acknowledged the presence of the emeralds and will be mindful of them if there is any concern about an unnatural death at the inquest."

"Thank you," Jane said, knowing there was nothing more she could do right now.

"Please excuse us," Mr Gillingham said, bowing to Jane and Cassandra before turning to their uncle. "Thank you for your help."

There was a long silence as the two men were shown out, broken only when their aunt and uncle came back into the drawing room.

"I will accompany you this afternoon," Mr Leigh-Perrot said, his normally jovial face grim.

"I am sorry if I have caused you trouble." Jane knew this death would be the subject of gossip for months amongst Bath society and her aunt and uncle would not welcome being part of it. Yet they were reasonable people and would understand her need to ensure justice was done.

"Do not fret, Jane," Mrs Leigh-Perrot said, taking her hand. "We shall all come with you. There is nothing that shows solidarity more than a family united."

At her aunt's words Jane thought of Lady Waters, likely sitting alone in that big house in The Crescent. Now her husband was dead, she had no family locally and no friends to comfort her. The only people she would have contact with would be her husband's family, who openly despised her.

The inquest was to be held in the middle of town. At short notice twelve gentlemen of good standing had been selected from the local community and summoned to attend.

"This is hardly fair," Jane said. They had just watched Mr Fortescue nod in greeting to many of the assembled jurors as he took his seat in the front row. "Mr Fortescue knows all these men; they are his friends and business associates. They will find it hard to come to a conclusion he does not support."

"You must have more faith in people, Jane," Cassandra said.

"I have exactly the right amount of faith in people, as they deserve."

Any further discussion was limited by the entrance of Lady Waters. The whole room fell silent, everyone's eyes following the widow's progress. She was dressed completely in black, the collar of her dress high on her neck and the hem sweeping the floor. The dress itself was simple but well made, with no show of ostentatiousness. She wore a simple string of pearls about her neck, and her hair was pinned back in an uncomplicated style. Even more telling were the red and puffy eyes and the pallor of her complexion. No one could doubt that this was a woman in mourning.

After a few moments the chatter started up again. Jane would have liked to have the opportunity to reach out to Lady Waters in support, but the young widow kept her head bowed and her eyes fixed on the floor. Other members of the family took their places, with Mrs Upton and her husband sitting beside Mr and Mrs Fortescue, leaving a noticeable empty space around their stepmother.

"I've always found inquests fascinating," Dr Black said as he slipped into the chair beside Jane. "How are you, Miss Austen? I hope the strain is not too much?"

"I am as well as can be expected, thank you. Are you here in a professional capacity?"

He shook his head. "Do you know, I am not sure. It is not the first time I have attended an inquest, but previously I have always been confident of the questions I will be asked before they leave the coroner's mouth. Today I am not certain what my role is."

The young doctor was prevented from speculating further by the entrance of Mr Gillingham, who introduced himself to the assembled mix of witnesses and jurors before taking his seat behind a raised desk. Mr Winters, the local magistrate they had met earlier in the day, sat to one side inconspicuously.

After a brief introduction and a word of thanks to the jurors for giving up their time to be there today, the coroner asked Dr Taylor to come to the front of the room. Jane was pleased she did not have to be questioned first. It would be easier if she could see how the proceedings worked before she was called to give evidence.

"Dr Taylor, how long were you doctor to the deceased?"

"Twenty-five years, on and off," Dr Taylor replied. "I understand Lord Waters consulted a colleague of mine when he resided in London, but whilst he was in Bath I looked after his health."

"Can you tell us about Lord Waters' health?"

Dr Taylor nodded, spreading his hands in front of him. "He had the normal complaints of a man of his age. Some trouble with gout, a stiffness in his joints in the mornings, one or two other age-related issues." He paused, glancing over at Lady Waters. "I was also concerned about his heart. Lady Waters sent for me on a few occasions after her husband collapsed quite suddenly. On each occasion he recovered quickly with no ill effects, but we were starting to see him slowing down a little. He would become breathless if he walked too far, and he needed lots of pillows to prop him up in bed at night."

"Would it surprise you to hear Lord Waters had collapsed and died suddenly, given what you had seen in the last few months as his doctor?"

"No, not at all."

"Thank you, Doctor, please take a seat. I would be grateful if you would stay until the end of the inquest in case we have any more questions for you. Dr Black, would you come forward."

The two medical men nodded at one another as they crossed paths, and Dr Black took his place facing the coroner.

"Thank you for coming today, Dr Black. I understand you were present yesterday during the festivities at Parade Gardens?"

"Yes, I was escorting my sister."

"Can you tell us what happened?"

"The music had just started, and everyone was gathered in a crowd. I heard a commotion, a few screams and then a request for space. Most of the people in attendance started to move away, but I thought I might be able to be of assistance if it was a medical matter." He paused and glanced at Jane and Cassandra for a moment. "At first I couldn't move against the crowd of people, so I escorted my sister to the edge of the park and then made my way back to where I saw Lord Waters' family gathered."

"Lord Waters was dead by this point?"

"Yes, I checked his pulse and for signs of life, but unfortunately there was nothing to be done."

"What happened next?"

"Miss Jane Austen, a friend of the deceased, approached me and said she was worried it may not have been a natural death." This blunt declaration prompted a murmur to run through the room. "She told me of how Lord Waters stumbled before his death, how he looked panicked, and she spoke of a darkness in his eyes."

"You examined the body?"

"Yes, briefly. There were no external signs of anything suspicious except a dilation of the pupils."

"In layman's terms, what does this mean?"

Dr Black cleared his throat and looked around the room before answering. "I was concerned Lord Waters might have been poisoned."

"Thank you, Doctor. Please have a seat. We may need to come back to you later. Miss Austen, please step forward."

All eyes were on Jane as she rose and smoothed down her dress. She glanced at Lady Waters, but the young woman was staring at her hands. Jane walked slowly, wanting to use the time before she had to turn and face the jurors to compose herself.

"You are visiting your aunt and uncle in Bath — is that right, Miss Austen?"

"Yes."

"You arranged yesterday to meet Lord and Lady Waters?"

"Yes. No…" Jane took a deep breath to compose herself. "My sister and I received a note from Lady Waters inviting us to join her at Parade Gardens yesterday afternoon. I was not aware Lord Waters was going to be in attendance."

"Please tell us what happened to make you concerned Lord Waters' death was not natural."

"I had accompanied Lord Waters to help carry the drinks. We returned to Lady Waters and my sister, Miss Cassandra Austen. Lord Waters seemed comfortable and in good spirits. The music started, and very soon after he spun around. There was a look of pure fear on his face and his eyes were unfocussed. His pupils were huge and made his eyes look completely black." She did not compare them to the dark pits of hell, not wanting to sound hysterical, but that was what she thought of when she pictured Lord Waters' final moments. "Then he collapsed."

"Thank you, Miss Austen. I am sure that was not easy to recount. Before Lord Waters collapsed, he was drinking wine — is that correct?"

"Yes, sparkling wine. It was part of the festivities, and he collected a glass for him and one for Lady Waters whilst I carried one for myself and one for my sister."

"Did you see him eat or drink anything else in the time you were with him?"

"No."

"Thank you, Miss Austen. That will be all for now."

Jane hesitated, sure there must be more to say. She wanted to tell them about how Mr Fortescue had been in the crowd, and how Mrs Upton had brushed past them and stood close to her father. It would have been easy for either of them or their spouses to put something into Lord Waters' drink. Yet she pressed her lips together, keeping quiet, aware her aunt and uncle would have to continue to socialise with these people. Today all the inquest needed to focus on was whether this was a natural or unnatural death. If it was deemed unnatural, then the coroner could order an investigation into the circumstances around it, and that would be the time to share her theories.

Jane walked back to her seat, pleased when Cassandra gripped her hand and murmured words of support in her ear.

"Next we will hear from Dr Tomkins," Mr Gillingham said, introducing a large, middle-aged man who walked through the courtroom with confidence, as if he had been here hundreds of times before.

"Good afternoon, Mr Gillingham, gentlemen," he said, turning to the jurors. "Thank you for being here. I am Dr Tomkins. I have practised medicine in Bath for twenty-four years and know many of you and your families. As part of my role, I also assist the coroner in his investigations into unnatural and non-accidental deaths." He spoke clearly, addressing the jurors in a way that showed he had been in this position many times before. There was no hesitation to his voice, no hint of nervousness. "I was informed by Mr Gillingham of the death of Lord Waters, and before I begin my account of the findings I would like to extend my sympathy to Lord Waters' widow and children."

Jane could not see Lady Waters' face, but she did not move and gave no sign of acknowledgement. However, Mrs Upton and Mr Fortescue both gave little nods in thanks.

"Please tell us what you found, Dr Tomkins."

"Of course. I was able to see the body of Lord Waters in situ, close to where he had collapsed in Parade Gardens. I understand he had been moved a little from his original position by concerned friends and family members seeking to confirm he had passed away. My initial impression was that he had collapsed suddenly and died quickly." Dr Tomkins cleared his throat and addressed the jurors directly. Jane got the sense he enjoyed this part of his work, however macabre, but she could not judge a man for seeking out a stimulating occupation for the mind. "Lord Waters' body was then removed from the park and taken to the undertaker's premises, where I examined it more closely."

Jane saw Mrs Upton close her eyes in anticipation of a description of what came next.

"After discussion with Mr Gillingham and the deceased's family, it was decided that a full post-mortem would not be conducted."

There was a ripple of surprise in the stuffy room. If the coroner thought there was even a chance of a suspicious death, normally everything was done to gather evidence.

"However, I was able to conduct a full external examination, and in so doing I discovered signs of poisoning. There was the dilation of the pupils, as mentioned by my colleague Dr Black, as well as some subtle discoloration around the lips and tongue. I believe this is enough to conclude that Lord Waters was poisoned with belladonna."

For a moment there was absolute silence in the room. Jane had not expected anything so definite. She had attended a few inquests before with Lord Hinchbrooke, and the medical men were always vague and uncommitting. Normally they would say there was a possibility of poisoning, or on balance a death was natural. They would not declare that they were without doubt looking at a murder and that they could be sure of the poison.

Beside her, Dr Black shook his head and started to rise.

"This is not a time for debate or questions," Mr Gillingham said, glaring pointedly at Dr Black. "Each witness has their appointed time to speak, and I expect everyone in this room to respect that."

Dr Black sank down again, still shaking his head.

"Thank you, Dr Tomkins," Mr Gillingham said, dismissing the doctor from his position at the front of the room.

Jane expected the coroner to address the jurors now, to remind them of the possible verdicts available to them. In every inquest she had been to the coroner influenced the jurors heavily, guiding them to interpret any evidence presented in a certain way. She was shocked when Mr Gillingham instead called another witness to testify.

"Gentlemen, I am sure you all know Mr Winters, our local magistrate," the coroner said in introduction. "Mr Winters, please recount what occurred just an hour ago."

"Thank you, Mr Gillingham. Earlier today I was informed of Dr Tomkins' conclusions, and after discussion with Mr

Gillingham I decided it would be wise to search the deceased's house." He paused and Jane saw him cast an uneasy glance at Lady Waters. "In Lady Waters' bedroom we found a small bottle of belladonna, labelled as the poison and hidden amongst her personal effects in one of her drawers."

A gasp travelled around the room and all eyes turned to the petite woman in the front row. Lady Waters seemed stunned, not moving at first, and then shaking her head slowly. Jane clutched the back of the chair in front of her, shocked by the revelation.

"No," she whispered.

"Remember you have no authority here," Cassandra murmured in her ear. "Do not make enemies of these people."

Jane had been poised to rise, ready to object loudly and vehemently, but she knew Cassandra spoke sense. If she stood now, then she would lose any chance of uncovering the truth.

Lady Waters stood, swaying slightly, and turned a panicked face to the room. "It's not true," she said, the words barely audible over the noise of the crowd.

"Lady Waters," Mr Gillingham said, his tone cold and commanding. "Please come forward. You will have your opportunity to address the room."

The young widow leaned heavily on the arm of her maid, but as she turned to see all eyes on her, she collapsed to the floor in an elegant heap.

CHAPTER EIGHT

Dr Black moved first, pushing through the gawping crowd to Lady Waters' side and crouching down. He took one delicate wrist in his hand and counted under his breath.

"She has fainted, nothing more," he said after thirty seconds. "Give her some space, and someone fetch a glass of water."

For a moment no one moved, and then Mr Gillingham took charge, ordering his staff to clear the room.

Mrs Leigh-Perrot clutched at Jane, trying to lead her out when it was their turn to move, but Jane stood firm.

"Dr Black!" she called, catching the young doctor's attention. "I wonder if it would be beneficial for Lady Waters to see a friendly face when she comes around."

Dr Black motioned her over to where Lady Waters was just beginning to stir. Her eyelids fluttered prettily and although her complexion was pale, she looked beautiful and fragile all at once.

"Lady Waters, you fainted," Jane said softly, taking the baroness's hand in her own.

"I didn't do it, Miss Austen," Lady Waters said, her words barely more than a whisper. "I know what it looks like, but I didn't kill my husband."

"They will see their mistake," Jane said with more conviction than she felt.

"Has she recovered?" Mr Gillingham said, towering over where Jane and Dr Black crouched beside Lady Waters.

"She will need a few minutes," Dr Black said firmly. He was young for a doctor, in his late twenties or early thirties, but nevertheless he had a quiet confidence about him and did not seem in the least bit cowed by the intimidating coroner.

"This matter needs concluding."

"And it will be, but she needs a few minutes."

Mr Gillingham grunted and retreated, but only as far as his chair where he had sat to oversee the inquest.

"Are you comfortable? Shall we sit you up a little?" Jane helped Lady Waters to manoeuvre into a more upright position. The colour was returning to the baroness's cheeks now, and she looked a little less dazed.

"I feel like a fool," Lady Waters said quietly.

"Did you know they were going to accuse you?"

"No. I let the magistrate and Mr Gillingham into the house earlier. They told me they needed to conduct a search of my late husband's papers. I thought nothing of it and removed myself to the garden. I never thought they would search my belongings."

Jane desperately wanted to ask if it was true that she had a bottle of belladonna in her possession, but she was conscious of the coroner sitting close by.

"Drink this," Dr Black said, handing Lady Waters the glass of water that had been brought in by an assistant. "It will make you feel a little better."

Lady Waters sipped at the drink and after a minute nodded her head resolutely.

"You are ready to begin again?" Mr Gillingham said. There was no flicker of compassion on his face, nothing to suggest he felt anything but contempt for the young woman in front of him.

"Yes."

"Recall the jurors. Everyone except the interested parties can stay outside. This has become too much of a circus as it is."

Silently the jurors filed back into the room, their faces set. If they had seemed biased before Lady Waters collapsed, they looked positively against the young woman now. Jane wondered if they had been discussing the case and the evidence outside and knew this would not have been a good thing.

The room was much less crowded as Jane slipped into a seat beside Dr Black, and she was relieved when no one ordered her out of the room. Mr Fortescue had also re-entered and now sat glowering at his stepmother. Mrs Upton and her husband were also allowed back in and had taken seats to one side, near the jury.

"We will keep this brief, Lady Waters," Mr Gillingham said.

"Thank you."

"I understand Lord Waters was your third husband?"

"Yes."

"You have been widowed twice before?"

"Yes."

"You are awfully young to have been widowed three times."

"Yes." This was said much more quietly, and Lady Waters' face showed her anguish.

"Lord Waters was much older than you?"

"Yes." She inhaled deeply and turned to Mr Gillingham. "I hardly see why that is relevant. I thought the point of an inquest was to establish the facts around a death, nothing more. I do not see how your judgement of my marriage is relevant."

Jane felt a rush of elation for Lady Waters, but as she glanced at the jurors it was short-lived. These gentlemen were from the class of society that liked their women silent and obedient. Any show of resistance, any spark of character and they would not hesitate to let their prejudice cloud their judgement.

Mr Gillingham sat up a little straighter in his seat. "Please confine your answers to the questions asked, Lady Waters. It is vital the jurors are given the full information around a case so they can decide on the right verdict." He nodded officiously and then continued with his questioning. "Do you deny having a bottle of belladonna secreted in your chest of drawers?"

There was a long silence and Jane found herself holding her breath. What Lady Waters said next could damn her.

"I do not deny it."

A ripple of unease spread through the room, with many of the jurors leaning forward or shifting in their chairs.

"Where did you obtain the belladonna?"

"From a doctor. It was a few years ago, when I resided in London."

"Why did you have the belladonna, Lady Waters?"

"On occasion I would drop a small amount into my eyes as a beauty treatment — but I have not used it for years!"

Jane had heard of such nonsense: women who wanted their eyes to appear bigger and brighter would use tiny amounts of a substance like belladonna to obtain the effect. There were hundreds of similar remedies, many of them dubious in their success and perhaps even detrimental to the user's health.

"A beauty treatment," Mr Gillingham said, his voice thick with disbelief. "I will ask you directly, Lady Waters: did you add belladonna poison to your husband's drink yesterday with the intention of killing him?"

"No!"

Mr Gillingham grunted and shook his head. "That will be all, Lady Waters."

"I did not kill him — I loved my husband."

"I said that will be all."

It was a biased and unfair process, with the coroner only asking the questions that would push the jury into one verdict.

"Gentlemen of the jury, I would like you all now to follow me. We can retire to a private room and discuss the finer details of this case and the possible verdicts that can be given."

The wait for the jury and coroner to reappear was only a few minutes, but Jane felt her heart thumping the entire time. Dr Black gave her a reassuring little nod as the doors opened and the coroner re-entered the room, looking grim.

"Thank you for your patience," he said, addressing his comment to Mr Fortescue. "As you are aware, there are a number of different verdicts the jury can come to at an inquest. We have discussed the possibilities, including finding this was a natural death, an accidental death, or an unlawful killing either by person or persons unknown or by a specified suspect." He turned to the men of the jury. "Foreman of the jury, what is your verdict?"

One man stood, his eyes fixed on the coroner and Jane knew immediately what the verdict was going to be. If there was a reprieve for Lady Waters, the juror would have at least glanced at her, but instead he refused to acknowledge her.

"We find Lord Waters' death was unnatural. We return a verdict of murder."

"Thank you for your diligence here today, gentlemen," Mr Gillingham said. "Please go about your day knowing you have given great service to your community."

There was silence as the men of the jury filed out of the room, leaving only a select group to witness what was to follow.

The inquest was not a criminal trial and the coroner had no authority to declare Lady Waters responsible for the murder of her husband, but as the magistrate stepped forward, Jane saw how carefully this whole thing had been orchestrated.

"Come with me quietly now," Mr Winters said, reaching out to steady Lady Waters as she stood.

"Please, I don't understand," Lady Waters said, but the panic in her eyes showed that she understood only too well.

"I am taking you into custody to await trial for the murder of your husband."

"I haven't done anything. I didn't kill him."

"It will all come out in the trial, my lady," Mr Winters said politely. There was none of the coroner's brashness about him, but somehow his gentle manner made the situation worse.

With one hand on her arm, the magistrate guided Lady Winters through the middle of the room. As they passed Jane, the widow reached out desperately and clutched at Jane's hand.

"I didn't do this, Miss Austen — do you believe me?"

Despite hardly knowing the woman, Jane nodded. "I believe you," she said quietly. "You are not alone."

"Promise you will help me."

"I promise."

The words came out before Jane could think through the consequences, but as Lady Waters was led away Jane realised the magnitude of her vow. She was not in Hampshire now. She did not know the people of Bath; she could not use her lifelong friendships to ask for introductions or secure invitations to places she should not be in. What was more, here in Bath she did not have the protection of her mentor, Lord Hinchbrooke. For a terrible moment Jane felt completely alone, but as she saw Lady Waters being pressed into a carriage she rallied. She could manage to make herself a little unpopular around Bath if it meant saving her new friend from the noose.

CHAPTER NINE

It felt wrong to be sitting in the sunshine, revelling in the late afternoon warmth, when Lady Waters was incarcerated, but Jane tried to push any guilt from her mind. She was resting on a bench by the river, shielding her eyes from the glinting rays of the sun as they reflected off the water. Cassandra was perched quietly next to her.

Their aunt had wanted to sweep them into her protective embrace after the inquest had concluded, but Jane had pleaded a heavy head and persuaded her that a walk by the river with Cassandra would do her good, especially as they promised to be no more than an hour. So far they had spent much of the time in silence, Jane overwhelmed by the weight of the task on her shoulders.

"I do not think you have a choice," Cassandra said eventually.

"I cannot abandon Lady Waters, however recent our acquaintance."

Cassandra shook her head. "I was not suggesting you abandon her."

Jane looked at her sister sharply. Cassandra was normally the cautious one, the calming influence that curbed Jane's impetuousness. In the past when Jane had found herself embroiled in criminal matters, Cassandra had advocated for a distancing approach.

Cassandra fiddled with the ribbons of her bonnet, ensuring the bow was symmetrical before speaking again. "There was great injustice in that room," she said quietly. "It was an ambush, pure and simple. The facts arranged to make Lady Waters look guilty."

"You do not think she is guilty?"

"I do not know. Certainly there are a few factors that cast suspicion on her, but Mr Gillingham wove a story in the inquest that had everyone seeing the facts he presented from just one angle."

"Coroners are meant to start an inquest impartial," Jane said, thinking of the few others she had attended in Hampshire.

"Mr Gillingham's mind was made up before he even entered the room, and what is worse is that he worked to persuade everyone else to share his opinion."

"So you do not object to me looking into the matter?" Jane said.

"I think you are obligated to, but it will not be easy, Jane. We are outsiders here; we have no history with these people. They will not want to talk to you."

"No," Jane said, biting her lip. "It is a small community, and Mr Fortescue appears to have a lot of connections. You saw how he greeted the gentlemen of the jury. And we both saw how everyone treated Lady Waters, even when her husband was alive. She is a baroness, yet people barely acknowledged her."

"I wonder where the animosity stemmed from? Lord Waters held the power in the marriage. He had the money and the title. Mr Fortescue can hardly have been concerned his stepmother was unduly influencing his father."

"Perhaps he thought she was spending too much of the money he would one day otherwise inherit," Cassandra said, shrugging. "Or perhaps he did not like the fact his father had married again after the death of his mother, and he took that dislike out on Lady Waters."

"We will need to find out," Jane said. She was daunted by the prospect of investigating Lord Waters' death and was realistic about the obstacles she would face, but part of her felt that familiar thrill of anticipation.

"You can't do this alone, Jane."

"You wish to help me?" The idea was surprising. For the last year Cassandra had supported her in her dealings with Lord Hinchbrooke, mainly by acting as chaperon so their parents could not object too much, but never before had she shown an interest in actually assisting Jane.

Cassandra gave her a small smile. "We are a long way from home, Jane. I do not think you can do this alone, and I am not sure my conscience will allow me to stand by and do nothing."

Jane gripped her sister's hand and squeezed it tightly. "Thank you."

"Where do we begin? Aunt Jane will not be happy if we suddenly start gallivanting all over Bath, questioning suspects and pestering the local undertaker to let us view a dead body."

"Yet we do need to see the body," Jane said quietly, aware of the couples strolling arm in arm along the riverbank close by. "Dr Black seemed sympathetic to Lady Waters' plight, and from what I have seen so far, I think he is an honest man."

Cassandra tapped her fingers on the wooden slats of the bench. "He does not seem to be beholden to Mr Fortescue, nor in awe of him as are so many other people in Bath."

"I wonder if he might help us to secure a few minutes to inspect Lord Waters, perhaps tell us a little more about why he suspects poison."

"There is no harm in asking," Cassandra said.

Jane felt her mind begin to whir into action. She had been stunned by the events at the inquest, swept along in the confusion and uncertainty that followed the sudden death of

Lord Waters. For a whole day she had been forced into a passive role, only reacting to events as they happened. Now it felt good to be on the offensive, to start to plan what she might do to gain the upper hand.

"We need to talk to Lady Waters. I wonder where they took her? I do not know if there is a gaol in Bath."

"Our uncle will know. I will ask him."

Jane looked sideways at her sister. "If we ask for permission to visit Lady Waters, our aunt will say no."

"I know."

"I can live with telling a few little lies — my conscience is happy to weigh them against the greater good — but I do not wish to corrupt you, Cassandra. If you would rather I did not tell you my plans and went about this alone, I would not blame you."

"No," Cassandra said sharply. "It would be reckless. I know not where this will lead us, but for now I am happy to accompany you."

Jane felt the weight lift from her shoulders. It would be difficult to navigate through the connections and loyalties in a town where they barely knew anyone. Having Cassandra by her side would make things significantly easier.

"We must also speak to the other people involved, to see if they might be suspects or to uncover anyone else who might have wanted to cause Lord Waters harm." She checked them off on her fingers. "Mr Fortescue, Mrs Fortescue, Mrs Upton."

"Mr Fortescue is the new Lord Waters now," Cassandra said. "It will make him even more influential."

"I think we need to get a better picture of his relationships before we speak to Mr Fortescue," Jane said. "Otherwise he will dismiss us; there will be no reason for him to speak to us."

"Mrs Upton will not be easy either. She is hardly likely to let anything slip — she's sharp and calculating."

They lapsed into silence, the enormity of the task ahead of them only just starting to register.

Cassandra stood and held out her hand to Jane, her face more animated than it had been in weeks. "Where to, Miss Austen?"

"Let us go and see a doctor about a dead body."

Dr Black lived in a smart townhouse on the corner of Great Pulteney Street and Henrietta Street, a sandy-coloured terrace that had four floors above street level and one below. It was an impressive dwelling for a man who could have only been out of medical school for at most ten years, and Jane wondered whether family money was involved in his being able to afford such a property. There was a shiny plaque next to the door stating his name and qualifications.

The downstairs of the house was set up as his consulting rooms. What would have normally been a drawing room was set with comfortable chairs and decorated in light, calming colours. A set of doors were flung open to reveal another room, but Jane could see they would be closed for privacy. In the second room she caught a glimpse of an examination couch as well as a huge desk and shelves filled with heavy books lining the walls.

"Can I help you?" A woman glided out of the inner room. She was tall and thin, a pair of spectacles perched on her nose and her hair drawn back into a tight bun.

"We're looking for Dr Black," Jane said.

"Dr Black's consulting hours are from nine until one every weekday. He only sees emergencies after this time. Is this an emergency?" She eyed them dubiously.

"No, we do not need medical attention," Jane said.

The woman looked at them with a frown. "Wait here, please. Can I take your names?"

"Miss Jane Austen and Miss Cassandra Austen."

"Ah, the Austen sisters," the woman said, her expression brightening. "You should have said." She gripped the banister that lined a sweeping staircase, threw her head back and called out, "John, the Austen sisters are here to see you!"

There was a brief pause followed by the sound of footsteps before Dr Black appeared on the stairs.

"Miss Jane Austen and Miss Cassandra Austen, what a delightful surprise. I do hope neither of you has been taken ill? Although after that farce of an inquest I would not be surprised."

"John," the woman said, a warning note in her voice.

"My sister thinks I speak too freely," Dr Black said, guiding all three ladies into his consulting room and motioning for Jane and Cassandra to sit on the two comfortable chairs opposite the desk. He perched on the edge of the desk and motioned for his sister to take the straight-backed chair that would normally be his. "But I think I am amongst people who are of the same opinion, Caroline. The inquest was a shambles. Mr Gillingham only asked the questions that gave a very specific answer, those that would add to the carefully curated picture he was trying to build."

"That is exactly what I said," Jane murmured in agreement.

"I beg you not to think of us as an entirely unscrupulous lot here in Bath," Dr Black said with a rueful smile. "It is only our officials who are corrupt and self-serving." He paused and looked at the two sisters, his eyes flicking over them, making an assessment. "Correct me if I am wrong, but I do not think you came to call this afternoon merely to discuss the unfairness of that debacle of an inquest."

Jane cleared her throat, sitting up straighter. "I understand my request to be unorthodox, but I beg you to at least listen to what I ask," she said, trying to instil a note of confidence into her voice.

Dr Black raised an eyebrow and his sister leaned forward in her chair.

"My sister and I live in a small village in Hampshire, and a little over a year ago a good friend of ours was killed. She was murdered at a ball we were attending."

Miss Black exclaimed softly, but Jane pushed on. It still made her uncomfortable to receive condolences over the loss of her friend. The crime was solved and the perpetrator had faced justice of sorts, but Jane didn't think she would ever shake the feelings of guilt and regret over her friend's death.

"It brought us into contact with our local magistrate, a decent and conscientious man. Lord Hinchbrooke allowed me to assist him in seeking justice for my friend, and since then he has been kind enough to provide guidance and wisdom on a number of criminal matters I have come across."

"What interesting lives you lead in Hampshire, Miss Austen."

"You would be surprised," Cassandra murmured.

"I do not profess to be an expert on crime or the law. I have no authority whatsoever, but I do have determination and a desire to get to the truth."

"You plan to help Lady Waters?"

Jane hesitated for a minute and then shook her head. "I plan to investigate the death of Lord Waters. There is a chance Lady Waters did kill her husband, and if that is the case I will not shy away from the truth. However, I think there could be another explanation, another culprit. I also believe that if I do not investigate this matter, no one else will. In the eyes of the coroner he has a suspect locked up with at least some evidence against her. There is nothing pushing him to look for another suspect, to question the facts that have already been presented."

"I applaud your spirit, Miss Austen. Our justice system is complex and superior to many throughout the world, but it is not infallible."

"Lady Waters may be a baroness, but she has no one to advocate for her. She is young, and I do not believe she has any family. It is all too easy for someone to arrange the facts so they point at her and be confident there is no one who will challenge them." Jane paused, glad to see Dr Black was sympathetic to her cause. He had not laughed her out of his consulting room as many men would once they heard she proposed to investigate a murder with only the help of her sister.

"There is something you need my help with?"

"Yes," Jane said slowly. "I need to see Lord Waters' body."

Dr Black's eyes widened and his sister shifted uneasily in her chair.

"Surely that is not necessary," Miss Black said. "My brother and Dr Tomkins both examined the body."

Jane bit her lip. It was difficult to explain how important viewing the body in a murder case was. Lord Hinchbrooke had taught her how to observe, how to look for the tiniest of details. Only by looking at a man's hands could you see if his nails had been broken as he fought off an attacker. Only by looking into a man's eyes could you observe the minute red spots that were present when someone had been asphyxiated. Often a doctor would approach things from a medical point of view. He might note the faint yellow tinge to the person's skin that hinted their liver was starting to fail, but he might miss the threads caught under their fingernails if they had clawed at their assailant.

"Sometimes there are clues that can only be found when you are looking specially for them."

"I am eager to help you, Miss Austen," Dr Black said, a note of caution in his voice. "But I am not sure I can arrange a viewing of the body. Lord Waters will still be on the undertaker's premises now, as I doubt Mr Fortescue will want the body returned to the house. They will be preparing him for burial. The weather is such that they will not want to delay more than a few days before the funeral."

"If you could accompany us to the undertaker's, I am sure they would let us in," Jane said. She knew she was asking a lot. "I only need a few minutes, but it would be helpful if you were there."

"You do not think Lord Waters was poisoned? I thought that was your concern when he died yesterday."

"I feel almost certain he was poisoned, but there might be other things to consider." She looked up at Dr Black and bit her lip. "I can investigate Lord Waters' death without seeing the body, but it will make it harder."

For a long moment Dr Black did not move or speak, and then he gave a short, sharp nod.

"John, do you think that is wise? If people find out…" Miss Black said.

"My sister is right to be cautious. I have resided in Bath only two years. Even with the influx of new residents and all the building that has taken place over the last few years, it is difficult to build a business here. People consult the doctors they have known for years, and when they become too old or infirm they consult their sons."

"You are not from Bath, Dr Black?"

"No. My sister and I spent our early years in Cornwall, and then I went to study medicine in London. Once I qualified, I practised in London for a few years but we wanted a change of scenery. Bath seemed the ideal place."

"I would not want to put you in a difficult position," Jane said, knowing Dr Black would be risking his reputation if he helped her.

The doctor stood and paced the room for a minute, his eyes cast down at the floor. "Yes, I will help you, Miss Austen," he said eventually.

"Thank you."

"Let us go now, before I come to my senses."

"I will accompany you," Miss Black said, ignoring the horrified look her brother gave her. "Miss Cassandra Austen and I can distract the undertaker whilst you and Miss Jane Austen inspect the body."

Jane didn't argue, knowing Miss Black would likely be able to dissuade her brother from helping them if she desired.

They waited whilst Miss Black fetched a bonnet and Dr Black his hat and cane, and then they set out along the streets.

The undertaker's shop was situated about half a mile away, tucked behind the imposing buildings of the town centre in the smaller, older passageways beyond. This was the Bath that would have stood a hundred years ago, before the building of the grand townhouses and the impressive public buildings.

Despite being tucked away, the undertaker's shop had a smart front that looked as though it had been recently painted. The woodwork was a glossy black and below it were spotless windows. A sign in the window welcomed people inside and gave a list of some of the services provided.

Dr Black stepped forward and rapped on the door with the top of his cane. Jane watched as the young man straightened his back and squared his shoulders as the door began to open. Despite his confident demeanour, it seemed that Dr Black was feeling nervous.

"Dr Black, this is a surprise." The man who opened the door was tall and thin with a gaunt face. His long hair was tied at the nape of his neck and only served to make him look even more like a ghoul. Jane had to suppress a shudder at the thought of meeting him in a graveyard at dusk.

"I was at the inquest earlier this afternoon and I wanted to clarify something before making a written report for the magistrate. It will take a few minutes only."

The undertaker hesitated, looking at the three women standing behind him.

"I agreed to escort my sister and her friend to the shops after," he said in explanation. "If you would be so kind as to let them wait in the shop, Mr Hempshaw."

Mr Hempshaw duly stood aside, letting them all in.

"This is my assistant," Dr Black said, indicating Jane. "She takes notes for me and will take dictation for the report for the magistrate. Would you show us to Lord Waters' body?"

Mr Hempshaw hesitated again, but Dr Black made the request sound so reasonable, so routine, that the undertaker nodded and led the two of them through the dark passageway from the shop at the front to the working areas behind. Off to one side were small rooms with a stout table and a few chairs, for the purpose of letting relatives view or sit with the deceased when they did not want to have them in their home before the funeral. On the other side of the passageway the heavy wooden doors were firmly closed, but from the faint aromas that were drifting out Jane assumed this was the working part of the undertakers, the place where the bodies were prepared for viewing and burial.

It was outside one of these doors that Mr Hempshaw paused and took out a large set of keys, going through them methodically before he selected one to fit into the lock.

"Are you sure your assistant wants to see this?" He spoke quietly, his eyes flicking to Jane and then away again.

"She has a strong stomach," Dr Black assured the undertaker. Leaning towards Jane, he murmured in her ear, "You do have a strong stomach, don't you?"

"I do."

There was an overpowering chemical smell in the room. Jane saw a casket on a bench, the only one in the room, although the lid had not yet been secured and was propped up against a wall.

"Lord Waters is going to be interred in the family tomb," Mr Hempshaw said, standing sombrely in the doorway. "I believe the funeral is tomorrow."

"Without his wife," Jane murmured. Right now it was the least of Lady Waters' concerns, but if she did manage to survive this, the widow would always be haunted by the fact she had missed her husband's funeral.

"Good," Dr Black said, his tone professional and brusque. "I just need a few minutes, Mr Hempshaw." He looked at the undertaker pointedly, but Mr Hempshaw seemed reluctant to leave them.

Jane began fanning herself with her hand. "I do feel a little warm, and I would hate to be overcome by the … scent. I don't suppose I could trouble you for a glass of water, Mr Hempshaw?"

The undertaker grunted but disappeared from the doorway. Jane quickly pushed the door to, leaving it open only a crack so they would hear his footsteps approaching.

"Well done, Miss Austen. I feel this is not your first time dissembling for the sake of a worthy cause."

"I do believe sometimes the ends justify the means. Mr Hempshaw was expecting me to swoon and so I played to that expectation." Jane hesitated before approaching the casket on the bench. She had seen dead bodies before, but it wasn't something she thought she would ever become accustomed to. "Will you talk me through your findings, Dr Black?"

"Of course. There isn't all that much to see, and I understand they did not conduct a post-mortem to view Lord Waters' internal organs."

"Is that usual?"

Dr Black thought for a moment and shrugged. "Post-mortems in themselves are rare. They're mostly done for scientific discovery, the furthering of our medical knowledge. At the medical schools in London, the dissection of a body after death is one of the main ways anatomy is taught, and surgical skills as well. Yet these are normally poor people, either criminals who have been executed or those desperate enough to sell the bodies of their relatives to the medical schools for a few coins. Post-mortems as a means to discover the cause of death is not a widespread practice, but there was a doctor at Guy's hospital, a mentor of mine, who advocated for them when a death seems suspicious. Slowly that practice has trickled out here to the provinces. I know of two such cases in Bath over the last couple of years, similar cases to this one where it was not entirely clear on first look whether the deaths were natural or unnatural."

As he spoke, Jane suppressed the roil of nerves deep in her belly and peered over the edge of the casket. At first glance it looked as though Lord Waters might rise up at any moment and berate someone for leaving him in such an uncomfortable place to sleep.

"He looks peaceful, does he not?" Dr Black said.

"Yes, more so than at the moment of his death."

Dr Black leaned in closer and lifted the old man's left eyelid. "Look, here are the dilated pupils we talked about before." The pupil was large, much larger than was natural, the blue of the iris only a small sliver around the outside.

"Could it have been caused by anything other than belladonna?"

"Yes, a few things. There are other poisons. I have also seen it when there has been massive trauma to the head, but that obviously isn't the cause here." He leaned over a little more, and with a grimace manoeuvred the corpse's jaw open a little. It was stiff and Jane felt herself clenching her own jaw in sympathy.

"Is there something in his mouth?"

"Look at his tongue and the inside of his lips. The signs are very subtle, even more so now some time has passed, but at the park I thought his lips and tongue looked dry. However, from what I understand he had drunk well with lunch and there is no reason for him to look dehydrated."

Jane nodded thoughtfully but wasn't sure she could see the subtle sign Dr Black was pointing out to her. "Is there anything else?"

"Not really, nothing definite. He has some swelling around the ankles that indicates a weakness in his heart and some discoloration in his legs, which I often see in elderly patients when their blood does not flow through the veins as easily as it does for a young man."

"Does that mean anything?"

Dr Black shrugged. "I would have been surprised if he survived for more than a few years. He was an elderly man with a weak heart and poor circulation. Whoever killed him must have had a pressing reason. Anyone close would have been aware of his failing health and the fact that he was likely to pass away in the relatively near future, yet they still decided to murder him."

"That is helpful," Jane said, nodding. Ever since Lord Waters' death, her mind had been filled with possible motives. Money was the obvious one, the inheritance Lord Waters would leave behind. As his only son, Mr Fortescue could expect to inherit the title and any property that was tied to it, but Lord Waters could have made any number of bequests, leaving his wife or his daughter a substantial amount. "So anyone hoping to inherit something from Lord Waters wouldn't have had to wait too long, even without taking it upon themselves to murder the old man?"

"Unless there was a pressing need for money, it would be foolish to do so."

Jane nodded, glancing at the empty doorway behind her and quickly continuing with her inspection of the body. She checked Lord Waters' hands and felt in his pockets, but everything had been removed by the undertaker, no doubt set aside to be returned to Mr Fortescue.

"The emeralds have gone, Miss Austen," Dr Black said as he watched her search.

"Yes, that magistrate said he returned them to Mr Fortescue to keep safe until the will is read." She paused, her mind still on the gems. "Why would Lord Waters take an expensive emerald necklace out with him to the park of all places?"

"It does seem odd," Dr Black said with a frown.

A few seconds later they heard the sound of footsteps on the flagstones that lined the corridor outside. Jane quickly took a step back, assuming a demure, slightly horrified expression as she retreated into the corner of the room.

"Here," Mr Hempshaw said as he threw open the door and thrust out the cup of water he had collected for her.

Jane took it, peering at the dirty water, discoloured and with grime floating around the edges.

"Thank you," she said, raising the cup to her lips and waiting for Mr Hempshaw to look away before lowering it again. She didn't know where the undertaker had got the water from, but it looked as though it had been collected straight from the river Avon.

"Thank you for your assistance, Mr Hempshaw," Dr Black said, stepping away from the casket and holding his hand out to shake the undertaker's.

"You're welcome," Mr Hempshaw said, bowing his head, still looking at them suspiciously. Jane wondered if he had lingered and listened at the door, overhearing the first part of their discussion. If he had, then no doubt Mr Fortescue would hear of it shortly.

CHAPTER TEN

Jane and Cassandra left Dr Black and his sister at the bottom of New Bond Street and walked arm in arm up George Street to The Paragon. Their pace was slow, and to the casual observer they looked like two ladies enjoying a pleasant afternoon stroll. In truth they were deep in discussion, their heads bowed together and their voices hushed so no one could overhear them.

Before they had parted, Dr Black had promised to write out a list of possible poisons. He assured Jane there were a few others that could produce the same effect as the deadly belladonna, but he had wanted to consult his medical books before he gave her a definitive list.

"What do we do next?" Cassandra said as they neared the top of the hill. Her expression was animated, and Jane was thankful that something had managed to rouse her sister from her melancholy. She knew it was a temporary effect, that as soon as their investigation was over and they returned to the routine of day-to-day life Cassandra's thoughts would once again slip to Thomas Fowle and the life they should have had together, but for now it was enough to have her sister distracted.

"I think we need to see Lady Waters. We know only a little of her past, of her marriages before she met Lord Waters. And we have made assumptions about her relationships with her stepchildren, but it would be good to hear about them from her."

"Let us find where she is likely to be held, and then we will decide how to approach our aunt and uncle."

"They will not let us visit her in prison," Jane said, feeling nauseous at the idea of even asking.

Cassandra pressed her lips together. "No, they are not as susceptible to your words of persuasion as our parents."

Jane smiled, knowing her sister was right. She knew how to appeal to their father's sense of justice, his need for order, and then she would change tack entirely when dealing with her mother and use a more emotional approach. Their aunt and uncle were not used to her methods of persuasion, which could work to Jane's advantage. However, they were also adamant that it was their responsibility to protect Jane and Cassandra from the cruel realities of the world and at the same time safeguard their reputations.

As they approached number one, The Paragon, they paused at the sight of an unfamiliar carriage outside. There were no markings to indicate who it belonged to, but the exterior was freshly painted and the horses well groomed.

The maid, Mary, opened the door, as if she had been sent to look out for them. As she ushered them in, she nodded towards the drawing room.

"There is a guest, Miss," said Mary, directing her words at Jane. "She is waiting for you."

Jane took off her bonnet and passed it over to Mary. She took a moment to smooth down her hair and then glanced at Cassandra, who nodded to show she would be right behind her sister.

"Sorry we are so late," Jane said as she breezed into the room. "Cassandra and I had a stroll by the river and completely lost track of time."

Mrs Upton was sitting on one of the comfortable chairs, sipping from a dainty teacup. She smiled indulgently at them.

"Mrs Upton has come to call," Mrs Leigh-Perrot said, rising from her chair and fussing around Cassandra and Jane.

"I am sorry we were out when you arrived," Cassandra said.

They all sat in a rustle of fabric and Jane looked appraisingly at their guest.

"Now you are here, I will speak bluntly," Mrs Upton said. "I wanted to apologise for allowing you to be dragged into our family drama." She leaned forward, an expression of concern on her face. "I have daughters of a similar age to you and I know only too well how important it is that not a whiff of scandal should attach itself to you."

Jane tried to keep her expression neutral, aware that Mrs Upton was trying to put them off.

"Unfortunately, my brother and I have been at odds with our stepmother ever since she married our father. It comes from a place of love, of course. We hated seeing our father duped in such a way, but it *is* a family matter."

"Do you think Lady Waters killed your father?" Jane said, ignoring the horrified gasp that came from her aunt.

Mrs Upton reacted well, smiling indulgently and holding out a restraining hand to Mrs Leigh-Perrot. "Please, do not chide Miss Austen on my account. I understand it is an unsettling matter to be caught up in, especially when you were beginning to view Lady Waters as a friend. Of course you have questions."

Jane summoned her most demure smile but didn't say anything, hoping Mrs Upton would continue.

The older woman sighed and nodded, a look of reluctant acceptance on her face. "Yes, I think there is a good chance Lady Waters killed my father."

"I know I do not know her as you do," Jane said, aware she was going to have to tread a careful line here to ask the questions she wanted to. "But I struggle to see what she would gain from it."

"Money," Mrs Upton said grimly.

"But she lived a life of luxury with your father. Surely there would be no need for her to kill him?"

Mrs Upton shrugged. "I do not pretend to understand her. Perhaps she did not like being tied to an old, infirm man."

Jane shook her head, realising this was something that had been bothering her about the whole affair. Everything they had seen showed how Lord Waters had doted on his wife. She wore luxurious gowns and lived in comfort, with a degree of freedom many women did not enjoy. Her husband indulged her, showering her with gifts and urging her to redecorate her new home so she might feel more comfortable in it. With Lord Waters' death she might get an allowance, but even if it was generous it was unlikely to match what she had had access to before his death.

"I am aware I have not known Lady Waters long, but she seemed most content with her life and doted on your father."

Mrs Upton stood, unable to disguise the irritation that crossed her face. "You're right, you have not known her long. Perhaps we should leave speculation to the judge and jury at her trial and stop this idle chatter."

Mrs Leigh-Perrot rose, smiling apologetically. "Thank you for your call, Mrs Upton. We appreciate your kindness."

Jane forced herself to smile and nod, though there were a hundred other questions she wished to put to the woman.

Mrs Upton left, striding from the room without a backwards glance. For a long moment no one spoke, all waiting for the front door to click closed and for Mrs Upton to walk far enough down the street that there was not the slightest chance she could hear them.

"Jane Austen, what were you thinking?" Mrs Leigh-Perrot said, starting to pace in front of the mantelpiece. "That was an incredibly rude way to talk to a woman who is in mourning."

"I am sorry, Aunt," Jane said, looking down. It had been a little insensitive. Ideally she would liked to have sat down with a willing and cooperative Mrs Upton to discuss the family structure and put together a picture of the animosities within the Fortescue clan. That was never going to happen, and it meant that either Jane had to content herself with working in the dark, or she had to ask difficult questions at inopportune times. "It was insensitive. My mind has been elsewhere today with the shock of everything that has happened."

Mrs Leigh-Perrot softened and reached out to pat Jane on the shoulder. "Of course, it has been a difficult day for you." She paused. "Your uncle and I were discussing the best thing to do before Mrs Upton arrived."

Jane nodded, her mind already elsewhere, wondering how best to confirm where Lady Waters would be held awaiting her trial.

"We think it might be for the best if you return to Hampshire," Mrs Leigh-Perrot said.

Jane's head shot up and she jumped to her feet. "No."

"Listen to me, Jane. It is not a punishment; we just feel that after a shock like this, it would be better if you were to return home."

Frantically Jane looked across at her sister, silently appealing for her to step in. Their aunt was more likely to listen if Cassandra objected too.

"We love having you girls stay with us, but perhaps it is better if you return home for a few weeks, until after the trial. It would give everything a chance to settle down, and then you could return to stay with us in July or August."

"No, please do not send us away."

There was a chance Cassandra would agree with their aunt and uncle. She had never asked to leave home, to come to Bath, and in her state of grief she might want to return to the familiar and routine. Jane hoped not. For two months Cassandra had sunk deeper and deeper into grief and melancholy. Here in Bath there had been a flicker of her former self, and since Lord Waters' murder she had been more interested in the world than she had been since the news of Thomas Fowle's death.

"We understand your concerns," Cassandra said softly. "But I hope you agree to let us stay a little longer. I feel my mood is lifting here in Bath, and I fear if we return to Steventon I might slip back into melancholy."

Mrs Leigh-Perrot quickly stopped her pacing and sat down next to Cassandra. "Of course, my dear, whatever you need. We only wish to do what is best for you girls."

"You are too good to me, Aunt," Cassandra said.

"Thank you," Jane added.

"You do need to be careful, though. Your poor mother would never forgive me if you returned to Hampshire with a stain on your reputations."

"Of course," Cassandra said. "We are making sure we go everywhere together and we will be careful of the company we keep from hereon in."

"You will give up this notion of looking into Lord Waters' death?"

Cassandra looked uncomfortable for a moment. Jane knew her sister did not like lying.

"I know you have had a certain involvement with the local magistrate in Hampshire, Jane, but you have no such connections here. It would be better for you to leave it to the authorities to investigate."

Jane suppressed a snort. She doubted the authorities were doing anything except adding to the evidence against Lady Waters.

"Both Jane and I can see the sense of allowing the experts to investigate," Cassandra said firmly. "Can't we, Jane?"

"Er, yes."

"Good. I will write to your mother, of course, and inform her of everything. She may decide it is best for her to come to Bath."

"We will write as well."

"I am sorry about how I spoke to Mrs Upton," Jane said after a moment. "I know I shouldn't have questioned her like that. I just feel for Lady Waters being thrown into a dungeon in some dank prison."

Mr Leigh-Perrot chuckled, but not unkindly. "Do not fret, Jane. They do not throw people of Lady Waters' status into dungeons. She is still a dowager baroness, even if she does not have the support of her late husband's family."

"Perhaps not a dungeon then, but into a dank cell?"

"She will be taken to the prison in Ilchester, but I doubt they will put her in a cell. I expect she will live quite comfortably in some rooms in the warden's house. Under lock and key, but otherwise able to maintain her dignity."

Ilchester was a place Jane had scarcely heard of, although she knew it was some distance away. It was in the county town of Somerset, and its distance from Bath meant Lady Waters was even more isolated from everyone and everything she knew.

"I wonder..." Jane began, knowing it was a risk to suggest her idea so soon after her aunt had urged her to drop the matter entirely. "I agree the investigation needs to be left to the authorities, but I do feel for Lady Waters, alone in Ilchester and thinking she has not a friend in the world. I think it would be the charitable thing to visit, to take her some clothes and food, and to let her know that not everyone has forgotten her."

"I'm not sure, Jane," Mrs Leigh-Perrot said, frowning.

"Our father is always talking about looking for those situations where it is difficult to be charitable, where it takes that little bit of extra effort," Jane said, wondering if their aunt would see through her manipulation. "I do not wish to visit to interrogate the woman, but I would like to visit her to show she is not alone."

Mrs Leigh-Perrot hesitated and Jane felt a flicker of hope.

"I shall think on it, Jane."

"Thank you."

"Would you excuse us?" Cassandra said, standing. "It has been a long and tiring day, and I think it would do us good to rest before dinner."

They took their leave of their aunt and hurried upstairs, Cassandra exhaling heavily as they closed the door behind them.

"Thank you for persuading our aunt we should stay here rather than go home," Jane said as her sister collapsed onto the bed.

"I do long for the fields of Hampshire," Cassandra said wistfully, "but I know how important this is."

"It is."

"We do need to be careful, though, Jane. The Fortescues and the Uptons are powerful as well as influential. They have a coroner and a magistrate within their circle, and who knows who else. We do not want them turning their focus onto us." As always, Cassandra spoke sensibly. Yet Jane knew she would choose the truth over keeping her distance from these people.

CHAPTER ELEVEN

It was another glorious day, and the sun was beating down on Jane and Cassandra's bonnets as they stood across the road from number seven, The Crescent. The evening before, Mrs Leigh-Perrot had informed them she would accompany them to Ilchester in two days' time for a short visit to Lady Waters whilst she was being held in custody. She had arranged with a friend to borrow a carriage for the trip so they would be travelling in comfort, but the thirty-five-mile journey would still take much of the day, so the plan was to stay in an inn overnight and return home the next day.

Jane had suggested they make an early start and walk up to The Crescent to collect some clothes and other personal items to take to Lady Waters, anything that might make her incarceration a little easier.

"He can't have moved in as yet, surely?" Jane murmured. They were debating whether Mr Fortescue might have moved from his own residence to his father's luxurious townhouse.

"It would be presumptuous. The funeral has not happened yet and the will has not been read. Lord Waters might leave this house to his wife or his daughter."

"Yet I wouldn't put it past Mr Fortescue to assume ownership and move in."

"Nor I," Cassandra said quietly.

They watched in silence for another few minutes. The curtains were drawn, the plants outside watered, but that merely meant the servants were still in residence and doing some of the jobs assigned to them. In all likelihood they were remaining in place in the hope that Mr Fortescue would continue to employ them if and when it became his household.

"Come on," Jane said eventually. "We cannot wait here all day to see if anyone comes or goes. If Mr Fortescue is in, we shall offer our condolences and leave."

Despite her words Jane felt a gnawing sensation in the pit of her stomach as she approached the front door. She knocked and took a step back, grateful for Cassandra's reassuring presence.

It took a minute for the door to be opened by the maid that had served them on their last visit to Lord and Lady Waters' house. She looked pale and drawn and regarded them with a surprised stare before stepping aside to allow them into the house.

"Lady Waters is not here, Miss," she said, struggling not to let anything slip that she shouldn't. From somewhere deep in the house the dog began to bark, and the maid looked over her shoulder, checking that he had not escaped.

"We know," Jane said. "It is Sarah, isn't it?"

"Yes, Miss."

"We were with your mistress two days ago when Lord Waters died and yesterday, at the inquest."

The maid's eyes widened and her lip quivered a little.

"Have you been given instructions, Sarah? From Mr Fortescue, perhaps?"

"Briefly, Miss. He came to collect a few things and told us he would be back to sort out the household in a few days."

Jane glanced at the stairs. There did not seem to be any other staff around, and she wondered if they were taking advantage of their absent mistress.

"Where is everyone?"

"Mrs Hope, the cook, doesn't live in, so she's gone home. Then there's Bill, who's the footman and Lucy the other maid who helps in the kitchens and upstairs. They're both abed. There's not much to be done at the moment, Miss. Please don't tell Mr Fortescue. I don't want to get them into trouble."

"Do not worry, Sarah. We are not here to make trouble for anyone."

"Do you know what has happened to my mistress?"

"She has been taken to the gaol in Ilchester to await trial."

Sarah swayed a little on her feet and Cassandra reached out to steady the young maid. "Come, no one will mind if you sit. It has been a difficult few days."

They led the maid through to the beautifully decorated drawing room they had sat in when they had visited Lady Waters' only a few days earlier. The maid hesitated before sitting, but Cassandra gently pressed her arm until the maid forgot her reservations.

"Did you like your mistress?"

Sarah bit her lip and then nodded. "The other servants don't talk kindly about her," she said quietly, "but that is because they are snobs. They've been with the Fortescue family a long time and think that she is an interloper. You'd think she was after *their* money from the way they look down on her."

"You haven't been with the Fortescue family a long time?"

"No, Lady Waters appointed me last year. There was some problem with her lady's maid, I'm not sure what, but she wanted someone she could train up." Sarah shrugged. "The house is not huge and Lady Waters is not demanding in her requests from a lady's maid, so it was agreed I would do some work as a housemaid as well."

"Then it must have hit you hard to hear she had been arrested."

Sarah nodded. "I am devastated about Lord Waters, of course. He was the kindest man, always asking whether my family were keeping well. Some masters do not even acknowledge their maids, but Lord Waters would always say please and thank you and would let us know our work was appreciated."

Jane often marvelled at how poorly some people treated their servants. At home they had Mrs White, their cook, and Lizzie, the maid, who were treated as part of the family. Jane and Cassandra would help with the chores and Mrs Austen was in the kitchen most days, preparing one part of dinner whilst Mrs White did another. It seemed ridiculous to treat servants badly; these were people who prepared your food, who saw you at your most vulnerable. Not to mention the fact they had hopes and dreams and personalities of their own.

"Then I am sorry for your loss."

"I do not think Mr Fortescue will be the same sort of master," Sarah said and then quickly covered her mouth, as if trying to push the words back in.

"Do not fear, we are not going to repeat anything you say to Mr Fortescue," Cassandra said kindly.

"It will be Mr Fortescue who gets the house, then?" Jane asked.

Sarah shrugged. "I do not know, but I doubt he will keep most of us. He has servants of his own, and he isn't likely to keep two households in Bath. Mrs Hope is already looking for a new position."

Jane nodded, absorbing the information. Although the situation was unfortunate for the servants, it did mean they would feel no loyalty to Mr Fortescue, and that should help to loosen Sarah's tongue when it came to the gossip that was inevitably passed between the household servants.

"We are planning on visiting Lady Waters in gaol tomorrow, making the trip to Ilchester. We will tell her of your support and loyalty," Jane said.

"You are truly going to visit her?"

"Yes, that is the main reason for our visit. I wanted to ask you to pack a few things for her, a change of clothes and some home comforts to make her stay a little more bearable."

"Of course, Miss." Sarah went to rise, but Jane reached out and stopped her before she could stand.

"Thank you, but before you do there were a couple of questions I wanted to ask you. I am hoping we can help her prove her innocence, but I need your help."

Sarah's eyes widened. "Whatever you need, Miss. As I said, Lady Waters was always kind to me."

"You must have seen what Lord and Lady Waters were really like together, not the show they put on for the rest of the world," Jane said, leaning in a little closer. "How would you describe their relationship?"

Sarah shifted in her seat and looked a little uncomfortable, and for a moment Jane thought she had lost the trust of the young maid by asking too personal a question so early in their exchange.

"It wasn't an act, if that is what you are suggesting. I know everyone said she was only with him for his money, but she was kind to him. She made him rest when he was taken unwell, ensured he always had his cup of tea first thing in the morning and protected him from the worst of his children's quarrelling." She shook her head, a note of defiance in her voice. "She may have married him because he was wealthy, but she was a good wife to him."

"Was he a good husband to her?"

113

"Oh yes, he doted on her. He was always surprising her with gifts and arranging little trips out for her." She looked away for a second and then continued. "The only thing he didn't do was stand up for her to his horrible children."

"Lady Waters said to us she didn't want to come between them."

"She is a woman of great patience," Sarah said.

"It doesn't sound as though she is someone who would be eager to kill Lord Waters."

"Oh no, Miss, I don't believe what they're saying at all. Why would she?"

"There were no secrets, nothing she told you as her lady's maid?" For a moment Sarah's eyes flicked away. It was only an instant, the hint of something hidden that her conscious mind wasn't quite quick enough to conceal. The young maid shook her head. "No, Miss, nothing."

"Do you know why there was such animosity between Mr Fortescue, Mrs Upton and Lady Waters?"

Sarah shrugged again. "I don't know for sure. I wasn't employed when she first arrived, but the other servants talk."

"What did they say?"

"That the marriage was very sudden. Lord Waters goes off to Brighton to take the sea air on the instruction of his doctor, and a month later he returns with a new bride twenty years younger than his children."

"He hadn't expressed a wish to marry again? Many men do take a second wife after they have lost their first, and I understand she died a good number of years ago."

"I don't know, Miss. You'd have to ask one of the servants who was here then." Sarah stood, glancing at the door, and Jane wondered if she had heard the stirring of someone upstairs. "I should go and collect some things for you to take to her."

"Thank you," Jane said, unable to press the matter further as the maid hurried from the room.

They sat in silence in the opulent drawing room, listening intently to the creaks and scrapes coming from the room above. Jane cocked her head to one side and looked up at the perfectly plastered ceiling.

"Would it be terribly rude if I went upstairs?" she murmured. "I remember Mr Winters said the belladonna was found in a chest of drawers, and I thought it might be helpful if I could look."

"Jane," Cassandra said, reaching out and putting a restraining hand on Jane's wrist. "It is one thing to question the maids, but quite another to go rifling through a woman's personal possessions."

"I am sure Lady Waters would not object if it could help prove her innocence."

"No, Jane. One of the other servants could see you and raise the hue and cry, telling everyone who would listen that a stranger has been digging around where their mistress kept a bottle of poison. You would end up in Ilchester County Gaol alongside Lady Waters, and what use would you be then?"

There was a murmur from outside the room, followed by the door being pushed open and a dishevelled footman and maid entering.

They drew up short at the sight of Jane and Cassandra.

"I am sorry," the footman said, recovering first. "I wasn't aware we had visitors."

The pair were dressed in their uniforms but not turned out anywhere near as smartly as they would have been if their master and mistress were in attendance. Jane could not blame them for taking advantage of a few easier days before the new master arrived or they had to go out and look for new positions in unknown households.

"We are collecting a few things for Lady Waters," Jane said, summoning her most friendly smile. "Sarah is just organising it for us."

"Sorry to disturb you," the footman said, already halfway out the door.

"It is Bill, isn't it? And Lucy?"

"Yes." Bill's tone had a curt edge to it now.

"Mr Fortescue said we would find you looking after the house," Jane said, silently acknowledging she would have to pray for forgiveness for her lies.

"You've spoken to Mr Fortescue?"

"Of course. He did not wish to select the items to be sent to Lady Waters himself, but he was happy for us to do it. He also said you would help us with any questions we had."

"Questions?" The footman looked unconvinced and Lucy the maid was hovering by the door, looking eager to escape.

"We will be seeing the magistrate later," Jane said, lowering her voice as if afraid someone could be listening, "and I told Mr Fortescue we would pass on any information that was helpful to the case."

"You are friends of Lady Waters?"

Jane smiled tightly. "We met Lady Waters for the first time a few days ago, and we were most devastated by the death of Lord Waters, as I am sure you were."

"Of course," Bill said stiffly.

"Good, then we are all on the same side."

"Sit down, Bill, Lucy," Cassandra said softly, her quiet voice carrying such authority that even Jane started in her seat.

The footman and maid complied, both perching on the fine furniture and glancing at the door. Jane was aware Sarah might come back downstairs at any moment. She needed to get to the important questions without any delay.

"Mr Fortescue implied that you were a good judge of character, Bill," Jane said, noting how the footman didn't swell with pride but instead kept looking at her cautiously. Sitting in on interviews with the magistrate Lord Hinchbrooke, Jane had seen how different people needed a different key to unlock them. For some it was flattery, for others it was allowing them to have a sense of superiority, and for a few it was bribery, pure and simple. The art came in assessing each person and finding their weakness, that one thing that made them want to talk. "And of course in your position, an observant man would be privy to all sorts of information."

"I also know how to be discreet."

"I am sure you do." Jane bit her lip, knowing she was going to have to take a gamble. Thinking of the flicker in Sarah's eye when Jane had pressed her about secrets, she said, "Mr Fortescue thought you might be the best person to speak to about this secret of Lady Waters'."

"Secret?" Bill said, frowning.

"Yes, he was sure she had one, something she was keeping from Lord Waters. Something significant."

Bill began to shake his head as Lucy murmured, "The man."

"The man?"

The young maid's eyes widened and she looked at Bill for reassurance. The footman cleared his throat and considered for a moment.

"This is for Mr Fortescue?"

Jane nodded.

"You will not present it as gossip?"

"No. If you help with this matter, he will know you are loyal and deserve a position in his new household." Jane felt the lie pricking at her conscience, but she forced herself to smile reassuringly.

"There was a man," Bill said quietly. "A few months ago. He came to the house and was hanging around outside."

"He was a rough sort," Lucy said, her eyes lighting up at the gossip. "He came to the kitchen door and Mrs Hope sent him away with a flea in his ear."

"He was here to see Lady Waters?"

"Yes, he asked to see her."

"He left, but later that afternoon when Lord Waters was resting, Lady Waters went out by herself. Lucy was coming back from the shops with a few things for Mrs Hope, and you saw Lady Waters talking to this man a few streets away, didn't you?"

Lucy nodded. "They looked uncomfortable, as if neither was at ease."

"What did this man look like?"

"He was of average height, strong-looking, with brown hair and an unshaven face."

"Have you seen him again?"

Lucy shook her head. "No, but after that Lady Waters pestered Lord Waters to buy her a dog. I always thought it was to give her an excuse to go out for long walks unaccompanied."

Jane raised her eyebrows. It was an impertinent suggestion from the maid, even with everything that had passed these last few days.

"You don't like Lady Waters?"

Lucy sniffed, trying to seem older than her years. "She is not like the rest of the Fortescues," she said haughtily.

Jane was stopped from asking any more by the return of Sarah. The lady's maid was carrying a soft bag which was bulging at the seams.

"I might have put too much in," she said as she entered the room, coming up short when she saw Bill and Lucy sitting on the sofa.

"Is that everything?" Bill asked, his manner cautious now.

"Yes, thank you."

They all watched as the two servants hurried from the room, waiting until their footsteps had receded.

"I didn't know what to pack," Sarah said, looking at the bag in her hands with uncertainty. "What do you send to a woman in gaol?"

"I am sure that whatever you have chosen, Lady Waters will be grateful."

"You will give Lady Waters my best wishes?"

"Of course," Jane said, standing. She had the sudden urge to get out of this house. No wonder Lady Waters had been unhappy. Not only had her husband's family been against her, but many of the servants had held her in contempt as well. No doubt they had been stiffly polite to her face, but it was easy to tell when someone had little respect for you. "Thank you for all your help."

Sarah saw them to the front door and Jane and Cassandra left the house in silence, neither daring to speak until they had left The Crescent and were walking along Brock Street.

"Jane Austen, I never knew you could be so economical with the truth," Cassandra said, giving her sister a stern look.

Jane felt the heat in her cheeks. It had been a necessary lie, but not something she was particularly proud of.

"What happens if that footman tells Mr Fortescue he answered all your questions because he thought it was *his* bidding?"

Shrugging, Jane walked a little faster. "Hopefully it won't happen, and if it does then I will deal with the consequences. There is no point in worrying about it now."

"I do not think that is what our aunt and uncle would say."

Jane grimaced, aware she was putting their future in Bath at risk. Changing the subject, she asked, "What did you make of this mysterious man they spoke of?"

"It could have been anyone, and it sounds as though it were months ago."

"You don't think Lady Waters was going out to meet him on her dog walks?"

"She would have to be supremely foolish if she were. She had a doting husband and her every need taken care of."

"People do foolish things for love."

Cassandra wrinkled her nose. "From the description the maid gave, he hardly sounds like the sort of man a woman would risk her marriage and her reputation for."

"No," Jane mused, a more disturbing thought coming to her mind. "But what if he is the one who supplied her with the belladonna?"

CHAPTER TWELVE

Lord Waters' funeral was to be held in St Michael's Church in the centre of Bath. There was to be a procession to the church, with the coffin transported in a black carriage pulled by two sleek horses. Family members and friends would follow behind, the whole thing a spectacle that would bring the streets of Bath to a halt.

Jane and Cassandra had taken up a position a little way from the church on a conveniently placed bench. They were close enough to see who was in attendance, but with their bonnets shading their faces from the sun and their heads bowed a little, it was unlikely anyone would notice them.

"Do you really think this is necessary?" Cassandra said, her expression drawn. "It feels as though we are intruding on this family's grief by being here."

"We're not in the church, Cassandra. We're sitting on a bench a good distance away, merely observing the proceedings. I doubt we shall be seen and if we are, no one will care."

Cassandra didn't say any more, her expression glum.

There had been no funeral in England for Thomas Fowle. He had been long dead and buried by the time the letter notifying his family of his passing had made it to England, and then it had been another week before his parents had sat weeping as they imparted the news to Cassandra. Jane knew the value of a funeral, the importance of having a dedicated time to mourn alongside the other people who cared for the deceased. It was another cruelty of Thomas Fowle's death thousands of miles away in the Caribbean.

"I am sure Father could arrange a memorial service for Mr Fowle," Jane said as they sat waiting.

Cassandra shook her head. "If his family had wanted that, they would have asked."

"They may still be in shock."

"I cannot impose my wishes on them, Jane. We were not married." That was one of the cruellest twists for Cassandra. She had been in love with Thomas Fowle for years, betrothed for almost as long, yet because they had not stood in front of a vicar and said their vows, her pain was seen as lesser. She mourned him as if she were his widow, but in the eyes of society their connection had been nowhere near as important.

They were saved from debating the matter further by the clatter of hooves on the cobbles as the horses approached, pulling the black carriage behind. It was by far the grandest funeral procession Jane had ever seen. Her father had officiated over many funerals, but most of the time the deceased was transported in a borrowed cart with the villagers trailing behind in their Sunday best. Here everything was orchestrated to show the wealth and status of Lord Waters and his family. Mr Hempshaw, the undertaker, walked in front of the carriage dressed in sombre back, and behind was a great procession of family members and friends.

"An expensive funeral," Cassandra muttered, her eyes darting over the crowd and settling on the carriage. "I have never seen anything like it, but it reminds me a little of the description Henry gave in his letter when he spent a week in London and saw Lord Wilson's funeral procession then. He said the mourners took an hour to get into the church, there were so many."

"Perhaps this is how all the titled and wealthy have their funerals," Jane said quietly, unable to tear her eyes away.

"Somehow it makes it worse, this ostentatious show. It is as if they are blanking Lady Waters out of Lord Waters' life, pretending she never existed. He will be laid to rest next to his first wife, and Lady Waters will probably not even get a mention."

"At present everyone thinks she murdered him."

"Am I being blind here, Cassandra?" Jane asked suddenly. "Am I letting my affection for the woman cloud my judgement?"

"No," Cassandra said slowly. "I was at that inquest. I saw how they pulled together all the evidence and formed it into a shape that would fit their narrative. There are questions for Lady Waters to answer, but I do not think she should have been hauled away on the evidence presented at the inquest."

"Good. Sometimes I think I form my opinions of people too quickly, good and bad."

"My opinion of Mr Fortescue was set in stone within ten seconds of meeting him," Cassandra said with a shudder. "The way he shouted at Lady Waters in her own drawing room showed a complete lack of manners, as well as a complete lack of sense."

"You're right. I question whether a man like that has the intelligence to put together the plan needed to allow the coroner to guide the jury to the conclusion they came to at the inquest."

They watched as Lord Waters' coffin was carried inside the church, followed by the mourners. Jane only recognised a few of them, the Fortescues and the Uptons as well as a few people she had met during her short stay here in Bath. She was surprised to see Dr Black there, walking sedately into the church with his sister on his arm, but she supposed as an active member of the community he would want to pay his respects, especially since he had been there when the old man had died.

Eventually the doors to the church closed and the soft notes from the organ drifted out. There had been no one else unexpected in the procession, no secret mistress come to declare her undying love for Lord Waters or secret child from an affair years earlier. Instead it had looked a sober occasion, with the gentry of Bath paying their respects to a man who had been part of their circle for many years.

"Come on," Jane said. "There is nothing to learn here. It is too hot to wait for the funeral to finish."

"It is hot," Cassandra murmured, taking out her fan and flicking it backwards and forwards.

"I know it is highly inappropriate," Jane murmured, "but all I can think about is buying some ices."

"It is inappropriate," Cassandra said, "but I would do almost anything for an ice right now."

"Strawberry," Jane said, closing her eyes. "Now, that would be refreshing."

"We have time. There is not much else we can do until we visit Lady Waters tomorrow. Everyone else connected with the case is in the church and will be for at least the next hour. We could go and buy an ice. I saw a shop close to the river."

Jane nodded, thankful Cassandra had come out of her melancholy a little. These past few days there had been a flicker of interest in her sister's eyes, an acknowledgement that the world was still going on around her. Jane was desperate to keep that; she would do anything that would keep Cassandra from withdrawing again.

They began to stroll in the direction of the river, passing the front of the church. Jane happened to glance down the dark alley at the side of the building and was surprised to see a door opening and Mrs Fortescue stumbling out. Her face was pale and drawn, her fingers clutching at her chest. For one awful moment Jane was back in Parade Gardens, watching Lord Waters die, but with a jolt she forced herself back to reality.

Mrs Fortescue leaned her head back against the wall of the church and closed her eyes, breathing deeply. Cassandra stepped forward, as if to go to the woman, but Jane caught her arm, motioning for her sister to stay silent as the door at the side of the church opened again. Jane frowned as Dr Tomkins, the doctor the coroner had called on to examine Lord Waters' body and give his expert opinion, slipped out.

"I need something," Mrs Fortescue said, her voice pleading as she turned to the doctor.

"Here is not the place, Mrs Fortescue."

"Please. I cannot..." She trailed off as the door opened again and Mr Fortescue stepped out.

"Inside," he snapped at his wife. "Now."

Mrs Fortescue scurried in, her expression unreadable, but before she passed through the door her eyes came up and met Jane's. Never before had Jane seen such desperation on a woman's face.

The doctor followed the Fortescues back inside and the door clicked closed behind them.

For a long moment neither Jane nor Cassandra could move. Stunned, Jane turned to her sister and puffed out her cheeks. "What was all that about, do you think?"

Cassandra shook her head, concern etched on her face.

"Mr Fortescue looked livid."

"He always looks livid," Cassandra said quietly. "There he looked apoplectic."

Jane replayed Mrs Fortescue's words. "She was asking Dr Tomkins to help her, to give her something, before her husband came out."

"Do you think she was asking for medication?"

"Possibly, but why would he refuse her request? He is a doctor."

Cassandra shrugged. "Perhaps it is a medication she is not supposed to have."

Jane nodded slowly. It would explain the furtiveness of the meeting they had just witnessed.

"We need to speak to Mrs Fortescue," Jane said.

"That will be close to impossible. You see how she trails after Mr Fortescue. I doubt he lets her out of his sight. Even there at the funeral of his father he left the church to drag his wife back inside."

"I have an idea, although if it goes wrong it will likely mean trouble."

Cassandra glanced at the church again. "I think we have to speak to her."

"I agree."

Jane's heart was pounding as she looked up at the Fortescue townhouse. They had a large residence on Beauford Square, nowhere near as exclusive an address as The Crescent, but the houses were grand and well kept.

Through the windows Jane could see a crush of people. Many of the mourners at the funeral had returned home with the Fortescues and were taking refreshments, no doubt whilst reminiscing about Lord Waters.

Looking down, Jane checked her appearance one last time, wondering if she would fool the servants. She was dressed in a sober, black, high-necked dress of medium quality, borrowed from one of the maids at her aunt's house. Jane had paid a princely sum to borrow the dress and to ensure the woman's silence on the matter. It had depleted her pin money, but she was hoping it would be worthwhile.

Jane adjusted the package in her arms and made her way to the side of the house, where there was a narrow alleyway containing steps down to the kitchen. She descended and knocked quietly on the door, hoping no one would hear. As she had expected, all the servants were far too busy catering for the huge number of guests upstairs to notice her at the door. Slowly she turned the handle and stepped inside.

The kitchen was medium-sized and currently chaotic. The cook was bent over the table, adding finishing touches to a plate of pastries whilst maids and footmen bustled up and down the stairs, taking plates and trays to the guests above.

"Who are you?" a middle-aged woman with a pinched face and permanent frown asked as she noticed Jane.

"Mary King, maid to Mrs Leigh-Perrot," Jane lied, hoping Bath was big enough that the servants wouldn't expect to all know one another.

"We're a little busy here today. What do you want?"

"My mistress is lending yours a few pieces of mourning attire," Jane said. "She asked me to bring them round." She motioned to the parcel she carried.

"Leave them here. I will take them up when the guests have all gone."

Jane hesitated and shook her head. "There are a few delicate items in there that need hanging immediately. If they are not, they will be ruined."

"I don't have time right now," the woman said, exasperated.

"I could take them upstairs and hang them?"

The woman started to shake her head and then thought better of it. "Fine. Use the back stairs. Second floor, first door on the left."

Jane hurried off before the woman could have second thoughts about letting a stranger into the private areas of the house, bowing her head in the hope no one else would pay her any attention. She made her way to the back stairs and ascended quickly, hearing the swell of chatter as she passed the ground floor.

It was quiet upstairs, since all the servants were occupied with the guests. Jane wondered how long she could linger without the woman she had spoken to becoming suspicious. She hoped the chaos of the kitchen and the demands of the guests would mean she would assume Jane had left without being observed, but there was a possibility someone would come looking for her.

Remembering the instructions, she tried the first door on the left on the second floor, opening it up to find a large room that was plainly decorated. There was none of the style or comfort that Jane had seen in Lady Waters' house; here the room was designed with practicality in mind. There was a large wardrobe and a chest of drawers next to it along one wall and a small dressing table opposite. The bed had a carved wooden headboard, but it looked old, as if passed down from previous generations.

Jane slipped into the room and pulled the door almost closed behind her. She didn't want to close it completely — some warning of anyone approaching would be ideal.

Now she was here, Jane was beginning to question her plan. She'd known getting Mrs Fortescue on her own to ask her about the encounter they had seen in the alley beside the church would be difficult with Mr Fortescue's overbearing presence. Jane also thought the woman might have some useful insights into the relationship between Mr Fortescue and his father. All of this could be very useful in piecing together the family dynamic, but perhaps the risk she was taking here was too much.

Feeling a little light-headed, she perched on the edge of the bed, forcing herself to take some long, deep breaths. She was keen to get to the truth in this matter, and sometimes her eagerness clouded her judgement. The longer she thought about it the more foolish she felt, sitting in a stranger's house, uninvited and unexpected.

Jane stood and began pacing the room, wondering if she should abandon her plan and call on Mrs Fortescue formally, as would normally be expected in polite society.

The decision was taken from her as footsteps approached along the hallway outside. Jane held her breath, her heart hammering. She almost cried out when the door began to open.

Mrs Fortescue looked petrified when she caught sight of Jane standing in her bedroom. She opened her mouth and for one terrible moment Jane thought she was going to scream, but no sound came out.

"Mrs Fortescue…" Jane began, but she struggled to find the right words to explain her presence.

"You can't be here, Miss Austen," Mrs Fortescue said, her voice shrill.

"I am sorry for coming into your house like this."

"You can't be here."

"I wanted to talk to you, alone."

"You can't be here," she repeated for a third time. "What if he sees you?"

"Your husband?"

Mrs Fortescue nodded then took a step back, peering out into the hallway. "You have to leave."

"We need to talk," Jane said, aware she was pressing a woman on the edge of hysteria.

"You don't understand," Mrs Fortescue said, her voice a mere whisper now. "Please, Miss Austen. I need you to leave. I will tell you anything you want, but not here, not now."

Jane saw the panic in the older woman's eyes and nodded. "Can we talk later, after your guests have left?"

"I don't know if I can get away."

"Mrs Fortescue, it is important."

"This evening. I will tell my husband I am returning something to a friend. Meet me at the gardens at the end of the road at seven o'clock."

It was late, later than her aunt would be happy for her to stay out, but Jane knew she would find an excuse to be there.

"Did anyone see you come up?"

"One of your maids. I said I was delivering some mourning clothes my mistress wanted you to have. I can go out the same way."

Mrs Fortescue clasped her hand, squeezing hard. "Do not let my husband see you, Miss Austen."

"I won't. I will see you at seven o'clock."

Mrs Fortescue didn't answer, instead moving to look out into the hallway. "It is empty. Go down the back stairs and straight out."

With one final nod, Jane hurried past her and made her way to the back stairs. It was quiet on the way down until she reached the lower level and the hustle and bustle of the kitchen. Jane bowed her head and walked quickly through the busy kitchen.

"You found it alright, then?" the woman she had spoken to earlier called as Jane's hand was on the door handle.

"Yes, thank you," she said, and then without turning she pushed the door open and walked up the outer steps to ground level.

CHAPTER THIRTEEN

"She's not going to come," Jane said, pacing back and forth.

"Have a little patience, Jane," Cassandra urged. "It can only be a few minutes after the hour."

They had left their aunt and uncle's house at a quarter to seven, walking briskly through the streets of Bath to reach the gardens near Mrs Fortescue's house a little before seven. They had been waiting for over ten minutes, although to Jane it felt like much longer.

"You should have seen her face, Cassandra. She was terrified. I think she would have said anything to get me out of her house."

"It was a foolish idea," Cassandra murmured. "I should never have agreed to it."

Jane fell silent and began pacing again. This investigation was not going as she had hoped. It showed how much she normally relied on local connections, on introductions to friends of friends, to propel her enquiries forwards. Here in Bath she felt a little out of her depth.

"If she doesn't turn up..." Jane muttered, knowing they would be reprimanded by their aunt whatever the outcome of this evening. They had decided to leave without telling her, hoping they would be back for dinner at half past seven with no one any the wiser, but as time ticked on without any sign of Mrs Fortescue, it was looking less and less likely.

"Someone is coming," Cassandra said.

Jane spun in time to see Mrs Fortescue hurrying into view.

"Good evening," Jane said when the older woman arrived, breathless from moving so fast.

"Good evening. I cannot stay long, Miss Austen."

"Thank you for coming."

"It wasn't as though I had a choice," Mrs Fortescue said primly. There was something slightly bolder about her out here, away from her Mr Fortescue's influence, although she did keep looking over her shoulder as if expecting to be hauled back to her house by her husband at any moment.

"We don't want to cause trouble for you, Mrs Fortescue."

She looked at Jane long and hard, blinking rapidly. "I don't believe you, Miss Austen," she said eventually.

"All we want to do is find the truth of this terrible matter with Lord Waters."

"You talk as if there is a question hanging over it; Lady Waters has been accused and will be tried in due course."

"I think we all know that is because of the influence your husband holds over this town, rather than any true justice."

Mrs Fortescue blanched, but Jane could see her words had struck a nerve. "I do not know what I can help you with."

"Sit with us for a moment," Jane said, motioning to a bench to one side of the gardens.

"I really don't have much time."

"It will not take long, Mrs Fortescue."

Reluctantly she sat, fussing with her skirts and glancing around, no doubt to check no one she knew was passing.

"You seem very nervous. Are you afraid of your husband?" It was a direct question, not one that would normally be asked in polite society, but Jane was too tired to tiptoe around the questions she really wanted to ask.

Mrs Fortescue shook her head forcefully, but a few seconds later her shoulders sagged. "My husband would not approve of my meeting you."

"Why is that?"

"He has strong views on what is a suitable use of my time and who I should spend my days with."

"I assume Lady Waters was not one of these people."

"No, she most certainly was not."

"Do you like her?"

"I hardly know her."

"Is that because your husband forbids an acquaintance?"

Mrs Fortescue sighed. "You are not married, Miss Austen, but when you do decide to become a wife, you will find it is not unusual for a husband to have a view on aspects of his wife's social life."

"A view is very different from telling you who you can and cannot spend time with."

"My husband does not like Lady Waters," Mrs Fortescue said, her eyes darting all over the place. "I respect his feelings and have kept my distance."

Jane felt the wall coming up between them and knew she had to do something quickly to knock it down. "We saw you outside the church this afternoon, meeting with Dr Tomkins."

"That was a private medical matter."

"I don't think it was, Mrs Fortescue," Jane said, knowing she was going to have to gamble on what she thought she had seen in order to get Mrs Fortescue to open up. If she was wrong, the older woman was likely to walk away without answering the rest of her questions. "I think you sat in that stuffy church surrounded by mourners, everyone's eyes on you and your husband, and you were overcome by anxiety. I am aware of the symptoms: a racing heart, sweaty palms, a feeling that the whole world is going to come crashing down around your shoulders."

Mrs Fortescue's breathing was becoming a little more rapid as she listened to Jane, her chest rising and falling with increasingly shallow breaths.

"I think you sat there in that church until you couldn't bear it any longer, and then you fled. Dr Tomkins was aware of your symptoms because you have discussed it with him before, and he followed you out."

Cassandra laid a hand on Mrs Fortescue's arm, bringing her back to the present. "Many people suffer with an attack of nerves," she said reassuringly.

"In that alley you asked Dr Tomkins for something, something he was not happy to give. When you husband burst out through the door he was livid, but I do not think it was because you had left, but because he found you out there with Dr Tomkins."

"You are not suggesting anything inappropriate?"

"I think you know exactly what I am suggesting, Mrs Fortescue," Jane said with a sigh of exasperation. She had imagined this interview would go differently, with the nervous woman giving up all her secrets easily in a bid to finish quickly and get back home before she was missed.

Mrs Fortescue looked down at her hands for a long moment and then nodded, her face falling. She looked once again the defeated, timid woman they had first met trailing behind her husband.

"You are right. I suffer from my nerves. It has always been a problem, but when I was younger I could cover things more easily. It has only been in the last few years that it has been more of a problem." There was much unsaid in those few sentences, but Jane could imagine the pressure she was under. Mrs Fortescue was younger than her husband, but not by much. She was fast approaching the end of her child-bearing years, and as yet there was no sign of an heir to the Fortescue title or fortune. Jane could not imagine Mr Fortescue being pleased by the thought of the title passing out of his direct family once he passed away. "Last year I found myself in turmoil. I could not leave the house without feeling as though my heart was going to burst from my chest and my head spinning. Our usual doctor, Dr Wilcox, attended me a few times and prescribed a tincture of laudanum."

Jane nodded. It was a strong medication.

"He gave me one small bottle, which I used within a few days, and then another. By the time a week had passed, I felt as though I could not function without it. And by the time two weeks had passed, I would feel terrible if I missed just one dose."

Jane remained silent. It was an all too familiar story. They all knew people who had sustained a terrible injury falling from a horse or in some household accident who had taken a little too much laudanum. When the pain improved and it was time to stop, they found it impossible to go without, suffering from all sorts of awful symptoms because of their body's need for the medication.

"Dr Wilcox said he was concerned about how much I was taking. He spoke to my husband and they agreed between them it wasn't good for me, that I shouldn't have any more."

"They stopped it, just like that?"

Mrs Fortescue nodded, her expression pitiful. "They didn't understand how much I *needed* it, that even getting out of bed without it was close to impossible."

Jane could imagine what had happened next. Mrs Fortescue might live her life in her husband's shadow but she had friends and acquaintants, and someone would know who to talk to about getting the medication she needed.

"I had heard rumours that Dr Tomkins was sympathetic to this sort of thing and made contact with him. He agreed to supply me with one bottle a week, without my husband knowing. It was hard at first, rationing myself, but I knew it was better than having nothing at all."

"That was what you were arranging outside the church? For him to give you your medication?"

Mrs Fortescue grimaced. "This past week has been very trying," she said quietly. "I have used more of my medication than I should, and on the morning of the funeral I took my last dose. I asked Dr Tomkins for some more, just this once, but my husband interrupted us before we could agree."

"Your husband knows now?"

"He suspects, I think. I told him Dr Tomkins was in the alley to check I was not unwell, but my husband is no fool, Miss Austen. He will have heard the rumours about the doctor."

Jane nodded. It was much as she had suspected when she had seen Mrs Fortescue in the alley outside the church. She found she was not surprised Dr Tomkins was supplying Mrs Fortescue with medication her own doctor had refused to prescribe and wondered if he could have been the one to give Lady Waters the belladonna. It was an unusual medication to have, but it had to have come from somewhere. Lady Waters might have procured it in London as she had said at the inquest, or she might have got it more recently.

"Thank you for being so honest," Jane said, seeing Mrs Fortescue begin to shift in her seat. Her next questions would have to be quick, as the woman had been away from home for fifteen minutes now. "Can I ask you about Lady Waters?"

Mrs Fortescue nodded but looked wary.

"Do you think she killed Lord Waters?"

"I don't know. The evidence…"

"I'm not talking about the evidence. I want to know what you felt about her, your own opinion."

Mrs Fortescue sniffed, looking down at her hands before speaking. "It was a surprise when Lord Waters turned up with her on his arm thirteen months ago. He'd only meant to be going to Brighton to take the sea air and recover his health after a bad chest, and he returned with a wife."

"He hadn't expressed a wish to remarry?"

"No. Quite the contrary. He always said there was just one woman for him, and when he was widowed we all expected him to live out the rest of his life alone."

"He seemed devoted to Lady Waters," Cassandra said.

"He was completely besotted with her. My husband always used to say it was as though she had cast a spell over Lord Waters, beguiled him."

"Perhaps they really did fall in love."

"Perhaps," Mrs Fortescue said and then shook her head. "If it was an act, then I commend Lady Waters. She must be a consummate actress, for I never saw her drop her guard once. No look of disgust when he kissed her, no impatience at the speed of his walking. She was always most patient."

"Your husband and your sister-in-law did not like her, though."

"No."

"Despite how happy she made Lord Waters."

"They didn't believe it was true. They thought her intention was to worm her way into his affections and spend his money."

Jane thought of the tastefully decorated drawing room and the expensive clothes Lady Waters wore. None of that would be cheap, but if Lord Waters was as wealthy as his reputation suggested, then it shouldn't put a big dent in Mr Fortescue's inheritance.

"What do you think, Mrs Fortescue?" Jane asked, regarding the middle-aged woman as she wrung her hands in her lap.

Mrs Fortescue sighed. "I think Lady Waters saw Lord Waters for what he was, a kind old man, and after two marriages she decided this time she would choose a comfortable life rather than a young man to keep her occupied."

It was a much more charitable opinion than anything else Jane had heard so far.

"You do not dislike her, then?"

"She has always been kind to me, even though I am bound by my duty to my husband to keep my distance."

"Do you think she killed Lord Waters?"

Mrs Fortescue frowned, some of the uncertainty back in her demeanour. "I do not know. He was a kind man, and I hate to think of anyone killing him."

"Someone did," Cassandra said.

"I know. But I can't understand why."

"What motive does your husband think Lady Waters has for killing his father?"

"I do not know, but he believes she is capable of it." Mrs Fortescue shrugged. "He worries about the inheritance."

"Lady Waters cannot take that from him."

"Not the ancestral home or the title, but my father-in-law could do whatever he wanted with the money."

"Surely he would plan for most of it to go to his heir, your husband?"

Mrs Fortescue grimaced. "It would be the sensible thing, but my husband worried it wouldn't be so. He worries about everything. Now he is agitated about these dratted emeralds. He took them to a jeweller to have them valued, and he was told they were fakes. He was apoplectic, as you can imagine, and insists he will need to inspect everything at number seven, The Crescent after the reading of the will. He thinks Lady Waters has conspired to hide some of Lord Waters' valuable possessions to stop him from getting his rightful inheritance."

Jane sat back on the bench, her mind spinning. She was struggling to find any motive for Lady Waters to kill her husband. Everyone they spoke to said how devoted she was to the elderly man, and how he loved her in return and showered her with gifts and affection. There would have to be a strong motive for her to jeopardise her comfortable life.

There was the matter of the fake emeralds as well. It explained why Lord Waters was happy to walk around Bath with them in his pocket, but Jane wondered who had known they were just paste and glass.

Mrs Fortescue stood up. "I have to return home, Miss Austen. My husband will already be wondering where I am."

Jane was aware of the time herself, knowing their aunt and uncle would be sitting down to dinner right now, wondering where Jane and Cassandra were.

"When is the will being read, Mrs Fortescue?"

"When the solicitor arrives from London. In a few days, I should imagine."

"Lord Waters didn't have a copy kept locally?"

Mrs Fortescue looked away, her expression shifty, and then she laughed bitterly. "He said the professional men of Bath were all in his son's pocket, so he couldn't trust any of them."

Before Jane could ask any more Mrs Fortescue hurried away, head bent and shoulders hunched.

Exhaling loudly, Jane sat back on the bench. It was a lot to take in, but she wasn't sure they were any further forward with their investigation.

"I didn't get a chance to ask her to confirm her movements when Lord Waters died."

"We know she was in the crowd at the Parade Gardens," Cassandra said. "If we are thinking someone slipped something into Lord Waters' drink, it is going to be impossible to prove where anyone was in the few minutes before he died. There were so many people there."

"All of his family."

"It is interesting that Lord Waters did not trust the solicitors here in Bath with his will."

"We have seen what Mr Fortescue's network can do. Lord Waters was right not to trust someone local."

"It would be useful to be in the room when the will is read," Cassandra said.

"It might be the key to this whole thing. If someone found out they were being pushed out in favour of Lady Waters, it could be a motive to kill Lord Waters and frame her."

"A condemned murderess would forfeit any inheritance."

"And her share would be split between the remaining beneficiaries."

For a minute the two sisters sat in silence, contemplating Mrs Fortescue's information before Cassandra sprang to her feet.

"We're late for dinner, Jane. Our aunt will be worried."

Quickly they hurried from the gardens, both holding their bonnets on their heads and picking up their skirts with their free hands.

CHAPTER FOURTEEN

It was another stiflingly hot day for May, and the air inside the carriage was close and stale by the end of the journey to Ilchester. They had broken the journey twice to stretch their legs, but as the carriage rolled to a stop Jane was eager to climb down and escape the enclosed space for good.

They emerged outside the Ilchester Arms, one of the coaching inns dotted along the main street. Ilchester itself was a little town that after the fine Bath architecture made Jane feel as though she were stepping back a hundred years. The buildings were low and squat, many of them leaning precariously into the middle of the road.

"I suggest we find a room and freshen up," Mrs Leigh-Perrot said as she eyed the coaching inn suspiciously.

A stableboy ambled out and helped the driver unload the few small bags they had brought with them for the overnight trip. He then directed the carriage through an archway to the small yard at the back of the inn.

Inside was tidy but gloomy, with hardly any natural light. Whatever did manage to filter through the small windows was immediately absorbed by the dark furniture and heavy wall hangings.

Mrs Leigh-Perrot arranged for them to have a room with a large bed that they would all share, and once negotiations were complete the landlady showed them upstairs. The room itself would be cramped with three, but it was only for one night.

"Let me lie down for a few minutes, girls, and then we will see about arranging a visit to Lady Waters."

"Of course, Aunt. You rest as long as you need to."

Mrs Leigh-Perrot was not a good traveller, which was one of the reasons they normally visited her in Bath rather than her making the trip to Steventon. She had been pale and quiet the whole journey, resting her head on the upholstered seat as the carriage rocked from side to side. By the time they had arrived in Ilchester, she had looked positively green.

Jane and Cassandra took off their bonnets and made themselves as comfortable as they could in the small room whilst they waited for their aunt to recover.

In ten minutes Mrs Leigh-Perrot's breathing had deepened, and after fifteen she was snoring softly.

"We should leave her to sleep," Jane said, quietly pleased by this turn of events. She had dreaded taking their demure aunt into Ilchester gaol. No doubt she would be scandalised by the conditions and urge them to hurry through the visit so they could return quickly to the more civilised Bath.

"She told us in no uncertain terms we were not to visit the gaol without her."

"It will be much more difficult to talk to Lady Waters if our aunt is there too," Jane said, her voice barely more than a whisper.

"Jane, she has been very tolerant of our escapades so far. We do not wish to repay that tolerance with betrayal."

"I know, but perhaps we could just pop into the gaol for a quick visit and tomorrow we can return with our aunt for the proper talk."

Jane could see her sister considering. With a final glance at Mrs Leigh-Perrot, dead to the world on the bed, Cassandra nodded reluctantly.

"A quick visit," she said.

"Thank you." Jane grabbed her bonnet from where she had set it down and hurried from the room before her sister could change her mind.

The gaol was easy to find, housed in an old building near the river. Jane had visited Winchester gaol with Lord Hinchbrooke, but even with his protection it had not been a pleasant experience. The gaols were designed to be dirty and depressing, and Ilchester gaol was no different, with a thick door in a stone outer wall and darkness inside.

Jane hammered on the door and waited, knowing there would be some sort of gatekeeper or guard tasked with opening the door to visitors as well as keeping the prisoners secure.

"What do you want?" A burly man with a ripped shirt and food-stained trousers growled as he flung open the door. He had rosy cheeks and Jane caught a whiff of alcohol on his breath.

"Miss Jane Austen and Miss Cassandra Austen to visit Lady Waters," she said, wrinkling her nose at the smell.

The guard smiled, revealing two rows of cracked and missing teeth. The result was a menacing grimace, and Jane had to steady her nerves to stop herself from recoiling.

"This isn't a fancy parlour," the guard said. "Visiting costs money."

"How much?"

He regarded them for a moment, taking in their simple but well-made clothes and freshly shined boots. "A shilling."

"That is extortionate!"

"It is the going rate. Take it or leave it."

Jane grumbled, reaching for her coin purse. It was over double what she had expected and budgeted for. At this rate she would spend all her pin money on bribes.

"Anything you take in costs extra," the guard said.

"We have nothing to take in today." Jane thought of the heavy bag the maid had packed at Lady Waters' house and dreaded to think how much that would cost her to bring in.

"Suit yourself. This way."

They entered the yard area of the prison, but instead of heading towards the main building that must have housed the majority of the inmates, they turned towards a house built within the walls of the gaol.

The guard thumped on the door and waited, his manner changing as the door opened to reveal a portly man of middle years.

"Visitors to see Lady Waters, sir." He stood a little taller as his spoke, his voice losing the leery edge and becoming respectful.

The warden was eating, but he quickly swallowed and then smiled at Jane and Cassandra. "I was wondering if she would get any visitors. Come in, come in."

They were ushered into the dark house and found themselves standing in a busy kitchen. There was a large table to one side with six children sitting around it. An exhausted-looking woman stirred a pot on the stove and filled up bowls. An older child stood next to her, taking each bowl once there was food inside and placing it in front of the younger children.

"Visitors for Lady Waters," the warden said to her in explanation.

"You find us in chaos," the woman said with a cheery smile. "Although with all our children, I think this place is always in chaos."

"I am Mr Scadding, warden of Ilchester gaol. I am in charge of the security and welfare of the prisoners."

"I am Miss Jane Austen, and this is my sister Miss Cassandra Austen. We are friends of Lady Waters."

"I am pleased she has someone visiting her. She has been very melancholy," Mrs Scadding said.

Jane frowned and Mr Scadding must have seen her expression, for he stepped in quickly.

"We are told to have a certain latitude with prisoners of rank. Lady Waters has been lodged with us. Ours is a humble dwelling and as you can see we are a little overcrowded, but I think she is more comfortable here than she would be in the gaol itself."

Jane felt a flood of relief. Ever since Lady Waters had been transported here, she had imagined her in a cold, dank room, at risk of gaol fever or any other illness that ran rife through the filthy prisons. This accommodation was not what Lady Waters would be used to, but it was a proper house with glass in the windows and home-cooked food.

"There we are," a familiar voice rang out as two small children toddled into the room. Their cheeks were rosy and they were smiling as they tottered on chubby legs. "They're all clean, Mrs Scadding." Lady Waters paused as she caught sight of Jane and Cassandra and then promptly burst into tears.

Instinctively Jane went to her and wrapped her arms around the widowed baroness. It was an overly familiar gesture, but she didn't doubt Lady Waters needed it. Lady Waters collapsed into her arms, sobbing softly.

"Lady Waters has been a godsend," Mrs Scadding said with an indulgent smile. "We've had three merchant's wives and the daughter of a wealthy landowner stay with us over the last year, and not one of them has offered to lift a hand to help. Lady Waters is wonderful with the children and is always quick to help, whatever the chore."

"You have been so kind to me," Lady Waters said, smiling at the warden's wife.

"I shall show you through to the parlour, where you can talk for a while," the warden said, looking a little embarrassed by all the show of emotion.

"Thank you," said Jane.

The parlour was another small room off to one side of the house with a window and three high-backed armchairs. Like the rest of the house the chairs looked as though they had seen better days, with patches on the arms and on the seat. However, the room was clean and quiet.

Lady Waters didn't sit down immediately, instead standing by the window and looking out into the yard beyond. It was hardly a scenic view and must have reminded the young woman that she was incarcerated without much chance of release.

"Are you well, Lady Waters?"

"Call me Arabella, please," she said with a tight smile. "You have travelled a long way to visit me." She sighed. "There are many things I regret, but not making the effort to form more friendships is high on the list. I have felt so very lonely these last few days."

"You have had no other visitors?"

"Who would visit me?" she said. "My parents are long dead, and my acquaintances in Bath have kept their distance."

"We are here," Cassandra said softly. "Are they treating you well?"

"Yes. I am pleased I do not have to stay in a prison cell; it is a little more dignified this way."

"You seem to have assimilated into the family well."

Lady Waters shrugged. "It keeps me busy, helping Mrs Scadding, and she does have so many children to cope with. I help where I can."

Many people would have retreated into themselves if they were thrown into gaol for a crime that would likely mean death if found guilty. They would lie in bed all day, refusing to do anything but ponder their fate. Lady Waters had refused to succumb to such melancholic thoughts and instead was keeping herself busy whilst ingratiating herself with the family who were in control of her accommodation. It was a wise move, and one Jane had to commend Lady Waters for making.

"We have brought you a few things from home, although the bag is still in our inn at the moment. We shall return tomorrow with it."

"You truly are angels sent from above."

Lady Waters sat down, perching on the edge of the chair. Close up, she was a little less put together than Jane had first thought. Her nails were bitten low and her hair was scraped into an untidy bun at the nape of her neck. Her eyes were red-rimmed and her skin had a sallow tinge, which was unsurprising if she had been cooped up inside for a few days.

"We don't have much time," Jane said, conscious of the small clock on the wall ticking away. "Our aunt accompanied us from Bath and we left her sleeping in the room, but I have so many questions for you."

Lady Waters nodded but looked a little perplexed.

"I hope you don't mind, but Cassandra and I are trying to look into this terrible affair. I have had a little experience assisting the magistrate in Hampshire in similar matters, and I think I might be able to help you."

"You truly want to help me?"

"Of course. There was something very wrong about the inquest, something orchestrated. We think Mr Fortescue used his influence to ensure the evidence was presented in a way that meant the men of the jury would come back with the verdict he wanted."

"It did all feel very surreal," Lady Waters said. She leaned forward, holding Jane's gaze. "I did not kill my husband. I loved him."

Jane nodded. "I believe you, but there is a lot of work to be done to prove your innocence. It helps that, here in Ilchester, the judge and jury are less likely to be friends or acquaintances of Mr Fortescue, but we still need to find out who did kill your husband to be certain of the right verdict at your trial."

"You think someone killed him?"

"Yes. I think his drink was poisoned whilst we waited in the crowd for the music in Parade Gardens."

"With belladonna?"

Jane shrugged. It wasn't something she felt she knew enough about yet. "Perhaps, or perhaps with something that has a similar effect."

"I do have a small supply of belladonna," Lady Waters said, biting her lip. "For cosmetic purposes. I haven't used it in years."

"For your eyes — to make your pupils bigger?"

"Yes. It was a trick I picked up from a young woman I used to know."

"You've had the belladonna a long time, then?"

"Yes, but as I say, I haven't used it in years. I didn't need to with Lord Waters. He always said I enchanted him with my beauty without the need for any cosmetic tricks."

"Did anyone know you had the belladonna?"

Lady Waters nodded. "It came up about a year ago. Elizabeth, one of Mrs Upton's daughters, came to borrow a pair of earrings for her coming-out ball. She saw the vial and asked what it was. I showed her the bottle and told her what it was used for."

"Do you think she told anyone?"

"Probably her mother. Elizabeth is a sweet enough girl, but with that woman as a mother I doubt she is allowed many secrets."

Jane nodded thoughtfully. If they were assuming Lord Waters had been killed by someone else, with the murder made to look like Lady Waters was the culprit, that person would have to know about the belladonna. It was the only way they could be certain Lady Waters would be accused.

"So anyone in the family could potentially know about that vial?"

"Yes, I suppose so. No doubt it was discussed and dissected like everything else I did."

"Did you see anything suspicious before your husband collapsed?"

"I've been thinking about this over and over. I didn't *see* anything definite. They were all there, though, all close enough to put something in his drink: Mr Fortescue and his wife, Mr and Mrs Upton and their two eldest daughters."

"Do you have any idea why any of them would want to kill him?"

Lady Waters closed her eyes for a moment and passed a hand across her forehead. "I'm sorry," she said softly, "I can't believe he's dead, much less that someone deliberately killed him. Of course I knew our years together would be short, he was not a young man, but I never thought it would happen like this."

"We are truly sorry for your loss," Cassandra said, reaching across and taking lady Waters' hand. "I can't imagine what you are going through."

Lady Waters rallied a little and gave a grateful smile. "Money," she sighed. "It is probably all to do with money."

"The inheritance?"

"Yes."

"Tell us."

She was silent for a few seconds, gathering her thoughts, and then sat up straighter. "My late husband was a very wealthy man, and over the years he has been very generous towards his children."

Jane shifted forward in her seat, hoping Lady Waters would go into specifics. People varied greatly in their interpretation of what was generous and what was barely enough to scrape by. It would be interesting to see what Lady Waters thought was the former.

"Lord Waters understood the challenges of maintaining one's standard of living without full access to the income that came with the lands and titles he held. He didn't inherit until he was in his forties, with children of his own to support, so he was acutely aware of some of the difficulties his children would face."

"He provided them with an income?"

"Yes, a generous one. He also gifted both Mr Fortescue and Mrs Upton a property each, with lands and income associated with it, to allow them to manage it themselves whilst earning from the rents and profits of the estates."

"A shrewd man. He did not just give them money, but a way to continue to make money."

"That was what he always said." Lady Waters grimaced. "It didn't work out quite as he'd hoped. Mr Fortescue is not as astute as my late husband with money. Over the course of his life, he has had a tendency to run up large debts." She lowered her voice. "Gambling."

Jane's eyes widened. Mr Fortescue would no doubt be keen to get his hands on his inheritance — money that would now be his without any conditions attached.

"My husband settled his debts numerous times, but last year he refused to pay out any more, saying he would continue to give him his monthly funds, but he would not settle any more of his debts."

"Was this your influence?"

"No, not directly. I never told him to cut Mr Fortescue off, but I think during our marriage he realised the importance of allowing his son to manage his own finances. Mr Fortescue was never truly going to be able to do that when he thought his father was prepared to rescue him from whatever predicament he got himself into."

"I can see why Mr Fortescue might resent you."

"Yes," Lady Waters said, shaking her head ruefully. "He blamed me outright. He even came to the house begging his father for money and shouting that I had ruined his life."

"It is unfathomable behaviour for a man of his age and station. I can see why he might be eager to get his hands on his inheritance if he had run up large debts."

"I don't know if he could do such a thing, though. His anger was always directed towards me, not his father."

"Killing you would not solve his money problems."

"No, I suppose not." Lady Waters sighed and sat back in the chair. She looked small, and Jane was reminded how young she was. "That is why he was so angry about the necklace, the emerald piece that I wore to Mr and Mrs Temple's ball. It is a very expensive piece of jewellery. Whatever trouble he has got himself into, the sale of that one piece would probably clear his debts."

"Yet instead his father gave it to you." Jane paused, wondering whether to say anything about the fake set of emeralds they had found in Lord Waters' pocket. "When Lord Waters died, he had an emerald necklace very much like the one you wore to Mr and Mrs Temple's ball in his pocket. I am told now it has been confirmed to be a fake, made of paste and glass."

Lady Waters looked intrigued but shook her head in disbelief. "Fake emeralds? I do not know anything about that."

"What about the rest of the family? Do they have any motive?"

Lady Waters tapped the arms of the chair. "Mrs Fortescue is a nervous wreck. She can barely leave the house without a dose of something illicit."

"You know about that?"

"Yes, she's a curious creature. Timid to the extreme and cowed by years of marriage to her husband."

"Did Lord Waters know of her addiction?"

"No, I don't think so. At least, he never said anything to me. I can't see how it would give her motive to murder him. Then there's Mr and Mrs Upton," she said. "They are troubled by money concerns of a different kind."

"Oh?"

"They have five daughters. Their eldest, Clara, is twenty and their youngest is fourteen. I know Mr and Mrs Upton are worried about the dowries needed for five young ladies to secure good marriages."

"It is a strain for sure, but surely not anything more than what a lot of families go through as their daughters reach a certain age."

"You're right, of course, and it wouldn't be so bad, but Mr Upton made some poor business choices and lost a lot of money a few years ago. The property my husband settled on Mrs Upton was forfeit, and I think there was some settlement that he is still tied to today to pay back what he owed."

"Lord Waters refused to help them too?"

"No, he helped them. I do not know all the details because it happened before I met Lord Waters, but I think he paid off a large proportion of the debt, but he also made it clear it would only happen that once."

"You would not know to look at them that either family were struggling."

"Their extravagance used to anger my husband. He would watch them attend the balls in expensive new clothes and he would shake his head and ask me where he had gone wrong."

Jane sat back and considered everything Lady Waters had told her. Money was an age-old motive for murder, especially if there were large debts involved. Either Mr Fortescue or Mrs Upton could have grown resentful of their father having the money to help them but refusing to do so in the hope they learned to deal with the consequences of their actions.

"Is there anyone else? Did your husband have any enemies? Anyone who might wish him harm?"

"No. He was an old man and lived his life quietly. He had no enemies."

Jane hesitated before asking the next question, knowing she had to ask it but not wanting to. She was aware there was a good chance Lady Waters would lie to her, and it would be the first crack in the fragile trust between them.

"What about you?" she asked, watching Lady Waters' expression. "Could this all be a ploy to hurt you, with Lord Waters as the unfortunate victim?"

Lady Waters' eyes widened as if she hadn't considered that possibility. Slowly she shook her head, but it wasn't a convincing denial.

"You've had a colourful life, Lady Waters," Cassandra said. Her normally soft voice had an edge to it that hinted she would not be fooled by honeyed words.

"I have."

"It is conceivable that someone from your past wishes to put you in the dock for murder. It is a convoluted way to kill someone, but the outcome is the same."

"Perhaps you should tell us a little about your life before you met Lord Waters," Jane said, smiling encouragingly. She thought of the well-built but scruffily groomed man who had visited Lady Waters at number seven, The Crescent. "We know someone turned up at your house a few months ago."

Lady Waters shook her head. "I never understood this urge to surround oneself with servants. They're always listening, always ready to betray. It is exhausting, never quite being able to relax." As she spoke, her voice lost some of its refinement, a London drawl elongating a few of the vowel sounds.

"This is not the world you grew up in?"

"Far from it, although please do not think I tricked Lord Waters into marrying me. He knew exactly where I came from. It amused him, I think, to see me dressed in my fine gowns, circulating amongst those who ten years ago wouldn't have given me the time of day." She looked between Jane and Cassandra and sighed. "I had better start with my first marriage. I was orphaned at fifteen. Before that, I lived in a poor part of London, on the edge of the St Giles' slums. It was not an easy life, and when my father died I knew I had a choice to make. Either I married or I sold myself to stay alive."

It was a world far removed from the genteel life Jane and Cassandra knew in Steventon. Of course, there were poor people, those who had fallen on hard times in the village and surrounding area, but country poor was very different to city poor. Jane had read about life in the London slums, and it seemed unbelievable that people could live in such a way.

"You chose marriage."

"I chose marriage," Lady Waters said. "I traipsed around London until I had holes in my shoes, looking for employment. Eventually I obtained a position as a servant to a lawyer. He wouldn't look twice at a lowly maid, but he had a young clerk who was kind to me. We were married on my seventeenth birthday."

"You were young."

"No younger than many girls. I was lucky. Will, my first husband, was kind. We didn't have much money, but we had a small set of rooms above his employer's office, and for a while we were happy."

"What happened?"

"He died of consumption two years after we married. I was nineteen and widowed." She shook her head at the memory, and Jane saw real sorrow in her eyes. "I was in a state of shock. I had fooled myself into thinking everything was going to be easy from thereon in and suddenly I was alone again."

"You married again?"

"Yes," she said slowly. "Only a month after Will died, his employer started to pester me. He told me I owed a lot of money for the rooms and if I didn't pay he would see me on the streets." She lowered her voice. "From the start it was clear what he wanted, but I held out for four months, scraping a living with casual jobs, none of which lasted long."

Jane felt a wave of nausea as she understood what Lady Waters had been pressed to do. She knew her life was sheltered in Hampshire. She was lucky to have two loving parents and numerous siblings who would provide for her in an instant if needed. Not many were as lucky.

"After four months, I gave in to him." Lady Waters looked away and Jane could see the pain in her eyes as she remembered sacrificing her dignity to stay alive.

"He wanted to marry you?" Cassandra said.

"No," Lady Waters said quickly. "He wanted me as a cheap and convenient mistress. After eight months he was starting to tire of me, when I discovered I was pregnant." Lady Waters closed her eyes and pressed her lips together, taking a moment before continuing. "He liked the idea of a son, someone to follow him into the law, so he told me we would be married."

"You didn't have a choice?"

"No. I lost the baby at six months but we were married by then, much to Bertram's disgust."

"I am so sorry," Jane said, reaching out and squeezing her friend's hand.

"I hated the man, but I would have loved that child." She took a shuddering breath and continued. "Bertram started travelling for work, and somehow I convinced him to take me with him. I studied people, knowing I didn't want to be trapped in this life forever. I would go into the best tea shops and hotels, order one drink and eke it out for hours, watching how the wealthy ate and drank, how they spoke, even how they sat. It was fascinating."

"What happened to Bertram?"

"We were only married for a little over a year. When he died he left me some money, not much but enough to live off for a few years, if I was frugal. He wasn't ever a kind man. I always felt as though he owned me. He used me when it suited him and looked down on me the rest of the time, but he did give me freedom once he died."

"You named your dog after him."

"Yes," Lady Waters said with a smile. "I wanted to call his name with the same expression of ownership as he had once called mine."

"You pass very well for someone not born into this life you live," Cassandra said.

"Thank you. I have studied hard and am on my guard every moment of every day."

"Is this why the Fortescues have never accepted you? Because you are not of their class?"

"They do not know, or at least neither I nor Lord Waters have ever told them. I am not certain, but I do not think I have ever slipped enough for them to be aware of my origins. However, the fact that I was married to a lawyer means that I am from a lower class in their eyes."

"Lord Waters knew, though?" Cassandra said.

"Yes. I met him in Brighton. I was husband-hunting, looking for the wealthiest, oldest man I could find." Lady Waters laughed at the shocked expression on Jane and Cassandra's faces. "Do not judge me too harshly. I had been married to a brute of a man, and I realised I was good at pretending to be a doting wife. It seemed like the sensible next step — to find myself a husband I could pretend to love for a few years before he died of old age." Lady Waters smiled, shaking her head. "I know, I know. Do not think too poorly of me. I had survived on my wits for a long time, and I was reeling from suddenly being alone and free from Bertram."

"That's why you married Lord Waters?" Jane said, not wanting to believe everything the Fortescues thought of Lady Waters to be true.

"No, although that is why I struck up a conversation with him. He was in Brighton taking the sea air, and I was aware he was a wealthy widower." Lady Waters looked down at her hands and smiled sadly. "I tried to charm him, but the reality was that he charmed me. There was something so kind about him, so reassuring. Within an hour of meeting him, I had told him my whole life story, warts and all."

"You fell in love with him?"

"Not then, and not how you mean. I told him of my plan to marry a wealthy man, and he said he felt sorry for me. He spoke of his first marriage, of the love and companionship he had shared with his wife, and he told me there was no greater gift in the world." Lady Waters fell silent for a moment, as if remembering the conversation. "We met up every day that first week, and he made me see my worth. Then he proposed."

"You didn't know he was going to?"

"No, I was in shock, but he had it all planned out. He was lonely and yearned for company. I was looking to secure my future. All he wanted from me was companionship, friendship, and to have someone to look after."

Jane raised her eyebrows. "He didn't expect any intimacy?"

"No, our relationship was not like that. It was an ideal union. We truly cared for one another. I would have done anything for his happiness, his comfort. We played chess together, went for walks together, discussed current affairs. I gave him my arm to lean on when he was feeling weak and he built up my self-confidence, the knowledge that I could rise to wherever I wanted in the world."

"Did his children know?"

"No. We told no one. We thought it best, and Oliver used to say it was none of their business."

"That is why you allowed Mr Fortescue to speak to you as you did. You didn't want to cause any unnecessary upset for Lord Waters."

"My husband was coming to the end of his life; I was well aware of that. My role as I saw it was to make everything a little better for him, a little easier. If that meant listening to Mr Fortescue berate me every few weeks, I could tolerate that if it meant he was not directing his ire at his father."

"Did you not want to find love?" Cassandra asked, her voice quiet. Jane saw the shimmer of tears in her sister's eyes and knew she was thinking of all she had shared with Thomas Fowle, and all that she had lost.

Lady Waters shook her head. "I was loved. Lord Waters loved me, and I loved him. It might not have been a conventional marriage, but we knew what the other person needed and tried our very hardest to give that to them."

"People do marry for stranger reasons," Jane murmured.

"We also knew it was not forever. Lord Waters was aware his health was declining, and I knew one day I would be a widow."

"Do you know what was in his will?"

She shrugged. "Not specifics. He told me I would be provided for, and that was enough for me. I did not need to know the details; I trusted him to leave me something without jeopardising the inheritance he would leave for his children."

Jane sat back and exhaled. It was a relief in some ways to hear Lady Waters' story of her marriage. Their union had been one of convenience, but a convenience filled with love and companionship. It meant that unless she had missed something, Lady Waters did not have a motive for killing her husband. Her life was better with Lord Waters alive.

"You do believe me, don't you, Miss Austen?"

"Call me Jane," she said, leaning forward and clasping Lady Waters' hand. "Yes, I believe you, and I promise I will do whatever I can to prove your innocence." She paused and then pushed on. "What about the man who called at the house a few months ago?"

"Yes, there was a man," Lady Waters said. "He came to the door and was pestering the servants to be admitted. I believe Mrs Hope sent him away. I went out for a walk a little later on and he accosted me in the street. He claimed to know me from my time in London, but I spoke to him sharply and sent him on his way."

"You did not recognise him?"

"It was a different life," Lady Waters shrugged. "Perhaps our paths did cross in St Giles — there were many children in the slums — but I did not remember him. I expect he wanted to press me for money, but I sent him away. The Fortescues may not know of my origins, but Lord Waters did. There was nothing he could use to blackmail me."

"You didn't see him again?"

"No."

Out of the corner of her eye Jane noticed Cassandra shift in her chair, and she knew their time here was almost done.

Quickly she asked one final question. "Why would Mr Fortescue want to see you accused of his father's murder? I understand the money troubles, but why does he hate you so much?"

"In his mind the two things are linked. Mr Fortescue thinks I influenced his father, that I turned Lord Waters against him. He thinks the only reason I married Lord Waters was to get my hands on as much money as possible, and in the process cut him off. Take that jewellery he was raving about when you came for tea. He does not care about it for any sentimental reasons; he cares about it because it is valuable. He believes his father would have happily sold it and given the proceeds to him, but whilst I was draining money from Lord Waters it was never going to happen."

"It really is all about money," Jane murmured, wondering whether this could be as simple as Mr Fortescue killing his father for his inheritance and then making it look like Lady Waters was the culprit. "Do you know why Lord Waters had the fake necklace in his pocket on the day he died?"

"No, although it is less surprising than having the real emeralds with him. They were very expensive and very heavy."

"You weren't aware of a false set of emeralds?"

"No."

"Come, Jane, we can discuss this more tomorrow, but we have to get back now," Cassandra said, rising from her seat.

"Thank you for visiting," Lady Waters said. Now it was time for Jane and Cassandra to leave, she had tears in her eyes.

"Be strong," Jane said quietly. "You will prevail."

"Jane might be an unlikely investigator, but she is tenacious and bright and I promise we will do whatever we can to get to the bottom of this matter," Cassandra said as they made their way to the door.

"Thank you."

They made their way back into the overcrowded kitchen and thanked the warden and his wife for use of their parlour.

"We shall visit again tomorrow, if that is acceptable," Jane said as he walked them to the door. "We are only here for one night, but would like to see Lady Waters again before we leave. We have some clothes and personal items to deliver as well."

"Of course. I am sure Lady Waters will be happy to have you," the warden said genially. He seemed to hold no animosity towards his prisoner and treated her with courtesy and respect. Although it was not a situation Jane would ever want to find herself in, she took comfort in the knowledge that there were some good people in this world, and Mr Scadding appeared to be one of them.

CHAPTER FIFTEEN

Jane slept poorly in the cramped bed alongside her sister and her aunt. The room was clean and the bedding fresh, but all through the night she heard mice scurrying across the beams over her head. The bed didn't have a canopy, so Jane lay there waiting for a mouse to lose its footing and fall down on her.

She was grateful when the sun started to filter through the thin curtains and outside the birds began to sing a dawn chorus. She rose quietly. Cassandra had been tossing and turning all night too, but was finally settled, the bedclothes caught around her legs in a big ball.

Jane quietly pulled a chair across the room and positioned it in front of the window, looking out on the road below as the town of Ilchester awoke. At first it was just a couple of tradesmen ambling across the cobbles, carrying their tools or rubbing their bleary eyes. A little later the servants began to bustle from the houses, walking quickly with their heads bent as they went about their tasks for the morning. There was no heavy footfall on the streets until after eight, when carts started to roll through the town and horses clip-clopped across the cobbles.

"You're up early, Jane. Could you not sleep?" Cassandra said as she stirred, opening her eyes a little to look across at her sister.

"I got up a while ago. I didn't want to disturb you."

"Jane Austen, you need to quiet that brain sometimes."

Jane sighed, knowing it was true. The whole morning she had lain in bed puzzling over how to prove Lady Waters' innocence and bring the real killer to justice. She had concluded that the only way to succeed with the former was to push ahead with the latter. Somehow she needed to unpick the complicated web of motive and opportunity to see who had really slipped poison into Lord Waters' drink.

"I know, my head is throbbing this morning. I cannot function on no sleep at all."

"Perhaps you will rest in the carriage."

"Perhaps." Jane had planned to try to write in the carriage, although she knew it was a futile exercise. She hadn't written a single word since they had arrived in Bath. Although it was not unheard of for her to take breaks from her writing, normally these were planned. Over the last few weeks, she'd had this awful feeling of being stuck. Her current novel, 'First Impressions', was a good way along, but she felt as though something was missing. She'd puzzled over it and read through what she had and something just wasn't working. The family structure seemed all wrong. She hadn't brought the whole manuscript with her from Bath to Ilchester, but maybe in the carriage she might be able to clear her mind of thoughts of murder and poison for a few hours and think instead about the Bennett sisters for a while.

It took an age for everyone to get dressed, and Jane was ready to groan in frustration as Mrs Leigh-Perrot debated with the landlady as to what they might take for breakfast. Once a menu of toast and eggs was agreed upon, they settled around a table and waited, Jane tapping her foot impatiently. All she could think about was getting back to the gaol and talking to Lady Waters again. Her head was swimming with questions she needed the answer to.

It was almost ten o'clock when they finally left the inn and walked along the cobbled streets to Ilchester gaol. The stableboy from the Ilchester Arms followed after them, hauling the bag they had brought for Lady Waters.

Jane had the payment ready for the guard at the door, but as they approached he stepped out and barred the way.

"No more visitors," he said, folding his arms and squaring his shoulders, as if protecting himself from a possible attack from the three women.

Jane had hoped they might be waved on through without too much fuss so that Mrs Leigh-Perrot would not realise they had visited the day before. It was unlikely they would get away with the illicit visit completely, but it was worth a try.

"The warden said we were free to visit again today."

"Things have changed," the guard said, stepping closer to the door as if afraid Jane might try to slip through.

"What has changed? Is Lady Waters unwell?"

"No."

"Then why can we not visit?"

"No more visitors," the guard said. "Move on, Miss."

"If I cannot see Lady Waters, then I want to speak to the warden."

"The warden is busy."

"Then I shall wait."

"What is happening, Jane?" Mrs Leigh-Perrot said. Jane felt her heart sink at her aunt's expression. It had been difficult to persuade her to let them come to Ilchester to visit the disgraced Lady Waters in the first place. If there was a whiff of opposition or scandal, they would be on their way back to Bath immediately.

"The guard says we cannot visit."

"That is a shame," Mrs Leigh-Perrot said, looking relieved. "Perhaps we can just pass him Lady Waters' bag and then go back to Bath."

"I need to speak to her, Aunt Jane," Jane said, biting her lip. They couldn't go, not yet. It was likely the last chance they would get to talk to Lady Waters before her trial, and Jane felt the weight of responsibility pressing down on her to find some way to free her new friend.

"If the guard says no, then there is not much we can do," Mrs Leigh-Perrot said, taking Jane's arm.

"We've come so far. It would be a waste not to go in."

To Jane's relief Cassandra stepped forward, her presence immediately calming things as always.

"We are sorry to pester you," Cassandra said to the guard. "But my sister and I came a long way to see Lady Waters. Can you tell us why we are not allowed to visit today?" Cassandra discreetly took out a couple of coins from her purse and slipped them into the guard's hand. Mrs Leigh-Perrot gasped, aghast that her niece would know how to bribe a man.

"Mr Winters, the magistrate, arrived with another man. They are questioning Lady Waters." He pocketed the coins quickly so Cassandra would not have a chance to change her mind about the bribe.

"How long have they been in there?"

"Ten minutes or so. Not long."

"Can we wait?"

"It's your time you're wasting."

"I am sorry, girls. This was a terrible idea," Mrs Leigh-Perrot said firmly. "Give the bag to the guard and let us go home. We have done our Christian duty bringing that poor woman some clothes and personal items. Now I need to protect your reputations and get you back to Bath."

"We've come so far," Jane said, panic rising within her. "Don't let it be a waste. We could wait for an hour and then return. I am sure Lady Waters will be able to have visitors then."

"No," Mrs Leigh-Perrot said, with a resolute expression on her face. "I should have trusted my instincts. I knew this was a terrible idea and we should never have come. Your poor mother would berate me for allowing you into such a situation."

Before her aunt could protest any more, Jane turned back to the guard. "Here," she said, thrusting out her purse. "It is all I have. Please take it. Just let me in to wait for Lady Waters."

The guard looked at the purse, his eyes weighing up how much might be inside. Jane knew she had succeeded when slowly he reached out to weigh the fabric pouch in his hand.

"Please."

"Fine. You can wait inside. It's not up to me if you will actually get to see her."

To Jane's relief the guard unlocked the heavy door and let her step into the courtyard area, directing her to a rickety bench. He called over another guard, who had been patrolling backwards and forwards across the courtyard, to come and stand with her, and then disappeared outside.

As she sat and waited Jane heard raised voices, muted by the walls of the prison. Stretching, she stood and edged a little closer to the warden's house, just close enough to make out the words.

"You are a thieving harlot! Tell me what you have done with the jewellery." Even through a layer of brick and mortar, the voice was unmistakably Mr Fortescue's.

Lady Waters' voice was softer and the words inaudible from Jane's position, even though she strained to hear them.

"I don't believe you. No one else could have…"

Lady Waters spoke again, and then Jane heard the gravelly tones of Mr Winters. Only Mr Fortescue was audible.

"This is ridiculous. I will find out what you have done," Mr Fortescue said, and then the door flew open. Jane was in the man's direct line of sight and he frowned deeply when he saw her, turning to Mr Winters and murmuring something in his ear. Mr Fortescue then marched to the door to the street, banging on it until the guard on the other side opened up and let him out.

Mr Winters emerged a moment later, talking intently to the warden. After a minute, the magistrate bowed his head and made his way over to Jane.

"I am surprised to see you here, Miss Austen."

"I offered to bring Lady Waters a change of clothes and a few personal items," Jane said.

"That is very charitable of you, Miss Austen, but perhaps a little unwise. I understand you did not know Lady Waters before a few days ago."

"That is right, Mr Winters."

"Then can I urge you to be cautious. You do not know what you entangle yourself in. This is a very serious matter, and I would hate to see an innocent young woman's reputation tarnished."

Jane contemplated his words for a moment, studying the older man's face. She could not work out if he was complicit in Mr Fortescue's plan to destroy Lady Waters or if he was merely a little incompetent. It did not really matter; the result was the same, but it would be interesting to know his motivations.

"Thank you for your advice, Mr Winters. I will take note of what you say."

"Good. I knew you were a sensible girl, Miss Austen. Shall I escort you out? I have instructed that Lady Waters has no more visitors until her trial."

"Surely I could speak to her for a few moments without any harm?"

"I am sorry, Miss Austen, there are to be no exceptions. If you have the bag you brought for her I can see it is given to Lady Waters, after it is searched, of course."

"Of course," Jane murmured. There was no arguing with the man. Jane could see that from his set expression and the way he laid a gentle but insistent hand on her lower back to guide her from the gaol. "Do you know the Fortescues well, Mr Winters? It is good of you to accompany Mr Fortescue over here to Ilchester. The journey is arduous."

"I am just doing my duty, Miss Austen. I take my role as magistrate very seriously. I know many see it as a stepping stone to higher office, but I am aware of the importance of the role, especially to the common folk." He smiled benevolently at her as they stepped out of the gaol, the guard closing and locking the door behind them. "But in answer to your question, yes, I do know Fortescue well. We went to school together many years ago."

"I see." Jane would never have guessed. The years had been kinder to Mr Fortescue than to Mr Winters. "I attended a small school for young ladies for a few years," she said, as if making idle conversation. "My sister and I were not there for that long, but some of the friendships we made there will not weaken, even with the passing of years."

"Too right. There is no greater loyalty than to the men you grew up with," Mr Winters said. "Is that your aunt over there? Do me the kindness of waiting here, Miss Austen, whilst I talk to her for a moment."

Jane stayed where she was, not daring to look over to where the magistrate was no doubt telling Mrs Leigh-Perrot to keep her niece under better control. After this disaster, she would be lucky if she wasn't sent back to Hampshire in disgrace.

The magistrate disappeared round the corner after a few minutes and Jane reluctantly re-joined Cassandra and Mrs Leigh-Perrot. Their aunt was unusually quiet as Cassandra approached the guard for a final time, asking him to take the bag they had brought to Lady Waters.

"Aunt Jane?" Jane said as they walked back through the streets to the inn.

"Not here," Mrs Leigh-Perrot said, her tone clipped and her expression severe.

Cassandra stepped closer to Jane and took her arm and the two sisters walked in silence behind their aunt.

Not a single word was uttered until they were in the carriage and on their way out of Ilchester, when Mrs Leigh Perrot raised her head and looked directly at Jane.

"I have never been so embarrassed in my whole life."

"I am sorry, Aunt."

"I do not understand what it is you are trying to do here, but I am putting a stop to it right now. I have allowed you too much latitude, been too lax with my sympathies."

Jane knew this wasn't the time to point out that both she and Cassandra were grown women. They were not children any longer and should have at least some say in what they did and didn't do. Their parents allowed Jane and Cassandra more autonomy than many young women of their age, but they were still dependent on their father for everything financial and material.

"You are not a magistrate, Jane, and I know you have assisted your Lord Hinchbrooke with his enquiries in

Hampshire, but you cannot do the same here. A respectable young lady does not spend her time bribing guards to gain access to a gaol. Your mother would be horrified."

Jane nodded, knowing better than to argue. Perhaps when they had returned to Bath and Mrs Leigh-Perrot had calmed a little, putting the distressing events in Ilchester far behind them, she might broach the subject again, but right now she knew she had to appear apologetic and agree to any conditions her aunt set.

"We are sorry, Aunt," Cassandra said, her voice conciliatory. "This was not how we thought things would unfold, and we regret that you have been caught up in something so sordid."

"It is not *my* reputation I fear for."

They fell silent, Mrs Leigh-Perrot staring out the carriage window with a frown on her face. Jane knew her aunt was deciding what would be for the best, whether to send her and Cassandra home once they arrived back in Bath. She closed her eyes and thought of Lady Waters' brave but desperate expression, the flicker of hope in her eyes when Jane had promised to get to the truth. It was a matter of life and death, more important than reputation. She needed to stay in Bath and she needed a degree of freedom to allow her to continue her investigation.

The journey was even longer on their return and after about two hours Ms Leigh-Perrot nodded off, her head bobbing around for a while until she fell into a deeper sleep with her cheek resting on the side of the carriage close to the window.

Jane and Cassandra didn't speak for a while longer, not wanting to disturb their aunt, but eventually Jane could not hold things in any longer.

"When I went in the gaol, Mr Fortescue was shouting at Lady Waters about the jewellery," Jane said. "He accused her of stealing it."

"Surely that does not make sense. Why would Lady Waters' steal her own jewellery?"

"I am not sure, Cassandra. I cannot work this out. As I was listening, I wondered if Lady Waters had stashed away some pieces to ensure Mr Fortescue didn't get his hands on what was hers, predicting the hatred and vitriol she would receive from her step-son when her husband died."

"Lady Waters is an astute woman. I would not be surprised if she suspected Mr Fortescue might try something and hid some jewellery just in case."

"I suppose." Jane groaned, balling her fists in her dress. "If only I had been able to speak to Lady Waters after Mr Fortescue and Mr Winters had left. I would have been able to ask her exactly what they meant."

"It is too late now, Jane," Cassandra said, placing a calming hand on her arm. "You will just have to find out some other way."

"None of it explains why Lord Winters would be walking around Bath with paste and glass emeralds in his pocket."

Jane slumped back in her seat. She felt the pressure of the investigation was made worse by not knowing how to proceed. Normally in her dealings with Lord Hinchbrooke, the magistrate's name brought a certain respect and fear with it. People willingly sat and answered the questions put to them, wanting to assist the magistrate in any way they could. Here in Bath no one knew her and everyone underestimated her abilities.

"I need to talk to Mr Fortescue and Mrs Upton," Jane said.

"They will not welcome you."

"I know, but it has to be done. I hope to be able to goad Mr Fortescue into saying something he shouldn't."

"I am not sure goading a man like that is a sensible idea."

"What other choice do I have?"

Cassandra remained silent for a while and then shook her head. "I can see no sensible way to do this, Jane. It is impossible."

"There is a life at stake."

CHAPTER SIXTEEN

There was a parcel waiting for Jane when they arrived home. It was wrapped in brown paper and had a note folded and tucked under the string securing it.

"Do you have an admirer, Jane?" Mrs Leigh-Perrot asked, a note of excitement in her voice at the prospect of a suitor.

Jane took the note and unfolded it, smiling at the words.

Dear Miss Austen,

Forgive the unusual gift, but I have not been able to stop thinking about the question of what poison could have killed Lord Waters, if indeed it was not belladonna. I have marked a few possibilities and written some notes. I am happy to discuss this further with you if you so wish. Best of luck in your endeavours.

Dr Black

"It is a book from Dr Black," Jane said, choosing not to unwrap it in front of her aunt.

"That is very thoughtful of him." Mrs Leigh-Perrot's eyes narrowed and she looked at Jane with a calculating expression. "He is a respectable man, Jane, a most suitable suitor."

Jane pressed her lips together and tried not to laugh. Dr Black was hardly courting her by sending her a book on poisons. "Do you mind if I retire, Aunt?" she asked, eager to get to the book. "I am weary from the journey."

"Of course. Rest well this afternoon and then tomorrow we will discuss what is to be done about your stay here in Bath."

She didn't try to protest, knowing that conversation was best delayed for as long as possible. Instead, she clutched the book to her chest and hurried upstairs.

The room she shared with Cassandra was dark with the curtains half drawn, and Jane took a moment to fully throw back the fabric and let the sunlight into the room. She settled herself on the bed, and then with a surge of anticipation she tore off the brown paper wrapping.

The book was bound in brown leather with its title, *Book of Poisons*, written in gold across the spine and front cover. It looked well used but not old, and inside the cover she saw the year 1785 printed on it. It was probably from Dr Black's time studying medicine in London.

She was careful as she turned the pages, acutely aware of the cost of books. Her father was indulgent in many ways, but she had to be considerate of the family's finances. She often received a book on her birthday and perhaps if she were lucky one at Christmas, but most of the time she had to make do with re-reading those in her father's collection or borrowing from friends when she visited.

The book was about half an inch thick, the pages made of good quality paper. There were pictures of some of the plants and herbs discussed in the text, often with a page of writing next to them. Jane's eyes skipped over the words. There was a lot of specialist language used, and once she had looked at a few pages it was clear this was a book written for doctors, not just interested amateurs.

The first note was next to a plant called *Conium maculatum*, a plant with green, fern-like leaves and clusters of tiny white flowers. Dr Black had written *Poison hemlock — this can cause confusion and sweating before collapse after around fifteen minutes*. A few pages on there was another scribbled note in the margin next to *Digitalis purpurea — Foxglove — can be lethal if there is an underlying weakness of the heart. Causes sudden death.*

Dr Black had annotated about a dozen entries, picking out the features of the poisons that had made him consider whether they could have been used to kill Lord Waters.

"What book did Dr Black send you?" Cassandra asked as she entered the room and flopped down onto the bed. She looked exhausted, her face pale and drawn, and she closed her eyes as soon as her head rested on her pillow.

"*Book of Poisons.*"

"Only you could be so delighted with such a gift."

"He's annotated it."

"With herb and flowers for love potions?"

Jane snorted. "Don't you start. It is bad enough having Aunt Jane think there could be something romantic between us."

"Instead he's supplying you with expert information about the crime you are not meant to be investigating."

"It is enlightening."

"Have you found the likely poison?"

Jane paused, flicking back through the pages. "Do you know, it could be any number of these. I only saw Lord Waters briefly after we think he imbibed the poison, and no one ever had a chance to ask him what his symptoms were. The book talks of a racing heart, sweating, and a dry mouth, but who is to know what he felt?"

"So you are no closer?"

Jane considered for a moment longer. "I think I can conclude two things that are helpful." She held up her fingers and checked them off as she spoke. "One, belladonna certainly isn't the only poison that could have been slipped into Lord Waters' drink. Others could have given him the symptoms he exhibited in the minutes before his death and the signs present when we examined the body. Two, belladonna might not be the only poison, but it is the most likely. Readily available if you know where to look, easy to administer, and just a few drops would be enough to kill."

Cassandra frowned. "You seemed pleased by this."

"I think the information contained in this book would be enough to convince an intelligent jury that any number of poisons could have been used to murder Lord Waters. It may have been belladonna, but it could also have been one of these other poisons. The fact that Lady Waters had some belladonna in her possession isn't proof she murdered her husband with it."

"I can see the logic," Cassandra said. "But you are assuming the jury will weigh up such evidence. The story Mr Fortescue and Mr Winters have spun with the belladonna is one that is easy to believe. It makes sense, even if it is not the truth. You are asking the jury to find in favour of uncertainties. It might be different if you could say with conviction the exact poison that was used, but asking them to find Lady Waters innocent because it could have been something else is not going to be enough."

Jane felt her shoulders slump. Cassandra was right. Juries were notoriously fickle, and they enjoyed a good story above all else. It wasn't enough to show something *might* be the case; you needed a narrative to capture their imagination to make them believe it.

"If it comes to trial, do you think it will be fair?" Cassandra asked as she relaxed further into the pillows.

"No. The whole county will have heard rumours of Lord Waters' murder, and they will have already made their minds up. It is quite a sensational story, isn't it? The young wife who has outlived two husbands already, marrying an unsuspecting older man for his money — then a little over a year later he dies in suspicious circumstances."

"Then you cannot deal purely in supposition, Jane. You need hard evidence, something a juror cannot ignore or brush away. Otherwise Lady Waters will be convicted because people do not like a woman of a certain class getting above her station."

For a long moment Jane sat in silence, and then she gave a resolute nod. "Then we will find hard evidence, Cassandra. We must, or Lady Waters will die a horrible death."

CHAPTER SEVENTEEN

Everyone was subdued at breakfast. Cassandra pushed her eggs around her plate without once lifting her fork to her lips, and Mrs Leigh-Perrot winced every time Jane scraped her butterknife over her piece of toast. Jane was waiting for the inevitable discussion around sending her and Cassandra home. She knew she would have to fight it, and had spent the night tossing and turning, trying to work out both how to convince her aunt to let her stay in Bath and what she could do to convince the rest of Lord Waters' family to talk to her.

Mr Leigh-Perrot cleared his throat and glanced at his wife. "Cassandra, Jane," he said eventually. "Your aunt and I love having you to stay, but we are concerned about this terrible affair you have become mixed up in."

"I know you said it helped staying here in Bath, Cassandra, but I think it really is time for you to go home now," Mrs Leigh-Perrot said. "It does not need to be forever. I suggest we plan another visit in a few months, when all this trouble has passed."

Jane pressed her lips together, knowing she needed to keep her counsel now more than ever. She wanted to point out to her aunt and uncle that this *terrible affair*, this *trouble*, was no less than murder, and it could very easily result in an innocent woman losing her life. "Yes, Aunt," she said meekly, to the surprise of everyone around the table.

"You agree?"

"I do not wish to be a burden, and I understand this is your home. You have to socialise with these people. I know all this, Aunt Jane."

"You are happy to return to Hampshire, then?"

Jane inclined her head, unable to say the words that would end her trip to Bath. There was no point in arguing; she knew her aunt's mind was made up. Instead, Jane planned to agree to go home in principle but to find an excuse to put it off a little longer. At best she estimated she could add five days onto their stay, at worst probably only one or two.

"I shall make enquiries as to which coach you need to take to get home. Hopefully we can avoid you having to go all the way to London to go back out again to Hampshire."

"Thank you, Aunt. If you have no objections, I think I would like to spend today having a last stroll around Bath." Jane stood and excused herself, quickly followed by Cassandra.

"What are you doing, Jane Austen?" Cassandra whispered once they were out of the room.

"There was nothing I could say to persuade our aunt and uncle to let me continue with my enquiries. If I beg them to think of Lady Waters, they will tell me to leave any investigation to the officials. If I talk of my experience in these matters, they will remind me we are in Bath, not Hampshire."

"But you're not giving up?"

"No. Not whilst there is still hope of finding the truth. I thought it would be easier to agree to go home, but find a reason to delay our journey."

Cassandra nodded thoughtfully. "I see my theatrical skills will need to be brushed up if I am to convince Aunt Jane I have a debilitating headache or awful cramps and can't possibly travel."

"I do not know what I have done to deserve you, Cassandra, but you truly are the best of sisters."

"What is the plan for today?" Cassandra asked as Jane collected her bonnet, tying the ribbon beneath her chin.

"Today I am going to tackle Mr Fortescue and Mrs Upton."
Jane paused and tilted her head to one side. "I have another
favour to ask you."

"Yes?"

"Would you return to Lady Waters' house and question the
servants again? I believed everything Lady Waters said, except
perhaps the tale about the stranger who visited and pressed her
for money."

"You want me to see if I can find any more information?"

"Yes, please."

"Do you not think I should come with you? You are entering
the lion's den, after all."

Jane hesitated, knowing what a calming presence her sister
would be when she stepped into Mr Fortescue's house. "No,"
she said after a moment. "Time is limited, and we cannot
afford to waste even a few minutes. This will be more
efficient."

"Be careful then, Jane."

"I will."

They left the house together and walked the length of the
street arm in arm, but at the end of the road Jane turned left
whilst Cassandra headed off to the right. It was another
glorious morning, with the sunlight illuminating the sand-
coloured buildings and all the windows freshly washed and
glinting.

As Jane approached Mr Fortescue's house, she wondered if
the servants might recognise her from her visit on the day of
Lord Waters' funeral, when she had impersonated a maid. She
hoped not, but she resolved to keep her head bent and her
bonnet firmly on her head until she was inside.

It was too early for social calls, but Jane knocked at the door anyway, steeling herself for the icy response she was sure to receive. It took a while for anyone to open the door, and when the footman did he looked distracted, glancing over his shoulder.

"Miss Austen to see Mr Fortescue," she said, handing over her calling card.

"Is he expecting you, Miss?"

"We did not make an appointment, but I am sure he will want to speak to me."

"Mr Fortescue is a little busy at the moment, Miss."

"I can wait."

"It may be a while. The solicitor arrived this morning."

Jane's eyes widened and she boldly stepped inside. She was thankful the footman was young and inexperienced and didn't insist she leave immediately. "Perhaps there is somewhere I can wait? Do not disturb Mr Fortescue if he is with the solicitor, but when the solicitor leaves please give him my card then."

The footman still looked undecided and Jane adopted her most innocent expression.

"Would you care to wait in the drawing room, Miss?"

"Thank you."

Jane watched as he hesitated outside the door across the hall, looking at her card as if trying to decide if he was going to disturb Mr Fortescue in his important meeting. After a moment he placed the card on the marble-topped table in the hall and disappeared.

Moving quickly, Jane darted back out into the hall, wondering if there was somewhere she could conceal herself so she could hear what was happening in the study without anyone knowing she was there.

Before she could find anywhere she heard footsteps, and the door to the study opened. Jane dashed back into the drawing room just in time, turning to see Mrs Upton flinging open the front door, tears streaming down her cheeks. Her husband followed, a frown on his face as he muttered something under his breath.

A minute later an older man appeared, dressed in a sober black jacket, waistcoat and trousers. By his appearance Jane could assume he was the solicitor. He shook Mr Fortescue's hand before he left and then made his way out of the front door. Mr Fortescue looked serious, but not as upset as his sister had been.

As the solicitor left Mr Fortescue glanced into the drawing room, his expression darkening as he spotted Jane.

"What are you doing in my house?"

Jane squared her shoulders and drew herself up to her full height, but she was still a good foot shorter than Mr Fortescue. Sometimes she wished for just a few more inches to give her a little more physical presence.

She held up her hands in a placating gesture. "I came to apologise, Mr Fortescue."

This brought him up short. "Apologise?"

"Yes. I have been insensitive. The last few days must have been extremely difficult for you, what with the loss of your father and all the grief and uncertainty that goes with that. I am aware I have not made things easier for you."

"You have not, Miss Austen."

"Then I apologise, and my condolences on the death of your father." She took a step towards the door, hoping she had read the situation right and Mr Fortescue would call her back.

"Wait, Miss Austen. When I last saw you in Ilchester, you had travelled a very long way to see Lady Waters. Why was that?"

Jane lowered her eyes. "I am embarrassed by the depths of my foolishness."

"Please stay, Miss Austen. I think we have things to discuss."

With a show of reluctance, Jane turned and walked back into the room, perching on the edge of a sofa. She was aware she was alone with Mr Fortescue in the drawing room, but the door was open and there was no question of impropriety.

"You must know what a charming young woman Lady Waters can be," Jane said, looking down at her hands.

"Yes, I suppose it would be easy to fall for her charms, if you were not aware of the danger she can pose," Mr Fortescue said, puffing out his chest like some sort of superior seabird.

"You never fell for it?"

"No. She charmed my father, of course. He was a different man after he came back from Brighton with her on his arm. I lost some respect for him, falling for the oldest trick in the book."

"The oldest trick in the book?" Jane enquired mildly, surprised at how easily Mr Fortescue was opening up with minimal encouragement.

"The lure of a younger woman. She must have promised my father all sorts, and in exchange he gave her whatever she wanted, forgetting about those who really mattered in his life."

"You and your sister."

"Exactly, Miss Austen."

"You must understand, Mr Fortescue, I knew none of this when I befriended Lady Waters."

"Of course you didn't, Miss Austen. Lady Waters is a consummate actress. She thrives on taking in the innocent and pulling their strings until they are dancing to her rhythm." He sounded magnanimous now, comforting Jane for being foolish enough to be taken in by his stepmother.

"Lady Waters herself told me she always tried to keep the peace between you and your father, that she didn't want to come between you."

Mr Fortescue snorted and shook his head. "A fine job she did of that. She was always there in the background, whispering in his ear, exaggerating any little morsel of information she gleaned to turn our father away from us."

"You see why I feel so foolish. I heard a completely different story from Lady Waters."

"What made you change your mind, Miss Austen?"

"I was waiting for Lady Waters whilst you were in with her and the magistrate. You were talking about the jewellery, I think."

"Yes," Mr Fortescue confirmed. "The wretched business with the jewellery."

Jane knew she had to tread carefully here. There was an art to making someone believe you knew more than you actually did, but it was a fine line to walk. One wrong word and she risked putting Lady Waters in further peril, as well as losing Mr Fortescue as a source of information. Rather than saying anything that might show her complete ignorance of what had occurred, she stayed silent, hoping Mr Fortescue would reveal something more.

"Did she tell you anything about it?" Mr Fortescue asked.

"No, not then, but we had spoken about the emerald necklace that used to be your mother's on a previous occasion."

Mr Fortescue leaned in closer, his eyes shining. "Did she say anything then?"

Jane swallowed, fearing Mr Fortescue was going to work out at any moment what she was about and evict her from the house. "No," she said, drawing out the word. "She didn't *say* anything, but I got the sense there was something more to this dispute with the jewellery than she was telling me."

Mr Fortescue stood, thumping one fist into the palm of his other hand. "I knew it. The thieving harlot. She wasn't content with the luxurious lifestyle my father gave her; she was stealing from him, stealing from *me*."

Jane frowned, trying to follow the path of Mr Fortescue's thoughts, but she struggled to piece everything together. "When I was waiting to see Lady Waters in Ilchester gaol, I knew I had been duped, but I still cannot quite work out what exactly happened with the jewellery." It was a gamble, but Mr Fortescue seemed too caught up in his dislike for Lady Waters to realise Jane was being disingenuous.

"My man is looking into it, but he thinks she took the pieces one by one so they wouldn't be missed. She must have found some dishonest jeweller to make her a replica out of coloured glass and taken that home for the collection, leaving her free to sell the real pieces."

"What I don't understand is why she would go to so much trouble. Were the pieces of jewellery not hers anyway?"

"They were the family's. My mother's."

"I see."

It was an interesting piece of information, although not for the reason Mr Fortescue thought. "You're sure it was Lady Waters who swapped the genuine jewellery for the glass pieces? Not an unscrupulous maid or someone else who had access to the household?"

"A servant would not be that audacious."

Knowing she could not press her incredulity any further without Mr Fortescue becoming suspicious of her motivations, Jane ran her hands over her skirt and made to rise from the sofa. "Please accept my apologies again, Mr Fortescue. I can now see the error of my ways. I will call on your sister to express the same."

"I would not right now," Mr Fortescue said.

"Oh?"

"She is a little upset from the reading of the will."

"I am sorry to hear that. Was it not as favourable as she hoped?"

"No," Mr Fortescue said, pressing his lips together. Jane could see she would get nothing further from the man now and decided to leave whilst he was still in a forgiving mood. That way, the door might still be open if she did need to return with further questions.

"Thank you for your time."

"Good day, Miss Austen." Mr Fortescue escorted her to the front door himself, disappearing inside once she was safely back on the pavement.

Jane walked slowly, trying to make sense of everything she had gleaned from their short conversation.

She had reached the end of the street, head bowed and deep in thought, when she felt a light touch on her arm. Mrs Fortescue stood behind her, her face pinched with worry and her cheeks flushed.

"What were you doing in my house, Miss Austen?" She seemed agitated, her eyes wide and with a hint of wildness about them.

"Are you unwell, Mrs Fortescue?"

"Unwell?" she trilled. "I am sick with worry. What did you say to my husband?"

Jane knew she could take advantage of this situation, press the woman for information before giving her the reassurance she needed, but she was aware her conscience wouldn't let her. Here was a woman in distress, and she wouldn't add to it.

"Come, Mrs Fortescue, let us sit and talk," she said kindly, leading the older woman into the gardens where they had met a few days previously.

They sat on a bench, surrounded by beautiful flowers and green grass, but the atmosphere was close and anxiety-ridden rather than peaceful.

"I came to the house to talk to your husband about Lord Waters' death," Jane said, speaking slowly and holding Mrs Fortescue's eye. "I did not mention you once, and I certainly did not talk of your health issues."

For a long moment Mrs Fortescue's eyes searched Jane's face, and then she exhaled deeply, her whole body slumping.

"I am sorry to have been the cause of concern for you, but understand that I would not do anything that would put you in danger with your husband," Jane went on.

"When I saw you leaving…" Mrs Fortescue trailed off, shaking her head.

"You thought I had been to talk to Mr Fortescue about the medication you need to get through the day."

Mrs Fortescue nodded miserably. "He would be furious."

"Does he hurt you?" Jane asked the question in a low voice, even though there was no one around.

Mrs Fortescue shook her head. "Not really."

It was a difficult subject to discuss. Many marriages were harmonious, or at least civil, but the law was on the side of the husband if he did decide to beat his wife for some imagined or actual misdemeanour. The relationships Jane had seen in close proximity, her parents' marriage, that of the Leigh-Perrots and that of her dear friend Mrs Telford and her husband, were loving and caring, and each person brought their strengths to the union.

Mrs Fortescue's answer made Jane feel a stab of sympathy for the woman. It was clear she was unhappy, and no doubt her husband was unkind if not physically violent towards her.

"I said nothing," Jane reassured her. "I do not wish to make your life harder than it is."

"Thank you, Miss Austen."

"I was talking to your husband about the jewellery he thinks has been substituted with fakes."

Mrs Fortescue frowned. "He is convinced Lady Waters has sold all the real pieces and replaced them with glass replicas."

"I could not fathom why she would do something like that. Surely they were hers to keep anyway?"

"He thinks she wanted the money to build a life for herself after Lord Waters passed away."

"Was she not provided for amply in his will?"

"Lord Waters was generous but fair," Mrs Fortescue said after a moment's contemplation. "He settled an allowance on her of two thousand pounds a year as well as ten thousand pounds to be given immediately. He also left her the London property in the will."

Jane's eyes widened. She had known Lord Waters was considered wealthy, but these were huge sums that she could not even begin to fathom. She tried not to be naïve when it came to money, often helping her mother with the household accounts at home. She knew it was possible to live a good life, a comfortable life, on a fraction of what Lady Waters had been promised.

"It doesn't make any sense. By all accounts Lord Waters was besotted with his wife and would have given her anything she wanted when he was alive, and now he's dead he has settled a very good sum on her. There would be no need for her to steal the jewellery, jewellery that had been gifted to her anyway."

"I thought much the same, but my husband is insistent Lady Waters was blinded by greed."

Jane wondered if this was pure foolhardiness on Mr Fortescue's part, or if he was trying to deflect suspicion away from himself. They had heard of his gambling problems and seen his desire for the jewellery that had once been his mother's. Perhaps he had taken the jewellery himself and exchanged it for worthless replicas, pocketing the money to pay off his gambling debts.

"What about Mr Fortescue? He did not seem too unhappy after the solicitor left."

"He gets the rest of the property, the estate in Somerset and the house here in Bath, as well as another property in Surrey. The estates are well run and profitable. We will not struggle for money."

"Your husband must be pleased his father put his trust in him in the end."

"Indeed."

Mrs Fortescue shifted and Jane knew the timid woman would soon insist on returning home, so she pushed on quickly. "What about Mrs Upton?"

"There he was a little less generous, but it was not entirely unexpected. Mrs Upton was not the heir, and not his beloved wife. I think in Lord Waters' eyes his daughter was married and so her husband should provide for her, whereas Lady Waters was his responsibility."

"Did she get anything?"

"Five thousand pounds and a few pieces of jewellery and items from the house, mainly things that belonged to the first Lady Waters."

There was a stark difference between the generosity Lord Waters had displayed when providing for his wife and what he had given his daughter. It also puzzled Jane that Mr Fortescue, who had been openly hostile towards Lady Waters, had been left well provided for, whereas Mrs Upton, who had been more neutral in her opinion of her father's second marriage, had been left with very little.

"I must go," Mrs Fortescue said, standing.

"Tell me," Jane said, reaching out and placing a hand on the other woman's arm, "were there any other bequests?"

"A small amount for each of Mrs Upton's five daughters, not enough for a proper dowry. *That* was a surprise."

Mrs Fortescue hurried off, leaving Jane alone to ponder what the details of the will meant. She wondered if Lord Waters had meant it as a deliberate snub — a message he had wanted to send to his only daughter — or if it was merely a case of him leaving the majority of his estate to his son and heir and ensuring the woman who had looked after him this last year was well provided for.

CHAPTER EIGHTEEN

Jane had arranged to meet Cassandra close to the entrance of
Parade Gardens. She had hoped to have spoken to Mrs Upton
by now too, but the discussion with Mr Fortescue and the
subsequent talk with his wife had taken longer than she had
anticipated. She was eager to hear how Cassandra had fared at
Lady Waters' house with the servants and decided they could
discuss it on their way to Mrs Upton's house. If Jane was
honest with herself, she was secretly pleased Cassandra's
calming presence would be there when she confronted Mrs
Upton.

"Miss Austen," a familiar voice called, and Jane turned to see
Dr Black and his sister Caroline hurrying towards her. "How
do you fare?"

"I am well, thank you. How are you both?"

"We are well, Miss Austen," Dr Black said.

"Thank you for the book. It was a riveting read."

"I thought you would find it interesting. I am intrigued to
hear your conclusions."

Miss Black shook her head and smiled ruefully. "He has
spoken of little else. We even resolved to call on you at your
aunt and uncle's house so he might hear your thoughts."

"I would be grateful for your expert opinion too, Dr Black."

"It would be my pleasure."

"I am awaiting my sister. She should be here soon, but if you
have a few minutes to spare we could perhaps take a stroll
around the gardens?"

"That would be very pleasant," Dr Black said.

"I confess we have found this whole matter quite thrilling, although terribly sad, of course. It is not often one becomes entangled in a suspicious death," Miss Black said, her eyes shining and full of vigour. "Why don't I wait here for your sister? I can bring her down to the gardens when she arrives."

"If you are sure it is not too much trouble?"

"Not at all. I have heard all my brother's theories; I will let him discuss them with you."

Jane took Dr Black's proffered arm and together they descended the steps into Parade Gardens. It was a beautiful space, bursting with colour from the formal flowerbeds and with wide paths to meander along and enjoy the views. Despite the beauty of the park, Jane's eyes were drawn to the spot in front of the bandstand, the place where Lord Waters had been standing as he turned to her, his expression desperate as he took his last few breaths.

"I think it will be impossible to come here and think of anything else but that poor man's death," Dr Black said, following Jane's gaze.

"I doubt Lady Waters will be able to stay in Bath when she is released," Jane said, forcing herself to remain optimistic. "The memories will be too painful for her."

"It makes it worse that Lord Waters died in such a public and dramatic way."

Jane considered his words for a moment. "It was rather a spectacle, wasn't it?"

"You think it was designed that way, to be witnessed by as many people as possible?"

"I do wonder," Jane mused. "I think in a public venue it was more likely someone would notice something amiss, something they thought pointed to an unnatural death."

"Whereas if Lord Waters had died in his bed, it would have been assumed that his heart merely gave out."

Jane had a sick feeling in her stomach as she realised that she had likely played the part the murderer had hoped someone would, declaring the death of Lord Waters suspicious and allowing Lady Waters to be accused.

"The evening before Lord Waters died, he collapsed whilst attending Mr and Mrs Temple's ball in town. His doctor declared him fit the next day, but I have been wondering if it could have been a first attempt on his life."

"Depending on the poison used, it may have been difficult for the murderer to know the correct dose to give him. Some poisons can cause collapses and convulsions at a certain dose, but not death unless more is given."

It was something Jane suspected they might never know for sure. It didn't help all that much either, for the people highest on her list of suspects, Mr and Mrs Fortescue and Mr and Mrs Upton, had been in attendance at both events. It didn't narrow things down at all.

"Do you have any thoughts on the poison used?" Dr Black asked.

"The book was very detailed," Jane said, casting a brief smile in Dr Black's direction, "but your notes helped me to build a list of possible poisons. There were a few things that interested me."

"Yes?"

"Well, firstly, the poison didn't have to be belladonna."

"I agree," Dr Black said. "But it could have been."

"Exactly. And not only could it have been belladonna, it is quite high up on the list of likely poisons."

"I thought the same."

"Many of the other poisons that could cause similar effects were from plants, and it got me wondering who would have the knowledge to procure something like that."

"Such knowledge is often passed from person to person within a family. There are still village wise women out in the countryside where modern medicine is viewed with suspicion," Dr Black said.

"But it is unlikely any of the people close to Lord Waters would have such knowledge. They have no need for it. If they have an ailment, they consult a doctor."

"That is true, and the knowledge is written in books such as the one I gave you, but they are unlikely to fill the shelves of the average man's library. It is quite a specialist field."

"I think most of the Fortescue family knew of Lady Waters' stash of belladonna. She said one of Mrs Upton's daughters spotted it one day when she was in the house and enquired about it."

"Many people have heard of belladonna, at least."

"Lady Waters said she has had the belladonna for years, that she used it for cosmetic purposes."

"A foolish thing to do, but not all that uncommon. There was a fashion for it a number of years ago, and every so often the women who sell beauty remedies try to promote it again as a way of making the eyes look big and innocent," Dr Black said with a grimace. "They are unscrupulous and do not seem to care that many of the things they recommend are later proven to be dangerous to the health."

"Is belladonna easy to procure, then?"

Dr Black considered for a moment. "I wouldn't say easy, but far from impossible. Whoever was buying it would have to be careful as well. The women who sell the beauty remedies are not known for their reliability. You could not guarantee you were getting actual belladonna from them."

"An apothecary, then?"

"That would be a more reliable source. They are used to handling herbs and medicinal plants, and they are often established in an area with a reputation to uphold."

"They supply doctors as well, do they not?"

"Indeed. I have a trusted man from whom I obtain many of my medicines, and if there is an ongoing need I direct my patients to him to deal directly."

"Are there many apothecaries in Bath?"

"Four," Dr Black said and then frowned. "At least, four reputable establishments. There are some that cater to the poorer population that are less reliable. They come and go."

Jane suppressed a groan. If the killer had purchased belladonna from one of the less reputable establishments, it would be more difficult to track.

"I have contacts amongst the apothecaries and I may get further than you on this matter, Miss Austen. Will you permit me to help? I can ask some questions on your behalf and see if any of the people connected to Lord Waters has been in to purchase belladonna or another poison that might give a similar effect."

"That would be most kind, Dr Black. I think you are much better placed to ask the right questions. I am indebted to you."

"Not at all, Miss Austen. I would like to do whatever I can to help."

Jane's attention was caught by the sight of Cassandra hurrying towards then, her cheeks red, one hand atop her bonnet to stop it from flying off. Miss Black followed a few paces behind, having to walk quickly to keep up with Cassandra.

"Is something amiss? Are you unwell?" Jane asked, searching her sister's face.

"No, Jane, I am in good health. I merely wanted to tell you what I found out as quickly as possible."

"You have come straight from Lord and Lady Waters' house?"

"I have. It was most enlightening."

"Tell me."

Dr Black led them to a bench, where Cassandra and Jane sat whilst he and his sister stood close by.

"The household was in a mess. The cook has found a new job and not been back, and the maid and footman we met the other day are out looking for work. They are not expecting Lady Waters to return and are convinced Mr Fortescue will move his own staff into the house when he takes possession of it."

"What about Sarah?" Jane felt sorry for the only maid loyal to Lady Waters in the place she had called home.

"Sarah was still there but distraught. Mr Fortescue was there a few days ago to collect some items of value. He took some of Lady Waters' jewellery, and there was nothing Sarah could do to stop him."

"Poor girl," Jane murmured.

"A few hours later apparently he returned and was shouting and raving about the jewellery being fake. He said it was all worthless, nothing more than cheap metal and coloured glass."

Jane nodded. It tied in with what Mr Fortescue had told her earlier. Someone at some point had swapped the real pieces of jewellery for fakes, no doubt selling the precious stones and the gold settings for a tidy sum.

"He threatened Sarah, saying she would not only lose her position but also be thrown in prison with her mistress and face the hangman's noose if she had any part in the theft."

"No wonder she was distraught."

"She told Mr Fortescue she knew nothing about it, that she just stored the jewellery as Lord and Lady Waters directed."

"She didn't notice any change in the jewellery? She had no suspicions the pieces were fakes?"

"No."

"They must have been well done," Jane mused. "I do not think Lady Waters suspected anything either, although I wonder if Lord Waters was suspicious."

"You think that was why he had the emeralds in his pocket the day he died?"

Jane nodded. "I wondered why he would be carrying such expensive jewels in his jacket pocket on a trip to the park, but I think he knew they were fake. He wouldn't have brought them out like that otherwise. I wonder if he was going to confront someone with them."

"It makes sense that Lord Waters would be the one to notice. He bought the jewellery and going by what Sarah said, much of it he hadn't gifted to Lady Waters yet. He liked to give her a piece on special occasions, something from the family collection that would then be hers to keep. Lady Waters would only have set eyes on the emeralds on a few occasions, whereas Lord Waters knew them well from when his first wife wore them." Cassandra shifted, her face animated and the colour still high in her cheeks. "I wonder whom he was going to confront?"

"Who would have had access to them?" Jane said. "Certainly Lady Waters and her maid Sarah."

"The whole Fortescue clan, I suspect," Cassandra said quickly. "Sarah told me that different items were loaned out to Mrs Fortescue and Mrs Upton, as well as to the eldest Upton daughters on special occasions. Both Mrs Fortescue and Mrs Upton had borrowed the emeralds in the last few months."

Jane groaned. "It doesn't get us any further, does it? It could have been any of them; they all had the opportunity. Mr Fortescue could have taken the emeralds when his wife borrowed them, and Mr Upton the same."

"And we know they both had money troubles."

"Might I interject?" Dr Black said, stepping forward.

"Of course."

"To arrange for the jewellery to be forged and the sale of the real pieces would require some connections I am not sure your suspects would all have."

Jane and Cassandra looked at each other and nodded. Jane would not know how to go about finding someone who could make a passable copy of a precious necklace, let alone where to sell the real thing without news of the sale leaking out.

"You are right. It is not something many people would have knowledge of, but if someone was very determined I suppose there are ways of finding out these things."

"There will be some jewellers in Bath," Cassandra said. "Perhaps they will be a good place to start. They may know who makes the sort of replicas our thief needed, and at the same time we can ask if they have heard anything about pieces being sold quietly."

"We will make a tour of the jewellers' shops after we have seen Mrs Upton," Jane said decisively.

"What thrilling lives you lead," Miss Black said with a shake of her head. "I wonder if I could be of some help, in a small way only, of course? I could make you a list of the places to visit here in town and where they are located."

"That would be most kind, Miss Black."

Jane felt a wave of optimism. They hadn't solved the case yet, but there were strands hanging loose, threads they could pull. She just needed to find the right one, and with a little luck and a good hard tug, hopefully the whole thing would unravel.

"There was something else Sarah told me," Cassandra said, placing a hand on Jane's arm to stop her sister from charging off. "I asked about the visitor Lady Waters had a few months ago, the one she denied knowing."

"Yes?"

"Apparently he has been back. He returned last night and thumped on the servant's entrance for ten minutes before anyone came downstairs to let him in. He was drunk, according to Sarah. He demanded to see Lady Waters and at first wouldn't believe Sarah when she said she wasn't at home."

"I find it difficult to believe he has not heard the rumours about Lady Waters' arrest."

"Eventually Sarah managed to convince him her mistress was not there, and he stumbled away just as the footman we met the other day finally roused himself."

"How strange. It seems odd he is still hanging around if what Lady Waters' told us is true." Jane leaned back against the bench and considered things for a moment. "The only reason he would still be here in Bath, approaching Lady Waters, would be if he thought he could get something from her."

"There is something of note," Cassandra said, the excitement evident in her eyes. "The footman followed him at a distance when he left. Sarah told him not to, as she was afraid he would be spotted and come to harm, but the footman insisted anyway. He followed him to close to The Saracen's Head, a tavern in town. He lost track of him, but Sarah thought there was a chance he might drink there."

Jane swallowed hard, wondering how much trouble she would be in with her aunt if Mrs Leigh-Perrot found out she was dragging her sister to taverns to search for a man of dubious nature.

"I cannot in good conscience let you go in search of this man alone," Dr Black said, his expression one of concern.

"Are you offering to accompany us?" Jane asked.

Dr Black blew out his cheeks and hesitated, nodding a moment later. "I believe you will go anyway, even without my escort. So yes, I will accompany you."

Feeling a surge of relief, Jane smiled her thanks to the doctor. She had stayed in a few coaching inns before when travelling long distances, but her life experiences did not include how to conduct herself in a tavern. She needed to be as inconspicuous as possible so she could ask the questions she needed to without drawing too much attention to herself. It would be easier with Dr Black by her side.

"We have a busy day ahead of us."

"Our aunt will expect us back at some point today," Cassandra said, reminding Jane of the time pressures they were working under.

"Yes, but perhaps it is wiser to stay away until all our tasks are done. That way, she cannot send us home on an afternoon coach if we are nowhere to be found."

"She will never invite us back to Bath after this."

"I know, but I find myself unable to care all that much. Once Lady Waters is out of gaol and the true culprit behind bars, I think I will be glad to bid this city goodbye."

Cassandra nodded in agreement. Jane stood and squared her shoulders, mentally preparing herself for the difficulties ahead.

"Dr Black, I would be grateful if you could make enquiries amongst the apothecaries, and Miss Black, if you could make a list of jewellers. Cassandra and I will call on Mrs Upton and put our questions to her, and then perhaps we could meet back at your consulting rooms in a couple of hours before we visit The Saracen's Head."

Dr Black and his sister set off in separate directions, and Cassandra took her sister's arm, a look of grim determination on her face.

CHAPTER NINETEEN

Mrs Upton's house was another example of fine Bath architecture, with an imposing façade, high windows and the characteristic sandy-coloured brick. Jane hesitated for a moment outside, remembering the fury and upset on Mrs Upton's face as she had fled Mr Fortescue's study earlier that morning.

"Courage, Jane," Cassandra said, but her anxious expression mirrored her sister's.

They were admitted into a good sized drawing room that was furnished with a few heavy pieces of furniture, but the walls and shelves were bare and it looked as though the Uptons were in the process of clearing the room.

Jane was surprised when instead of Mrs Upton a young woman breezed in to greet them.

"I am Miss Elizabeth Upton," she said, dropping into a pretty little curtsey. She was striking in her looks, although not what was normally deemed beautiful. Her face was just a little too long and her eyebrows arched a little too high, giving her a superior look, as if she were always looking down on her companion.

"I am Miss Jane Austen, and this is my sister, Miss Cassandra Austen. We would like to talk to your mother, if she can spare us a few minutes."

"My mother is indisposed," Elizabeth said, sitting down opposite Jane and Cassandra. "Is there something I can help you with?"

"Lizzie, I thought I heard you talking to someone." Another young woman sauntered into the room. "Who are your friends?"

"Mind your manners, Catherine," Elizabeth said sharply. She turned back to Jane and Cassandra. "Please excuse my sister. She is still a child."

"I am not. I am fifteen years old. Mary Hillwood was married at fifteen and mistress of her own household."

"I cannot imagine you being mistress of your own household at five and twenty," another young woman said, coming in to join them.

Jane and Cassandra were faced with three of the Upton daughters now, all looking alike with light brown hair and grey-green eyes. It was difficult to tell how much they differed in age, and Jane recalled Lady Waters telling her there were five Upton daughters, all in need of dowries.

"Lydia," Elizabeth chided, giving both her sisters a ferocious look. She turned back to Jane and Cassandra and then let out a groan as the discordant notes of a piano piece sounded from somewhere deep in the house. "Catherine, go and tell Mary to be quiet. Mama is not feeling well."

"Why should I go and miss all the fun?"

Elizabeth Upton looked to be at the end of her tether and spoke through gritted teeth. "Go and do as I ask, or Father will hear of it."

Catherine disappeared in a huff, and a few seconds later the house fell silent.

"Thank goodness," Elizabeth muttered under her breath. "I apologise again. What can I do for you, Miss Austen?"

"Do you know if your mother will be feeling up to callers later today?"

"I cannot say. Sometimes she gets one of her heads and is abed for a day or more."

Jane suppressed the feeling of panic. She needed to talk to Mrs Upton, and if she did not do so today there was a good chance her aunt would have organised transport back to Hampshire.

"I am a friend of Lady Waters," Jane said, deciding to push on and see what the Upton daughters knew. "I know there was some animosity between your mother and Lady Waters, but I believe she is innocent of the crime she is accused of. I am sure Mrs Upton would not want an innocent woman to go to the gallows whilst her father's killer remained free."

Lydia's eyes widened and she leaned forward, ignoring the admonishing look she received from her older sister. "I told you there was no reason for Lady Waters to kill Grandpapa," she said, clasping her hands together. "She would have to be a fool to do so."

"Be quiet, Lydia. We do not discuss family business with strangers."

"Oh stop it, Lizzie. Lady Waters was never anything but kind to us. She was always suggesting you go and try on some of her gowns, and she never objected to you borrowing her jewellery."

"She let you borrow her jewellery?" Jane asked.

"Yes," Elizabeth said after a moment. "She was quite generous with it. She had the most beautiful set of diamonds, a necklace and earrings that Grandpapa gave her when they first moved to Bath. She let me wear them for my debutante ball."

"It was her suggestion?"

"Yes." Elizabeth shifted and then sighed. "I know Mama disliked her, but she was only ever kind to me. She would often invite me or my older sister Clara round to take tea and talk about dresses and balls. Mama wasn't keen on us going, but sometimes she allowed it."

"Did she lend you other pieces of jewellery?"

"Yes, sometimes. I wore a beautiful ruby bracelet once and a pearl necklace. Mama borrowed the emeralds for some special occasion."

"When you borrowed these items, did you keep them for long?"

"No, a couple of days, perhaps, before we got around to returning them. It was not an issue — they always went back. There was no question of us keeping them."

"As much as Mama would have liked to," Lydia murmured from her position beside Elizabeth.

Elizabeth frowned but continued. "Mama felt some of the jewellery should come to us rather than Lady Waters. It was her mother's, after all, and Mama always said she wouldn't want a stranger to have it above her own flesh and blood."

Jane felt a stirring of excitement. Mrs Upton had a reason to want the jewellery that had been stolen. As well as the monetary value of the items, she felt they were hers by right. Perhaps she would think it was not stealing at all, just bringing the jewellery back to its rightful owner.

"Did the pieces ever go missing whilst they were in your house?"

Elizabeth looked shocked. "Of course not. They were kept in the safe in the kitchen."

No doubt Mrs Upton had a key to the safe.

"Thank you, Miss Upton, you have been most helpful."

"Do you think Lady Waters will be convicted?" Lydia asked.

"I think there is a lot of ill feeling and emotion surrounding this case, and when that happens sometimes facts are obscured by sentiment."

"If Lady Waters is found guilty, surely they will not hang her? She is a baroness."

"If she is found guilty of the murder of her husband, then I do not think the judge will have any option but to decide on the death penalty. What sort of message would it send otherwise?"

Lydia paled, her eyes widening.

"I understand there is some animosity between your mother and uncle and Lady Waters?" Jane said, using the shock the two Upton girls were displaying to press on with questions they might otherwise refuse to answer.

"Uncle Henry is a snob," Lydia said, the words coming out quickly and earning her an admonishing glare from her older sister. "Well, he is. Lady Waters made Grandpapa very happy, and surely that is what matters. There was all this talk of her being a money-grabbing harlot, but then all Mother and Father talk about is finding us the best matches for husbands. It is no different to what Lady Waters did. They would be delighted if we each found a wealthy baron to marry, even if we did not love him."

"That is enough, Lydia," Elizabeth said sternly. "I am sorry, we should not be talking of these things. They are private family matters. All families have disagreements."

"What is going on?" The sharp voice of Mrs Upton came from the hall as she descended the stairs. Jane and Cassandra quickly got to their feet, dipping their heads in greeting as the older woman glided into the room.

"Miss Jane Austen and Miss Cassandra Austen came to call on you, Mama. I was just telling them you were indisposed and not up to visitors at the moment."

There was a long silence as Mrs Upton regarded them. "Lizzie, Lydia, leave us. Take your sisters and practise your French grammar upstairs."

"Mama…" Lydia began to protest but was silenced by a firm look from her mother.

Jane and Cassandra sat in silence as the two Upton girls traipsed upstairs, and Jane had no doubt that at least one of them would be listening from the landing. Mrs Upton must have had the same thought, for after a minute she rose and closed the door to the drawing room.

"Miss Jane Austen, Miss Cassandra Austen, I cannot spare you long. It has been a trying day."

"I am sorry to hear that," Jane said diplomatically. "I understand the will was not quite what you hoped."

"You are a bold young lady, Miss Austen, but though boldness is sometimes applauded, it can also lead to rudeness."

"I am sorry to offend you." Jane sat bolt upright but held Mrs Upton's gaze. After a few long seconds of silence, Mrs Upton sighed.

"What can I do for you?"

"I went to see your brother earlier this morning," Jane said, knowing the ruse she had used on Mr Fortescue was not likely to work on his sister. She was too sharp, too observant. Jane would have to choose a different tactic to try and get Mrs Upton to speak. "I told him I had come to apologise for inserting myself into this matter and that I had seen the error of my ways."

"I suppose Henry believed you?"

"He did."

Mrs Upton shook her head. "When I was younger I used to write lists of everything that was unfair about being a woman. I am the oldest, you know, the first born, but because of his sex Henry inherits everything and I am discarded."

"It does seem unfair."

"He will squander the estate, the fortune my father amassed over his lifetime. In a way, I am pleased I have no sons. At least I do not have to watch as their inheritance gets depleted by my fool of a brother."

"Mr Fortescue may have children of his own yet," Cassandra said.

"Unlikely. He's been married to that useless wife of his for years with no sign of a baby. I doubt there will be a miracle now." Mrs Upton studied Jane and Cassandra. "But I do not think you came to gossip about my brother."

"He told me of the theft of the jewellery, the pieces that have been swapped for fakes."

"Yes, he was livid." Mrs Upton's expression was a mask; she was impossible to read.

"What I cannot fathom is his insistence that Lady Waters was the one to steal the jewels."

Mrs Upton shrugged. "She is not one of us, not from our world. I suppose it is possible she saw the emeralds and just couldn't help herself."

"She had no need to. Your father provided her with everything she could want or need."

"Perhaps we will never know her reasons."

"You believe she stole the jewellery, then?" Jane pressed.

"She is a murderer — why not a thief as well?"

"Lady Waters has not been found guilty yet, Mrs Upton."

"The evidence is there. She will be."

Jane looked into the older woman's eyes and saw the coldness. There was no sympathy, no flicker of emotion at the idea of an innocent woman going to the gallows.

"Why do you dislike her so much?" Jane asked, the words coming out before she could censor them.

For a moment it looked as though Mrs Upton wasn't going to answer, but then she gave a half smile filled with bitterness. "Do you know what my father left me in his will?"

Jane shook her head, aware that Mrs Upton wouldn't be pleased if she found out Mrs Fortescue had been gossiping.

"Five thousand pounds and a few trinkets. It is nothing, worse than nothing. It is a snub. He could hold a grudge. You think he was a sweet and even-tempered man, but he wasn't always like that. It wasn't fair that his second wife got the best of him. For years my husband and I have struggled because of an honest mistake, one business deal gone wrong. My father deigned to help us, but he has held it over us ever since. Then *she* waltzes in and bewitches him, and he's spending all this money on her when his own granddaughters don't even have a proper dowry."

"I can see how that would hurt, but surely it is your father your anger should be directed towards, not Lady Waters."

"If he hadn't met her, he would have come round. He would have provided for his granddaughters, at least. He always spoke of leaving enough of the family fortune to go with the title and estates to allow Henry to run everything properly, I understood that, but if *she* hadn't come along, that two thousand pounds a year he left her would have been mine, as would the ten thousand to pay for my daughters' dowries."

"It really is all about money," Cassandra murmured quietly.

"Just wait!" Mrs Upton exploded. "Just wait until you have the burden of children, and girls at that. Five girls, I need to see married off. Five girls, and they have barely a penny for their dowries between them."

Jane stood, aware they had outstayed their welcome and knowing Mrs Upton was hardly going to answer any more of their questions now.

"Thank you for talking to us today," Jane said as she and Cassandra edged towards the door. "I am sorry for any upset we have caused."

"Stop!" Mrs Upton commanded, her eyes narrowing. "I do not want to hear any of this repeated in the drawing rooms or Assembly Rooms of Bath. You might be from Hampshire, Miss Jane and Miss Cassandra Austen, but if I hear anything we have talked of today being discussed, I will make it my aim in life to destroy you and your family, starting with that aunt and uncle of yours."

"We will not say a word," Jane said, a chill travelling through her.

Quickly she and Cassandra left, not wanting to stay in Mrs Upton's presence any longer.

Outside they walked rapidly, putting some distance between them and the house. Only once they were a few streets away did Cassandra take Jane's arm and they slowed to a more leisurely stroll, their heads bent together, the rims of their bonnets touching.

"That woman is horrible," Cassandra said.

"I can understand being protective of her daughters, but she takes it too far."

"Everything she said, every view she held, was so self-centred. She does not care if Lady Waters goes to the gallows. All she can think about is herself and her daughters."

Jane nodded. "Do you think she has a motive for murder, though? Mr Fortescue inherited the vast majority of the fortune and the properties, while Mrs Upton gets barely anything. Is that enough reason to kill?"

"Five thousand pounds is not to be dismissed, especially if their circumstances are dire."

"That is true. I wondered as well if it could have been Mrs Upton who stole the jewellery. She could have easily sent her daughters to borrow the pieces and then a few days later sent back the fakes in place of the real thing. It sounds like many of the items of jewellery were in her possession at one time or another." Jane felt a frisson of excitement as the pieces all started to come together. There was no proof yet, but for the first time she could see a motive and opportunity linked to one person.

"It would also explain why Lord Waters had the fake emerald necklace with him on the day he died. Perhaps he had come to the same conclusion and was going to confront Mrs Upton with it," Cassandra said.

"If she thought her father suspected her, it could be a reason to kill him. And by using belladonna — which she knew Lady Waters kept in her room — it would point the finger of suspicion at the woman she disliked more than any other."

"We need to tread carefully, Jane. You heard what she said before we left. She is a woman with influence in society, and she will use it to blacken our names."

"I know. What we need now is proof. We need the evidence that ties her to both the thefts and the murder. If she is the murderer, there should be a trail."

CHAPTER TWENTY

Jane was thankful for the cup of sweet tea Miss Black set in front of her as she sank into the comfortable armchair. Dr Black and his sister lived above his set of consulting rooms. A sweeping staircase led up from the hallway below to an airy set of rooms on the first floor. Miss Black had shown them in and bade them sit whilst she arranged tea.

"Did you find out what you needed to?" she enquired as she handed Cassandra her cup.

"It was an enlightening visit," Jane said slowly. She was going over everything Mrs Upton had said, not wanting to miss any little clue that might lead to that vital piece of evidence.

"My brother has not yet returned from his hunt for an apothecary who might have supplied the murderer with the poison. The apothecaries are an unusual bunch and some do like to talk. Hopefully he will not be long."

"Were you able to make a list of the jewellers?" Jane asked, forcing herself to relax. It was a hot day, and she and Cassandra had walked quickly from Mrs Upton's house over Pulteney Bridge to the doctor's residence. The room here was delightfully cool, with the two big windows thrown open and a gentle breeze blowing through. Even though time was ticking away, she knew the importance of stopping every now and then, of letting her mind wander a little and her tired limbs rest. Lord Hinchbrooke often counselled her on the importance of giving the mind time to think, to piece together everything and dig out the little nuggets. He would often settle back in a comfortable armchair, steeple his fingers together and close his eyes, asking for a few minutes of silence. In that time, he told her, he would try to clear his mind and let himself drift away. Often after a minute or two he would sit up, invigorated, with some new clue or fact that he had heard but not acknowledged before.

"Yes," said Miss Black. "There are only three jewellers in Bath itself. Two are reputable establishments and cater to the wealthy. One is less so. It is located in the older part of the city, and I understand it deals a lot in buying the trinkets and family jewels of those fallen on hard times. It then resells them at a marked-up price."

"That could be the most likely place to start, then."

"Indeed, although I am not sure if there will be someone there who has the skill and knowledge to forge such precious and expensive jewellery. The other jewellers might have more of an idea of who would be a good contact to do that for their clients who wanted to appear wealthier than they were."

"We shall visit all three and put our questions to them," Cassandra said, her eyes flitting to the little clock on the mantelpiece.

"Time is running out," Jane said, feeling the pressure mounting. They had already stayed out far too long, and their aunt would no doubt reprimand them when they returned to number one, The Paragon. One solution was to stay out until they had finished conducting their enquiries for today, but Jane was aware that if they did that, Mrs Leigh-Perrot would be even more determined to see them on their way back to Hampshire as soon as possible.

"Has the trial date been set?" Miss Black asked, misunderstanding Jane's panic.

"No, I don't think so, but we should take time to find out from Mr Winters the magistrate. He is sure to know when it is likely to be."

"He warned us to stay away, Jane. I doubt he will be pleased to see us again, enquiring about the date of the trial."

"I know Mr Winters," Miss Black said. "He has been to dinner a few times. He is a dour sort, very serious, but we are on good terms. I could make enquiries if it would be helpful?"

"Yes please, that would be wonderful. I would prefer Mr Winters not to know we were still looking into the matter and advocating for Lady Waters," Jane said.

They all turned at the sound of the front door closing below them and waited as footsteps rang out on the stairs. Dr Black entered the room, removing his hat and flopping down into a free armchair.

"Good Lord, the hot weather has set in. It is unbearable out there."

"Did you find anything out from the apothecaries?" Jane asked, unable to stop herself from getting straight to business.

"Perhaps. Bath has six apothecary shops, situated all over the city. I've traipsed from up near The Circus all the way down to James Street."

Miss Black rolled her eyes at her brother. "Come, John, no one wishes to hear of your walking route around Bath. What did you find out?"

"All the apothecaries hold a small supply of belladonna. It is still used by a few young ladies for beauty treatments, but it is also the drug of choice by a few of the local doctors for treating joint pains and back pains. One of the apothecaries makes an ointment with belladonna as the main ingredient that he swears will cure any backache in three days."

"Did any of them supply anyone connected to Lord Waters with belladonna?"

"No, although they were all keen to point out that often their wealthier clients will send a servant or errand boy to pick up an item. The servant hands over the money and the apothecary will not always know who the intended recipient is."

"Surely that is a bit dangerous when it comes to such deadly poisons?"

"The apothecaries are largely unregulated. They were at pains to point out it was not their fault if one of their medicines had been used as a means to murder."

"Nice to see them taking some responsibility," Jane murmured.

"I gave a detailed description of all of Lord Waters' family members to the apothecaries, and no one recognised any of them as asking for a substance that could be used as a poison. But they all hold a supply of plenty of medicines that could, in the right doses, be fatal."

Jane closed her eyes for a moment, wondering if Mr Fortescue or Mrs Upton would take the risk of confiding in a servant and sending them to get a poison. It left a trail that could lead back to them. She was aware she didn't have the authority to question the servants in the Fortescue and Upton household, but if she could get the magistrate onside, he could work through them quickly to find out if anyone had been asked to visit the apothecary by their employer. She wondered quite how deep Mr Winters' loyalty to Mr Fortescue ran. He had already overstepped his professional boundaries as magistrate for his old school friend; he might refuse to entertain even the idea of questioning anyone who might provide evidence to show Lady Waters was innocent.

"We have to find a way to talk to the servants in the Fortescue and Upton households," Jane said. "It will be difficult, but I do not think we can entrust this matter to the magistrate."

Cassandra nodded. "It will be difficult. I am sure at least some of the servants are loyal to their employers and will run straight to Mr Fortescue or Mrs Upton the moment you start asking questions about poisons and apothecaries."

"Then we will leave it until we know more. It will be the last piece of the puzzle to slot in, that final piece of evidence to show Lady Waters' innocence and someone else's guilt."

"What is our next step?" Cassandra said. She looked exhausted, her face pale, but there was a spark in her eyes. Investigating Lord Waters' death had certainly brought her out of her melancholy. She had been forced to focus her thoughts on something other than the loss of the man she had loved so dearly.

"I think Dr Black and I should visit the jewellers and then take a trip to The Saracen's Head."

"Are you sure it wouldn't be wiser to let Dr Black visit the tavern on his own?"

"Yes," Jane said, despite her reservations.

"What do you need me to do?"

Jane contemplated for a moment, knowing she was giving Cassandra the hardest job. "I think you should go back to our aunt and uncle's house and see what plans Aunt Jane has made for our return to Hampshire. Perhaps see if there is anything you can do to delay them."

Cassandra nodded grimly. "I will try my best. When she asks where you are, I will tell her you were invited for a stroll with Miss Black and Dr Black. That should keep her happy for a while."

It was pleasant strolling through Bath, Jane's hand tucked into the crook of Dr Black's arm. Despite him protesting he did not know all that many people in the city, they were stopped on numerous occasions by grateful patients and acquaintances who wanted to pass on their thanks to the doctor.

The sun was at its height in the sky now and even Jane's bonnet did not give her much respite from the glare, so she was thankful when they came to the first of the jewellery shops.

They paused by the window, admiring the display of precious stones set around a stunning diamond necklace.

"I am surprised it is safe to keep a necklace like that in the window display. Surely someone could just come along, smash the window and grab it," Jane said, unable to tear her eyes away.

"I suppose they are unlikely to risk it in broad daylight with so many witnesses about." Dr Black indicated the busy shopping street behind them. "At night I assume the shopkeeper has a safe he moves everything into, leaving the windows bare."

Inside the shop was small, made up of a few counters and a couple of comfortable seats. Jane knew the wealthy would often request house visits, where a jeweller would bring an item for them to inspect, but the atmosphere in the shop was inviting and she could imagine Lord Waters bringing Lady Waters here to examine a set of diamonds or rubies before buying them.

"Dr Black!" a short, middle-aged man said, appearing from the back of the shop. "Welcome, welcome, please have a seat. I do not think I know your companion."

"It is my pleasure to introduce Miss Jane Austen, a good friend of mine," Dr Black said.

The jeweller eyed them appraisingly, no doubt trying to use his professional experience to decide what sort of item Dr

Black was in the market for. "It is lovely to meet you, Miss Austen. Is it a gift for the young lady you are looking for?"

"Alas no, Mr Cooper. Miss Austen and I were hoping you might help us with a most delicate matter. I am sure you have heard of the sad death of Lord Waters and the scandal of the arrest of Lady Waters."

Mr Cooper nodded, but there was a guarded expression on his face now.

"Miss Austen is a friend of Lady Waters, and the baroness has asked her to make some enquiries on her behalf. There are inconsistencies in the evidence against her and it is likely she will be released soon," Dr Black said.

Jane glanced at him. He was not lying, there were inconsistencies, but the way he spoke hinted at a more imminent release than they could honestly expect.

Leaning in closer and lowering her voice, Jane spoke. "Lady Waters is concerned that some of the precious pieces of jewellery her husband gave to her have been taken and swapped for fakes, items made of metal and coloured glass."

The jeweller inhaled sharply.

"She is unsure who could have done this, but she would welcome and reward any information that anyone could give on this matter, whether hard facts or mere insight into the world of jewellery."

"How do you think I can help you in this matter?" Mr Cooper asked.

"We wondered if anyone close to Lord Waters has approached you trying to sell any pieces of jewellery?"

"No, no one. At least not recently." He paused, as if trying to work out whether to go on. "A few years ago Mr Fortescue came to me looking to sell a few pieces of jewellery, but I understood they belonged to his wife."

"What pieces of jewellery were they?"

"A gold bracelet and a two sets of gold earrings. I gave him a good price for them."

"When was this?"

"Three years ago, perhaps four."

"There has been nothing since? No other pieces of jewellery?"

"No, nothing. Lord Waters himself did buy a beautiful gold brooch from me a few months ago — it was in the shape of a peacock's feathers and dotted with precious stones — but apart from that, I haven't had any contact with the family for some time."

"Mr Cooper," Jane said slowly, trying to work out a way to ask the question she needed to without causing any offence. "You must have come across some unscrupulous people in the years you have worked as a jeweller. I wonder, if you were looking for someone to create forgeries of some very expensive necklaces, to whom would you turn?"

Mr Cooper shook his head and then stopped, mid-movement. "I do not know, Miss Austen. Certainly there are people with the talent for such a thing, and there are many reputable jeweller's shops that specialise in creating pieces made out of coloured glass and cheaper metal to imitate more expensive items, but what you are asking is something entirely different. Jewellers are craftsmen, proud of what they create, and that is true even amongst those who cater to those with smaller budgets. If someone came to a jeweller asking for an *exact* replica, it would be difficult to create something like that and not have it weighing on your conscience, for you would know why it was wanted."

Jane doubted all jewellers were as conscientious as Mr Cooper, or as successful. It was easy to have strict moral standards when your income gave you a comfortable lifestyle.

"I understand," she said, holding Mr Cooper's gaze. "But if you were going to direct a customer to someone, who could do something like that...?"

"I would have to suggest they spoke to Havers and Meller."

Havers and Meller was the third name on their list of shops to visit, the establishment that Miss Black had indicated was less upmarket.

"Thank you for your time, Mr Cooper," Jane said, standing. "You have been very helpful, and I will ensure Lady Waters is made aware."

"Please give her my best wishes. It is a tragedy to lose a husband and be cast under this net of suspicion at the same time."

Jane started to walk away and then turned, realising there was another question Mr Cooper could help her with, albeit one that wouldn't further the investigation.

"Mr Cooper, you must come into contact with a lot of people in your line of work. What are people saying about Lady Waters? What is the opinion of the public?"

Mr Cooper looked down for a moment, studying the wooden countertop underneath his hands. "I cannot lie and say everyone is kind and charitable. There is a lot of gossip. In some circles she has gained the moniker 'Black Widow', what with her having three deceased husbands. Yet there is some sympathy for her as well. There are many in this town who have come up against Mr Fortescue or Mrs Upton and not come off well as a result. There is some awareness of the difficult family situation and the fact that things might be more complex than they seen."

"Thank you, Mr Cooper, for your honesty."

It was about as good as Jane could hope for. Public opinion mattered in these cases. Juries were told to ignore all speculation and gossip they had heard before a trial, but the jurors were only human and as easily influenced as everyone else. Jane hoped that Lady Waters would never have to stand trial, but if she did it was heartening to know not everyone thought she was guilty.

"I wish you luck, Miss Austen, Dr Black."

They left the jewellers and walked in silence along the street, having to sidestep a few times to weave their way through the crowds of people out and about. Bath was certainly popular at this time of year, and Jane wondered how many of these people would abandon the city for London during the Season and how many would stay.

The second jewellers they visited didn't supply them with any further information, the proprietor a stiff little man by the name of Mr Wendle. He denied contact with any of Lord Waters' family and did not deign to give an opinion on who might be called upon to make fake copies of the precious jewellery.

Their last stop was the shop of Havers and Meller. It had a tiny shopfront, the window filled with cheap-looking jewellery and a sign declaring that they bought as well as sold items.

The shop inside was gloomy, with two candles flickering away on the counter despite it being the middle of the day. Not much light filtered through into the depths of the shop from the one window, and Jane wondered if it was a deliberate ploy to keep the area poorly lit so the customers couldn't examine what they were buying too closely.

"Good afternoon," a cheery man said as they approached the counter. "What can I do for you today? Are you looking for a piece of jewellery for this beautiful Miss? I have a delicate gold bracelet that would look perfect on her dainty wrist."

"Is it Mr Havers?" Dr Black said.

"No, my business associate is away at the moment. I am Mr Meller."

"It is a pleasure to meet you, Mr Meller. I am Dr Black, and this is Miss Jane Austen."

Jane smiled and stepped forwards. "I am hoping you can help us, Mr Meller," she said, lowering her voice. She had decided to try a different line of questioning here than she had in the other shops, hoping to trap Mr Meller into a confession before he knew what she was doing. "I have come into a beautiful item of jewellery, a ruby necklace I inherited from a generous aunt. They are the most exquisite gems and it is a pretty necklace, but my sister and I have fallen on hard times. We need to sell the necklace in order to survive." She paused, dropping her voice to barely more than a whisper. "The rest of my family are already put out that I inherited the rubies over them. There would be outrage if they found I had sold them. I was hoping I could get a replica necklace made, perhaps with coloured glass, that would be enough to fool my family."

Mr Meller nodded, looking at her a little closer. "That is a service we can provide," he said slowly. "My colleague Mr Havers is the one who would actually make the replica."

"He is skilled?"

"Oh yes," Mr Meller said, smiling. "You would be surprised at the number of toffs walking round with glass around their necks and hanging from their ears rather than the precious stones they pretend them to be. It is virtually impossible for anyone to detect a difference between Mr Havers' work and the real thing."

Jane felt a mounting excitement. This was it, this was the final piece of the puzzle, the one that would allow everything else they had found out so far to slot into place.

"I think you have done some work for the family of Lord Waters before — Mr Fortescue, perhaps, or Mrs Upton. They were the ones who directed me here to speak to you."

A guarded look crossed Mr Meller's face. "As I said, Mr Havers deals with that side of the business."

"When will Mr Havers be back?" Jane asked, continuing quickly as Mr Meller's frown deepened. "I wish to show him the necklace to see if he thinks he can make a replica."

"He is visiting a client out of town today and will make the return journey tomorrow."

"Thank you. We will come back and show him the necklace then."

Jane turned, aware Mr Meller was more suspicious than the other jewellers they had spoken to and not wanting to spook him before she spoke to his business partner. To her surprise, Mr Meller called out just as they reached the door of the shop.

"Mr Havers will know more, but I do not think we have provided such a service for Mr Fortescue or Mrs Upton, although I do know who they are. It is in a jeweller's best interests to know the wealthy and influential in society." He paused, his eyes twinkling with something that looked like mischief. "We did provide a service producing replicas of some pieces for Lady Waters, though. Perhaps it was her you were thinking of?"

Jane felt as though she had received a blow to her gut. Only Dr Black's supporting arm saved her legs from buckling under her. "Lady Waters?" she said, trying to cover the quiver in her voice.

"Yes. Her man brought quite a few pieces to us."

"What man was this?"

"Tall, well built, with a few days' stubble about his chin. He never gave a name."

"And he said he was working on behalf of Lady Waters?"

"He did."

"Thank you, Mr Meller."

Outside, Jane had to lean against the wall to recover for a second.

"Miss Austen, you have gone dreadfully pale. Take some deep breaths and lean on me," Dr Black said, gripping her arm tightly. Quickly he weaved his way along the pavement to a bench and bid her sit down.

"It can't be true," Jane said.

Ever since the terrible death of Lord Waters and the inquest that had led to Lady Waters' arrest, Jane had been certain in her conviction that the baroness had been wrongfully accused. Despite their short acquaintance, she felt as though she knew the woman and could assess her character, but for the first time she had to stop and consider if she had been wrong. Perhaps all the convenient facts she had thought Mr Fortescue or Mrs Upton had arranged to show Lady Waters in a negative light were instead the truth. Lady Waters could have given the jewellery to the mystery man to commission replicas and then sold the originals. She could have slipped belladonna into her husband's drink. They only had her account of the relationship she and Lord Waters had shared. Perhaps it had been very different to the picture she had painted and she was unhappy, selling the jewels to build up a store of money for when she did become free of her husband.

"That is quite damning evidence," Dr Black said quietly.

"Yes."

"It does not mean she murdered her husband, though."

"If she swapped the jewellery, it gives her a good motive. I think we can assume Lord Waters had realised there was something wrong with the emeralds. He might not have known who had swapped them, but he would find out. If Lady Waters knew he suspected, she might have seen no other way out than to murder her husband." Jane groaned. She didn't want to believe it, even though the evidence was pointing in that direction. "Normally I am a good judge of character. Normally I can tell if someone is dissembling," she said, a lump forming in her throat. "But perhaps this time I overestimated my abilities."

"Do not despair just yet, Miss Austen. There is still more to unravel."

Jane nodded, but she felt like a fool as she desperately tried to cling onto the idea that Lady Waters was innocent, searching her mind for ways the baroness could have been set up.

CHAPTER TWENTY-ONE

The Saracen's Head was nestled between the church of St Michael's and a row of shops on Broad Street. It was well kept and from the outside looked a reputable establishment. The tavern windows gleamed in the sunlight and the door had recently been painted dark blue.

Inside was quiet, unsurprising for this time of day. The workers had not yet finished their labours and everyone but regular patrons would want to be out enjoying the sunshine on a day such as today.

Dr Black led Jane to a table near the window, tucked into the corner out of the way of the few solitary men who occupied the stools around a larger communal table. A serving girl wandered over after a few minutes and Dr Black ordered a beer for himself and a cup of wine for Jane.

It took a few minutes for the drinks to appear, and when they did Jane thanked the young woman and pressed a shilling into her hand.

"I wonder if you could spare a moment of your time."

"I'm not one of those girls," she said quickly, backing away a couple of steps. "I just do my work here and mind my own business."

Jane shuddered at the thought of what the young woman was suggesting and spared a thought for her on busy evenings, when she must be groped and propositioned by numerous drunken men.

"Nothing like that," Jane said, trying to give her a reassuring smile. "I am looking for a friend of a friend, someone I think has fallen on hard times. I promised my friend I would do my best to find this man, and I have been told he might drink here."

"I don't want any trouble."

"No trouble. All I want is a little information, and there is another shilling in it if you help." Thankfully she still had a little money stashed away after her trip to Ilchester, where she'd spent the contents of her purse on bribing the guard. She took out another shilling and saw the young woman's eyes flick to it.

"What's this man like?"

"He's tall, well built, often unshaven."

"That could be half our customers."

"He would have started coming here a few months ago, probably not before then, and would have been in yesterday afternoon."

The serving girl shook her head, not taking her eyes off the shilling. Jane saw her mind ticking over, as if assessing whether to make up a story.

"I am only interested in the truth."

"No, I was working yesterday afternoon. Only our regulars were in."

"Could someone else have served him?"

The young woman shrugged. "I can ask."

"Please do."

She slipped the shilling into her pocket and disappeared into the depths of the tavern. A few minutes passed as they waited, Dr Black sipping his beer in silence. Jane tried a mouthful of wine but it was too sour for her to drink.

She had almost given up hope of the serving girl returning when the waif-like figure slipped through the door that led to the back of the tavern and came over.

"No one knows of a man as you described him coming here regularly over the last couple of months."

"Thank you for checking," Jane said.

When they were alone Jane let out a sigh, shaking her head. She wondered who this man was. The thought crossed her mind that perhaps it was a lover, a man from Lady Waters' past who had followed her to Bath and stayed in the background whilst she gained Lord Waters' trust, stepping up when she needed him.

"I think I need to return home," Jane said, suddenly weary.

"Let me escort you."

There was a flurry of activity at number one, Paragon Street with Mrs Leigh-Perrot at the centre. She frowned at Jane when she returned home, but spared her any reprimand as Dr Black stepped into the hall after her.

"Thank you for a riveting afternoon, Miss Austen," Dr Black said with a smile, bowing over her hand. "My sister and I thoroughly enjoyed your company."

Jane nodded graciously, silently thanking Dr Black for his discretion and sensitivity when it came to how he acted around her aunt. It was better for Mrs Leigh-Perrot to think there was a possible romantic connection between them rather than realise he had been helping her conduct her forbidden investigation.

"Thank you," Jane said with feeling. "I am most grateful for you company today."

"It was entirely my pleasure. I know your travel plans are not set, but if you are in Bath for another few days, do let me know and hopefully we can arrange to meet."

He bowed to Mrs Leigh-Perrot and took his leave.

"Really I should reprimand you, Jane," Mrs Leigh-Perrot said. "I thought you were going against my strict instructions not to involve yourself in this matter with Lady Waters any further. But now I see you were with that charming young doctor, I cannot bring myself to be angry."

"Dr Black was kind enough to invite me for a stroll with his sister as chaperon."

"This is very exciting news, Jane. Do you have deeper feelings for the man?"

Jane had to suppress the urge to roll her eyes. "He is kind, but I barely know him, Aunt. If I were here for longer, then perhaps we would get the chance to spend a little time together, but you can hardly expect me to know if we would suit after a couple of brief meetings."

"He must like you, though, Jane. He would not invite you to spend time with him otherwise."

"Perhaps I can get to know him better if we return for a visit later in the year, if he has not found a wife by then."

Mrs Leigh-Perrot bit her lip, glancing over her shoulder to where her husband sat in his study, looking through some papers. "I had arranged for two tickets on the coach tomorrow, but I wonder if they will consider swapping them for a day or two later." She looked at Jane sternly. "But only if you give me your word you will not disappear off at all hours, tying yourself up in matters that do not concern you."

"I give you my word, Aunt," Jane said, a sinking feeling in her stomach. She believed in keeping her promises, yet she was deep in the investigation into Lord Waters' murder. "Do you mind if I go and lie down for a few minutes? It is so warm that I feel a little light-headed after being out in the sun."

"Of course, my dear. Shall I send up some tea?"

"Thank you, that would be kind."

Upstairs was a little cooler and Jane was pleased to find Cassandra in their shared room, sitting on the chair close to the open window, fanning herself lazily with her fan.

"Jane, you look terrible," she said, getting to her feet. "Did something happen?"

"I cannot believe it, Cassandra. I don't want to believe it." Jane felt a swell of agitation and threw her bonnet down on the bed.

"Be calm, Jane. Take a minute and gather your thoughts, and then when you are ready tell me all that has passed."

Jane did as her sister advised, lying back on top of the bedcovers and closing her eyes, letting all the conversations she'd had these last few days wash over her. She dwelled on the visit to Ilchester gaol, the nonchalant way Lady Waters had denied any knowledge of the scruffily dressed man. Jane thought of the look of affection that had passed between Lord and Lady Waters the first time she had met them on the grassy area below The Crescent. She couldn't believe that was the look of someone plotting to murder her husband.

Once the maid had brought in the tea and Cassandra had prepared her a cup, Jane sat up, determined to make sense of everything she had heard.

"We spoke to one of the jewellers, Mr Meller of Havers and Meller, and he confirmed they could make replicas of expensive pieces of jewellery for a fraction of the price. Apparently Mr Havers is the craftsman and the one to talk to about that side of the business, but he is out of town until tomorrow morning."

"Did Mr Meller know anything?"

Jane grimaced. "I asked him if Mr Fortescue or Mrs Upton had come in asking to have replica pieces of jewellery made. He told me they hadn't, but before we left he called me back and told me that Lady Waters had commissioned them to copy a few pieces."

"Lady Waters?"

"Yes."

"She went to the shop?"

"No. She sent a man to deal with it on her behalf."

Realisation dawned on Cassandra's face and she shook her head in disbelief. "Not the well-built man with the unshaven face?"

"The description matches."

Cassandra looked crestfallen and rose to her feet, pacing the room. "What does it mean, Jane?"

"The most likely explanation? I was wrong about Lady Waters all along."

Cassandra shook her head. "No, I can't bring myself to believe it."

"You warned me to keep my distance from her at first."

"Yes, but that doesn't mean I think she is a murderer."

"Let us revisit the facts. Pieces of her jewellery have gone missing, substituted for fakes made from coloured glass. The jeweller is under the impression Lady Waters is the one who has asked for the replicas. Lady Waters is seen with the man who has delivered the jewellery to Mr Havers so he can make these replicas." Jane took a breath. "Then there is the poison. I was twisting myself into knots trying to work out what it could be and how someone could have obtained it, but what is the philosophy Lord Hinchbrooke always likes to quote? Occam's razor — the simplest explanation is usually the correct one. Lady Waters had belladonna in her possession. She had access to it at all times and knew of its dangerous properties. She also had the best opportunity to slip it into Lord Waters' glass."

"Anyone could have slipped it into his glass in that crowd, Jane. You could have been standing next to one of our brothers and not known it, it was so busy."

"Still, it would have been easier for Lady Waters."

"We come back to the question of why, though," Cassandra said, echoing Jane's own thoughts from earlier.

"I was thinking on that. We only have Lady Waters' word for it that their marriage was a happy one. What if in private he was cruel, or he insisted on intimacy that she did not want to give? What if the mystery man we keep coming across is her lover and she wanted out of her marriage to be with the man she loved? She did not know when Lord Waters would die." As Jane said the words, she found she didn't quite believe them. She glanced over at Cassandra, who was also shaking her head.

"The jewellery that Lord Waters gave to Lady Waters, that was hers to keep, was it not?" Cassandra said slowly.

"Yes, I believe so. There were a few bequests in the will to Mrs Upton, pieces of the first Lady Waters' collection that Lord Waters left to his daughter instead, but the things already given to Lady Waters were hers."

"Then why make replicas of jewellery that was already hers? She had no pressing need for money in that instant, and when her husband died the jewellery would be hers to sell or do with as she pleased."

"Unless the mysterious man is someone from her past, someone blackmailing her," Jane said, but she didn't quite believe it. With a sigh, she took a sip of tea and closed her eyes. "I know all the evidence is there, Cassandra, but I still do not believe it. Am I being naïve?"

"No. What does Lord Hinchbrooke always tell you? Listen to your feelings, to your instincts: sometimes the hidden parts of your brain are trying to tell you something."

Jane rallied a little at her sister's words. "Shall we go through the suspects?"

"Good idea."

"First there is Lady Waters. She had the means to commit the murder with the belladonna, and the opportunity with easy access to her husband's glass in Parade Gardens. Her motive is questionable, but possibly something to do with this jewellery theft."

"We cannot forget that her two previous husbands died, although there is no evidence their deaths were suspicious."

"You are right. I am sure much of that will be made at her trial." Jane paused and considered the next suspect. "Mr Fortescue gains the most from his father dying. He has inherited a veritable fortune and will finally be able to step out from Lord Waters' shadow and show what sort of man he is."

"That is a motive indeed."

"We know he has a gambling problem, and that could be a motive for him to steal the jewellery, but his indignation at the discovery of the replicas seemed genuine when he was questioning Lady Waters at Ilchester gaol about them. It is possible the jewellery theft is a separate matter and Mr Fortescue is the killer without being the thief."

"We cannot forget he was at Parade Gardens and could easily have slipped something into Lord Waters' drink."

"As could any of our suspects. Mrs Fortescue is up next. She gives this air of being a pitiful creature, but sometimes they are the most dangerous. If Lord Waters had found out about her addiction, he could have threatened to tell her husband or convinced her he would ensure her supply was cut. Desperate people can be driven to do desperate things."

"Or she could have orchestrated the thefts to pay for the medicine she buys each week."

"That is true, and afraid of being found out, she killed Lord Waters to keep her lesser crime a secret."

They sat and contemplated this for a moment before Jane shook her head. "She has possible motives, and would have had access to the belladonna or even an alternative poison through her contact with Dr Tomkins, but I just cannot see it. Then there is Mrs Upton."

"I get the impression you would really like it to be Mrs Upton."

Jane wrinkled her nose. "The woman is not pleasant to be around."

"No, she is not, but that does not make her a killer."

"You're right. There is something of a motive there, though. I think the Upton family finances are in a worse state than even Lady Waters was aware of. Mrs Upton was very sensitive about the subject of her daughters' dowries, and it would not surprise me if they did not have the money to provide their daughters with the funds needed for securing a match worthy of their social status."

"It could be the reason they did not go to London for the Season this year or last. Perhaps they do not have enough money to travel there and maintain a household whilst financing dresses and carriages and all those other expenses one incurs as a debutante," Cassandra said.

"Mrs Upton could have wanted to stay closer to her father too, in the hope he would take pity on her daughters and give them the dowries she thinks they deserve."

"All this is very well and good," Cassandra said, pouring out another cup of tea, "but is it enough to accuse Mrs Upton of murder?"

"I wonder if she could be responsible for the thefts. It would be easy enough for her to push one of her daughters to borrow this piece of jewellery or that, and we know one of the girls spotted belladonna in Lady Waters' bedroom. What is more, she was in Parade Gardens, and I always wondered if Lord Waters was going to confront one of his children about the replica emeralds he had in his pocket."

They both fell silent, considering Mrs Upton as the villain.

"There is also Mr Upton," Cassandra said as she stirred her tea.

"Yes, not much has been said about him, apart from to remark on his foolishness in business."

"Is that enough to put him in with our other suspects?"

Most of the family had a motive of sorts, and the means and opportunity to carry out the attack in the park, but there was nothing that convincingly put one person above another.

"I need to think on this," Jane said, placing her cup on the tray next to the rapidly cooling teapot and kicking off her boots. "I think I have delayed our departure by a few days. Dr Black helped me with our aunt."

"Oh?" Cassandra said, tidying the rest of the tea tray away ready to place outside their door.

"Aunt Jane thinks Dr Black might be interested in courting me, and I in being courted."

Cassandra looked at her carefully. "He is an attractive man, and he has a good profession."

Jane didn't answer, instead closing her eyes and letting the cool breeze dance over her face.

CHAPTER TWENTY-TWO

Jane awoke early as usual, with the urge to throw off the bedcovers. It was stiflingly hot, the air close and the room humid. Outside it was beginning to get light, but dark clouds covered the sky and Jane wondered if the spell of hot weather might break with a thunderstorm. They had begun their stay in Bath with rain; it felt fitting they should end it with the same.

It had been three weeks since she had last picked up her pen and paper and written anything of use. She had been plagued with worry for Cassandra and stuck with her current manuscript, unable to work out what was missing from the Bennet family dynamics.

Now it was as though her brain were on fire, and she needed to get the ideas committed to paper before they burned.

She moved around silently, aware of Cassandra's still form in the bed and thankful that for the last few nights her sister had been sleeping a little better than previously. Once set up at the little writing desk, she emptied her mind of all other thoughts and let the words flow onto the paper.

She wrote quickly, scribbling snippets of prose and dialogue, finally realising what the manuscript had been missing. Originally the Bennet sisters had numbered two, just the eldest, Jane, and the second, Elizabeth, but now she added to the chaos of the family, drawing on the panic she had seen in Mrs Upton's eyes the day before at the thought of providing dowries for five daughters. Five Bennet sisters, all unique in their personalities, each influenced by their position in the family. The youngest would be spoilt and naïve about the ways of the world, desperate to break free of being the baby of the family. The eldest would be serene and fair, the middle one unaware of some of the social niceties, both happy and unhappy to be different to her sisters. She sketched out their characters. Elizabeth she felt she knew, but she was fast realising the depth of the book, the warmth of it, would come from the family interactions, the way the sisters loved but also irked each other.

Her pen scratched across the paper, never stopping, as the words flowed from her and the dry spell she had been experiencing came to a dramatic end.

By the time Cassandra had woken, Jane was surrounded by piles of paper and she was sitting back in her chair with a contented expression. The love story, that push and pull between Elizabeth and Mr Darcy, was the heart of the book, but the Bennet family would be the element that made it feel real.

"You're looking pleased with yourself."

"I realised what 'First Impressions' was missing."

"Oh Jane, I am pleased. I know it has been bothering you, and you are so much happier when you are writing."

"I think this one is good, Cassandra, better than my last."

"You know I love everything you write. Even your letters make me smile."

There was a knock on the door and Mrs Leigh-Perrot bustled in, looking cheery for the early hour.

"I had a thought, Jane. Why don't you invite Dr Black and his sister to take tea with us this afternoon?" She held up her hands to ward off any protests. "I know you have not yet decided whether you wish for the doctor to court you, but there can be no harm in getting to know him a little better."

Jane bit her lip and looked across at Cassandra.

"Do not mind me," Cassandra said with an encouraging smile. "I am not so self-centred that I think the whole world should stop because I am in mourning. I think it is a wonderful idea, Aunt Jane."

"Good," Mrs Leigh-Perrot said, clapping her hands together. "I will send a note. In the meantime, we should see to it that you are dressed in your finest dress and have your hair pinned in a way that shows your best features."

"What are my best features?" Jane murmured, horrified at the monster she had created. Her own mother was very patient, but Jane could see she despaired sometimes of her youngest daughter ever marrying. There had been the short courtship between Jane and Tom Lefroy which had left Jane broken-hearted, and since then she hadn't wanted to risk letting anyone close. She was still young, but many of her friends were married with a brood of children of their own.

Jane wasn't against the idea of a courtship, and of the gentlemen of her acquaintance she found Dr Black's company most enjoyable, but she didn't like the feeling of being pushed into something she wasn't yet sure of.

"I think the pale blue dress — you do look fetching in blue, although I have to say all of your dresses are rather practical and a little plain."

"Jane cannot be doing with lace trims and bows," Cassandra said, sitting back against her pillows. Jane had a sneaking suspicion her sister was enjoying this.

"The pale blue dress will have to do, then." Mrs Leigh Perrot turned to the door and raised her voice. "Polly, come and help Jane with her hair."

Polly was Mrs Leigh-Perrot's faithful lady's maid. She was approaching sixty and moved slowly, her back a little bent and her eyesight not what it once was.

"Jane has a suitor coming to call later," Mrs Leigh-Perrot explained. "I think she should have some ringlets around her face and then the rest of her hair curled and pinned, as is the latest fashion."

Jane groaned. Making her hair curl would take hours. She quite enjoyed the ritual of getting ready for a ball or dinner party, of choosing which dress to wear and helping Cassandra with her hair, but she always chose styles for herself that were quick to complete, not liking to sit still for long regarding herself in the mirror.

"Why don't you sit down, Miss," Polly said, pressing Jane onto the stool in front of the small dressing table and picking up a brush. "You can tell me how you like your hair once we've got it brushed."

"I haven't even had breakfast yet," Jane grumbled.

Despite her moans Jane found the gentle tug of the hairbrush in her hair quite soothing, and when it became clear Polly would do as she asked rather than spending hours crafting ringlets to pin, Jane relaxed a little.

"Have you thought any more on the business with Lady Waters?" Cassandra asked as she picked through her dresses and chose one for the day. It was one of the half-mourning dresses in light grey, a shade that made her look pale and thin.

Cassandra was being deliberately vague. They were both aware of Polly's loyalty to Mrs Leigh-Perrot. She had been her lady's maid for years, and they knew everything they discussed here might be repeated later. It made Jane think of the comment Lady Waters had made when they visited her in prison. *I never understood this urge to surround oneself with servants. They're always listening, always ready to betray. It is exhausting never quite being able to relax.*

Jane felt the same to a lesser extent. She and Cassandra had grown up with servants in the house, although the Austen income did not stretch to allow for a lady's maid. So many people conducted their business as if their servants did not exist, continuing private conversations in their studies whilst the butler served them whisky, or gossiping about their neighbours whilst the maid lit the fires. Jane had never felt like that, always addressing the servants they had working in the Austen household, aware that they were fallible like everyone else, and that if she said something foolish they probably would not be able to keep it to themselves.

Something pricked at the edge of her mind. She forced her body to relax, enjoying the tug and pull as Polly secured the strands of hair into a neat bun, letting her mind drift away.

After a minute, she sat bolt upright and turned to Cassandra. "I have it, Cassandra! I see how it all ties together. How could I have been so stupid?"

"Tell me," Cassandra said, her body tense with excitement.

"I cannot believe I was so trusting. I accepted everything everyone told me as the truth, when it is so easy to twist things, to add a suggestion that something is one thing rather than another."

The wait for Polly to finish her hair and leave the room was excruciating, the maid going slowly in the hope Jane and Cassandra might let something else slip in front of her. Once Polly had gone, Jane rose to her feet and quietly closed the door. In a low voice she outlined her theory to Cassandra.

Cassandra puffed out her cheeks and exhaled slowly, nodding. "How do we prove it?"

"We need to find the mystery man, and I think I know how."

"You cannot do this alone, Jane."

"I know. We need help from the magistrate, Mr Winters. I will speak to him and outline my theory."

"What if he does not believe you?"

"Somehow I need to make him believe me." She clasped Cassandra's hands. "I think this is the solution, Cassandra. I can feel it."

"If it is not, we will lose any vestige of goodwill with the magistrate. He will not listen to us a second time."

"I know."

Cassandra regarded Jane for a long moment and then nodded. "You speak to the magistrate. I will watch the house until you return. Once they lead us to the mystery man, I will send a note asking all the concerned parties to gather at Lady Waters' house."

"I wish she could be here for this, instead of locked in gaol, not knowing if we are still working to secure her freedom."

"If you are right then she will soon be out, Jane. That is enough for one person to achieve."

CHAPTER TWENTY-THREE

Jane rapped at the door of number seven, The Crescent. The door was answered quickly by Bill, the footman they had met on their previous visit to Lady Waters' house. He was dressed smartly this time, his hair groomed and his face freshly shaved. Jane wondered if he had done this to impress Mr Fortescue, in the hope the new owner of the house would keep him employed.

Inside there was a buzz of chatter, and Jane was pleased to see all the interested parties already gathered in the drawing room. On one side of the room were Mr and Mrs Upton and their two eldest daughters, Clara and Elizabeth. In the middle were Mr and Mrs Fortescue, the new Lady Waters looking petrified about what might be revealed here today. Dr Black and Miss Black had agreed to come without much persuasion, glad to see the conclusion of this affair they had become entangled in. Huddled in the corner were the two maids, Sarah and Lucy, and the footman who had just shown them inside. Cassandra was sitting directly in front of Jane, smiling up at her with encouragement.

"Thank you for all coming this afternoon," Jane said, looking round the room at all the hostile faces.

"I thought this was a summons from the magistrate," Mrs Upton said, rising from her chair. Jane fixed her with a hard stare.

"Please sit down, Mrs Upton. The magistrate is on his way — he just had to finish questioning the suspect first."

"Lady Waters," sneered Mrs Upton.

"Someone other than Lady Waters," Jane said coolly.

Mrs Upton let out a startled exclamation.

"Perhaps you would indulge me," Jane said, looking around the room with as friendly a smile as she could muster. "There is a suspect in the magistrate's custody, but there are a few questions that are still unanswered."

No one voiced an objection, so Jane began.

"As I am sure most of you know by now, my sister and I only arrived in Bath a couple of weeks ago. We are visiting our aunt and uncle and do not have many connections in the city. On one of our trips out, we met Lord and Lady Waters." Jane could see the contempt in Mrs Upton's eyes and the boredom in her husband's, but she pushed on. The assembled group of people didn't need to hear this part of the story, but Jane was playing for time. The magistrate had been reluctant to help at first, trying to dismiss Jane as she told him of her suspicions, but as she had outlined her theory he had become more interested. Once she had told him there was an easy way to verify her suspicion, he had agreed to at least make enquires. She had received word that the mystery man had been apprehended. All they were waiting for now was the return of the jeweller, Mr Havers, from his trip out of the city to confirm the man in custody was the one who had brought him the jewellery.

"Lady Waters invited us round for tea, and whilst we were here we first encountered Mr Fortescue. You burst into your father's house and insulted your stepmother, did you not, Mr Fortescue?" Although the rules of inheritance meant Mr Fortescue was the new Lord Waters, Jane could not quite bring herself to call him that.

"Not my finest hour," he murmured, but he did not look overly concerned. He was the most powerful man in the room, and his wealth gave him a degree of protection.

"That was the first time we heard of the conflict involving the family jewellery." Jane shook her head. "What a convoluted web that has become. It was clear there was some jealousy regarding the jewellery that had once belonged to the first Lady Waters. I understand neither you nor your sister wanted the collection to be given to the new Lady Waters."

"That jewellery should have been given to my girls," Mrs Upton said, her voice low and dangerous.

"Then we come to the night of the ball at Mr and Mrs Temple's townhouse. Lord Waters collapsed, and I wondered at first if it could have been an initial unsuccessful attempt on his life." She paused and regarded all the faces in the room. Now she had their attention. No one was muttering; no one was making moves to leave.

"But now I am not so sure. I think the collapse could have prompted Lord Waters to confront a matter he had been avoiding. Faced with the prospect of his own mortality, he knew it was the time to work out who had stolen the jewellery from his home. It would explain why he had the replica emerald necklace in his pocket when he went to the Parade Gardens that fateful day."

"He knew the jewellery was fake?" Mrs Upton said, a note of disbelief in her voice.

"I believe so. The emerald necklace was expensive, and I know Lord Waters was generally a very careful man. He would not have walked around a public place with such a valuable necklace stored carelessly in his jacket pocket. The only explanation is that he had realised the necklace was not as it should be and intended to confront someone about it."

"Surely he couldn't have thought any of us would have done something like that," Mrs Upton said, a note of doubt in her voice for the first time.

"I think you were his prime suspect, Mrs Upton. He knew of your need for money, the cycle of debt you were in, the ill-advised investment choices your husband kept making."

"Steady on," Mr Upton said. He fell silent with a glare from his wife.

"I would never stoop so low," Mrs Upton said.

"Not even for your daughters? For the sake of their dowries?"

The silence following the question was complete and Jane nodded, moving on.

"On the day of his death, Lord Waters took the emerald necklace from Lady Waters' jewellery casket and placed them in his pocket. I think he intended to confront both of his children about the theft of the real jewels at the event at Parade Gardens."

"I think this is all very conveniently twisted away from Lady Waters," Mr Fortescue said. "*She* is the interloper; she is the person no one knows anything about."

Jane ignored him. "Sadly, Lord Waters' decision to investigate the theft of the jewels sealed his fate. The murderer had already taken the belladonna from Lady Waters' room. They waited for their opportunity and when Lord Waters' attention was otherwise engaged, they dropped a few drops into his drink. The taste would have been bitter but disguised by the sparkling wine, and the murderer was counting on the fact that Lord Waters would not notice it."

"It is a nice story, Miss Austen, but where is your proof? And where is your suspect?" Mrs Upton said.

"I suspected you all at one point or another," Jane said, looking at Lord Waters' family. "And I had to think long and hard to ensure I was not being too lenient on Lady Waters because I considered her my friend."

Mr Fortescue grunted.

"You all had a motive. Mr Fortescue, you have been waiting a long time to inherit the Fortescue fortune, and I understand your debtors have been circling recently." Jane paused and looked at Mrs Fortescue. There was no need to make the poor woman's life even worse. She had considered Mrs Fortescue as the culprit, driven by her need for funds to continue buying the illicit drugs Dr Tomkins was supplying, but she had dismissed it. This crime could not have been committed by anyone of a nervous disposition. Moving on, Jane said, "Mrs Upton, you need dowries for your daughters. Mr Upton, your finances are in a mess. Your two oldest daughters visited Lady Waters and had access to both the jewellery and the belladonna." Jane held up a placating hand to ward off the onslaught she knew would be forthcoming. "I am not accusing Miss Clara and Miss Elizabeth of anything; I am just saying there was the opportunity."

There was a knock at the door and Jane felt her pulse quicken. Here was the moment of truth, the moment she had been waiting for. Bill, the footman, slipped from the room and opened the front door, before showing Mr Winters into the drawing room. He was accompanied by two men. The first was aged about thirty. He was tall, well built and unshaven, and looked exactly as Jane had pictured him from the various descriptions. The second man was around the same age, but of a smarter appearance.

"I am sorry I am late, Miss Austen. We were waiting for Mr Havers." The magistrate indicated the man Jane assumed was the jeweller.

"Thank you for coming," Jane said. She felt a swell of confidence. She had watched everyone's faces as the mystery man entered the room, and she had seen a flicker of shock on one in particular. It had confirmed her suspicions. "I understand you have men stationed outside the house, covering all doors and windows — is that right, Mr Winters?"

"It is, Miss Austen. There is no hope of escape."

"Good. Shall we continue?"

The magistrate pressed the unshaven man into a chair and stood looming over him.

"I am sorry, I do not know your name," Jane said, directing her words to the newcomer.

He looked as though he wasn't going to answer, but he spoke following a growl from the magistrate. "Ripon. George Ripon."

"Thank you for joining us, Mr Ripon." Jane turned back to the rest of the assembled group. "Mr Ripon here was the person that puzzled me most about this matter. When I came to talk to Lord and Lady Waters' servants, Lucy and Bill here mentioned a stranger approaching the house and asking to see Lady Waters. He was chased away, but later Lucy spotted him talking to Lady Waters when she was out running an errand."

Mr Fortescue snorted. "The company she keeps."

"That was my thought, Mr Fortescue, or at least something a little more charitable. I assumed it must be someone from Lady Waters' past. She grew up near the slums of St Giles, raised herself up and worked hard until she could pass as a suitable wife for a baron. I thought the most likely way she would know this man would be from her past." Jane paused, tilting her head to one side. "I asked Lady Waters about him when I went to visit her in gaol. She told me all about her past life, her relationship with Lord Waters. She was open and honest about everything, and I believed her. Yet when she denied knowing this man, I doubted her. I don't know why —

she'd told me the truth about everything else, yet on this matter I assumed she was lying."

"Who is he, then?" Mrs Upton said. "And how did he steal the jewellery if he was never allowed access to the house?"

"A very good question, Mrs Upton. Mr Havers, can you confirm this is the same man who brought you the jewellery he wanted replicas made of? A set of emeralds, diamond earrings and a bracelet, and an assortment of other items?"

"Yes. This is him," the jeweller said, looking a little bewildered.

"We can prove Mr Ripon was the one to approach the jewellers, the one to sell the jewellery that was not his. But he could not have taken the items in the first place. That needed someone with easy access to the house, easy access to the jewellery. Someone who could move around number seven and handle Lady Waters' jewellery with no questions asked." Jane paused and turned towards the servants. "Someone like you, Sarah."

A ripple of surprise spread through the room as everyone turned to regard the young maid. She was only about twenty, with mousy hair and a plain face. In appearance she was forgettable.

"Me, Miss?" she said, her eyes wide.

"Yes, Sarah. You."

"You're accusing the maid?" Mr Fortescue said, his voice incredulous. "It is a bold scheme, surely too bold for a maid."

"No," Jane said. "A maid is exactly the sort of person who has access to all areas of our lives. It was a comment made by Lady Waters that ultimately made me realise the truth of the matter. She said she never understood why people like to surround themselves with servants, for they were always there, listening in."

"It is true," Mrs Upton said slowly, eyeing Sarah with interest.

"Perhaps I can tell you a story, Sarah, and you can correct me if I get anything wrong."

The young maid didn't move. One hand was clutching the back of a chair, and Jane could see her knuckles were white.

"I think Mr Ripon here is your brother, and I also think that at some point in your lives you came across Lady Waters before she gained a title and a wealthy husband."

"Don't say anything," George Ripon growled.

Jane pushed on. "I think you knew her when she was in London. For some reason, life brings you to Bath and one day, Sarah, you find yourself applying for the position of lady's maid in Lady Waters' household. She doesn't recognise you, but I expect you were little more than a child when you last saw her. You tell your brother about the wealthy woman you are working for, how you are certain it is the same woman you knew in St Giles, and after he has been drinking he comes to the house. This is the time Lucy and Bill tell me about, where Mrs Hope turns him away from the kitchen door." Jane looked from Sarah to George Ripon and saw both shifting uneasily. Much of her speech was supposition, but she was confident that enough of it was true to make them feel uncomfortable. "You waited for Lady Waters to go out, didn't you, Mr Ripon, and you approached her."

George Ripon crossed his arms in front of his chest and looked at Jane defiantly. "I don't know what you're talking about."

"I wonder whose idea it was to steal the jewellery? Yours, perhaps, Sarah? Did you realise that no one looked at the pieces for weeks on end, that you had the perfect opportunity to smuggle them out of the house to your brother and get a replica made? You would place the fake piece where the real items had been, and no one was any the wiser.

"Lady Waters didn't notice; she had worn the pieces of jewellery a half dozen times at most. I expect you were careful not to choose any pieces that were particularly precious to her." Jane paused, her eyes fixed on Sarah now. "But Lord Waters noticed, didn't he? He had chosen the items, gifted them to his first wife and cherished them as memories of her, and then slowly, piece by piece, he was giving them to his second wife. He noticed that the green of the emeralds wasn't quite so vibrant, that the shape of the diamonds was a little different."

Sarah looked as though she was going to say something, but George Ripon gave her a vicious look in warning.

"I wonder which of you decided Lord Waters had to die? It was a bold move, but with the knowledge of the belladonna Lady Waters had in her room, I am sure you thought she would get the blame. After all, it was no secret the rest of the Fortescue family hated her."

"She deserved it," Sarah said quietly.

"Sarah, shut your stupid mouth. You'll get us both hanged!" George Ripon snapped.

"Walking around as if she were better than the rest of us," Sarah went on. "I knew where she had come from. I knew what she'd had to do to get out of that slum. She was greedy, unwilling to share any of her good fortune with the rest of us. Ordering me about as if she were better than me."

"It was the maid?" Mr Fortescue said, incredulous.

"It was the maid," Jane said, knowing the comment would anger Sarah but not anticipating quite how much.

Sarah lunged forwards, grabbing Jane's arm, her eyes wild and flashing with anger. "You don't understand," she said, her voice low. "None of you understand. You swan around with your expensive clothes and jewellery without a care in the world, whilst other people empty your chamber pots and get up at the break of dawn to light your fires. It is so unfair, and it is solely because you were born into one family and I another."

"Lady Waters wasn't born into this life."

"That made it worse," Sarah said, gripping Jane's arm so hard that she was sure to leave a bruise. "*She* should have understood. I didn't want much, just a little acknowledgement, but she was as bad as the rest of them."

"Which of you killed Lord Waters?" Jane asked, though it hardly mattered. They would both be facing the noose for their part in the theft of the jewellery.

"I did," Sarah said, drawing herself up. "No one notices a maid in the crowd. I slipped through and stood right in front of Lord and Lady Waters, and they didn't even notice I was there. It was easy putting the poison into his drink; the old fool only had eyes for his wife."

George Ripon leaned forward and rested his head in his hands, groaning softly. "You stupid girl."

The magistrate moved towards Sarah, who tightened her grip on Jane's arm.

"Stay back or I'll hurt her," she said, reaching out for a bottle of whisky that was tucked away on a shelf. With a deafening crash that silenced the room, she brought the whisky bottle down on a little side table, keeping hold of the bottleneck. Shards of glass shot in every direction, tinkling onto the floor and the maid was left with a jagged weapon in her hand.

"You don't want to do this, Sarah," Jane said, hearing the quiver in her voice.

"Don't tell me what I want. I've spent my whole life being ordered around. Sarah do this, Sarah do that. I can't stand it anymore." There was a note of hysteria in her voice, and Jane saw the smashed bottle in her hand waver.

"You don't want to hurt me."

"You forget I've killed before," Sarah whispered in Jane's ear.

"That was out of necessity. You knew Lord Waters would work out sooner or later that it was you who had stolen the jewellery. There was no other way out. The amount you had stolen meant it was a capital offence; you would go to the hangman if you were caught. And Lord Waters was a determined man; even if you disappeared, I expect he would have expended considerable time and money to hunt you down." Jane took a deep breath, her eyes coming up to meet Cassandra's, trying to reassure her sister when she felt terrified herself. "Killing me will not help you, Sarah, and I do not think you would do something so heinous out of mere spite."

The maid's hand trembled. No one else in the room moved.

"Go quietly with the magistrate. He will see you are looked after."

"They'll hang me," Sarah said, and despite the knowledge that this young woman had killed an innocent old man, despite the fact she was holding a broken bottle to Jane's neck, Jane felt a flicker of sympathy for her. She had seen Lady Waters with everything she had desired, comfort and wealth, and she had let her jealousy fester until it had blackened her soul.

"Wait," Mr Fortescue said, shifting in his seat. "Where is the money? Where is the jewellery?"

"That is what you are asking now?" Cassandra glared at him. "My sister is in peril, and all you can think about is the money?"

He had the sense to press his lips together and say no more, but Jane sensed it wouldn't be the last time he asked that question.

"Sarah, let me go," Jane said, wondering if she should just try to step away, but the maid tightened her grip on her arm.

"I want to leave," Sarah said. "You, magistrate, call off the men you have outside. George and I will leave without anyone trying to stop us."

Mr Winters hesitated and Jane felt Sarah press the broken glass of the bottle against her neck.

"Now!" Sarah demanded.

The magistrate left the room, returning after a few minutes. "My men have instructions to let you past."

"They will not follow us?"

"They will not follow you."

"Come, George," Sarah said, glancing desperately at her brother.

"They will catch us," George said.

"We have to try."

Sarah began backing out of the room, pulling Jane with her. She wondered how far the maid would take her and hoped she would be too burdensome to drag too far.

The front door was open, and outside Jane could see a collection of young men standing uncertainly a little way back. Sarah tightened her grip on Jane as they stepped outside, but none of the young men approached, all looking wary.

"What now?" George said as they reached the street. There were a few people strolling along The Crescent who glanced at the scene and hurriedly moved away.

"Keep walking," Sarah said, then raised her voice. "No one follow us."

The Crescent felt like it stretched on forever, even though the end of the street was in sight at all times. Twice Jane stumbled, her feet finding the uneven paving slabs, and in her terror she thought she might fall onto the jagged glass. Her heart was thumping and she felt her breath coming in short, shallow gasps.

As they neared the first house in the semi-circle, Jane felt Sarah's grip on her shift and then suddenly the young woman called out to her brother. "Run, George!" In an instant Jane was pushed away, stumbling and crashing into the black iron railings, and Sarah and her brother were darting off down the middle of the road.

Seconds later, the young men who had been gathered outside Lady Waters' house rushed past, following the two fugitives at a rapid pace. Jane clung to the railings, unsure if her legs would support her if she relinquished her grip.

Then she felt a reassuring presence beside her and Cassandra's arm looped around her waist, pulling her into an embrace.

"You're safe, Jane," her sister murmured over and over, and slowly Jane's pulse slowed and her breathing settled into a normal rhythm.

Jane let out a little sob and buried her head in her sister's shoulder. She was aware of the magistrate passing by, murmuring a few words to Cassandra, before continuing on, but all the time she kept her face pressed against her sister, inhaling her familiar scent and taking comfort in the softness of her dress.

"You are safe. They have both fled, and I am certain the magistrate's men will capture them before they can cause any more harm."

"Let us return to the house."

Slowly they walked down the street, arm in arm for support, and by the time they reached number seven Jane felt a little more composed. With a deep breath she walked through the front door, finding the assembled guests and servants talking excitedly.

There was a hush as Jane appeared and she could see they were waiting for her to speak, but for once her voice wouldn't come.

"The magistrate's men are chasing them," Cassandra said, squeezing Jane's hand. "I am sure the two criminals will be apprehended shortly."

Avoiding the smashed glass, Cassandra led Jane to a chair and pressed her to sit. Elizabeth Upton hurried over.

"Are you hurt, Miss Austen?" the young woman asked, genuine concern on her face.

"No, a little shaken but not hurt."

"I cannot believe what just happened. How did you know it was the maid?"

"I asked people questions and I listened to their answers," Jane said and then smiled at the young woman. "And then I looked for the inconsistencies between what people had said and the evidence."

The magistrate re-entered the room, looking harried. "I am going to raise a hue and cry for the maid and George Ripon," he said, coming straight to Jane. "Are you harmed, Miss Austen?"

"No, just a little unsettled."

"Then I am thankful. I am sorry, I never expected her to react like that."

"Nor I," Jane said, her hand fluttering up to her neck.

"I must go and organise my men. Do not fear, Miss Austen. We will catch them."

"I am confident you will, Mr Winters." She reached out and caught his arm before he left. "You will see to it that Lady Waters is released immediately?"

"Yes, of course. I will ride over there personally once Sarah and her brother are caught. If there is any delay, I will send an urgent messenger."

"Thank you."

As the magistrate left, Cassandra took her arm. "I think we should go home," she said, looking round the room at the stunned faces of the Fortescue family.

"Good idea."

CHAPTER TWENTY-FOUR

Jane smiled at the genteel scene as they entered the tearoom. There were nine or ten tables around which fashionably dressed women were seated, all talking softly and drinking from beautifully decorated, dainty teacups.

"Jane, Cassandra," Lady Waters said, standing to greet them as her little spaniel, Bertie, jumped down from her lap. She pulled them both into an embrace and held them tightly.

"You are looking well," Jane said. It was the truth. In a matter of days, Lady Waters had shaken off any hint of her time in gaol and was looking radiant.

"You are too kind, Jane." She lowered her voice. "I still feel I have the stink of Ilchester gaol on me, but I think that may be my imagination."

"I am so pleased to see you in better circumstances than our last meeting," Cassandra said, beaming at Lady Waters before adopting a more solemn expression. "I am sorry for your loss."

"Thank you. I miss Oliver so much." Lady Waters was dressed in a sober black dress, and despite her proclamations of good health there was a faint tinge of pink to her eyes. "I know his health was not robust, but I feel our time was cut cruelly short."

"It was an evil thing to do."

Lady Waters signalled for tea to be brought over. Once they were all sitting with a cup, she leaned forwards. "I owe you everything, Jane. I am eternally in your debt. I have no doubt whatsoever that if it were not for your diligence and your faith in me, I would be in that horrible place still, inching ever closer to the hangman's noose."

"I cannot lie and say it was an easy few days," Jane said, shaking her head as she remembered the moment she feared for her own life, the broken bottle pressed to her neck. "But we got to the truth in the end."

"Tell me, have you spoken to the magistrate? Has he told you the latest?"

"Yes, he called on us this morning. I doubted his competence at first, especially as he was so closely associated with Mr Fortescue, but he has been diligent since we exposed the true criminals."

"He has the brother and sister in custody?"

"Yes. They were caught trying to board a coach to London. They are both in Ilchester gaol now." Jane paused. "Now you know who they are, can you recall them from your life in London?"

"I've been thinking about that. I believe there was a young man called George who lived a few doors away. He had a younger sister, but I was only fifteen and she must have been about ten. I didn't really take much notice of her."

"You didn't recognise her when she applied for the job of lady's maid?"

"No. I think I didn't ever really expect to see anyone from my past here in Bath, and so my mind didn't ever make the connection. Do you know why they left London? It is difficult for people from the slums to ever get out."

"Their parents died a few years ago. Sarah took a position as a scullery maid and one night let George into the house. He stole a number of items of value and then they both disappeared. It happened more than once. Each time Sarah was only in the position a month or two before the burglary happened. Eventually they fled London and came to Bath."

"She was with me for ten months."

"The other households they targeted in London were respectable, but none as wealthy as yours. They must have decided to play a longer game when they realised what they could do with the jewellery."

"I don't understand why George Ripon came to the house, why he approached me in the street and asked for money. Surely that was a huge risk. If I remembered him, then it might prompt my memory of Sarah."

"He became greedy. The jewels were not enough. He thought he could blackmail you for more money. He didn't know that you had already told your husband everything about your past. Fortunately for him, you didn't recognise him."

"I do not see why they did not just steal the jewellery and flee."

"I expect the hope was that if they took things slowly, no one would ever know of the crime. Once the last of the pieces of jewellery had been swapped for replicas, I think Sarah would have handed in her notice and the Ripons would have disappeared to another city."

Lady Waters sat back in her chair, her slender fingers gripping her teacup. "All this for money."

"All this for money."

She sighed and closed her eyes. "The thing is, I do understand, a little at least. Unless you have grown up in complete poverty, never knowing where your next meal will come from and how you will pay for it, you cannot understand the desperation. I can remember the time when I would have done almost anything to survive."

"*Almost* anything," Jane said pointedly.

"Yes. I take your point. How did you work it out, Jane?"

Jane sat back in her chair and gave a rueful smile. "Do you know, I suspected every one of your late husband's family at one point or another. I made the mistake Lord Waters made, in looking at them to try to work out who needed the money the most."

"They all live beyond their means."

"Indeed. Mrs Fortescue with her addiction, Mr Fortescue with his gambling. Mr Upton with his unwise investments and Mrs Upton with her worry about dowries for her daughters. I have to admit that I also began to suspect you. It all fit. You could have seen Lord Waters with the emeralds and realised his concerns. You could have taken the vial of belladonna with you to Parade Gardens. Then we spoke to Mr Meller the jeweller, and he told us it was you who had ordered the replicas made."

"You truly suspected me?" Lady Waters looked amused, but Jane could see the shock in her eyes.

"I thought the facts were pointing in that direction, but I was troubled by one thing."

"What?"

"Your love for your husband. I believed it. I also couldn't reconcile the motive for stealing the jewellery with your circumstances. You were comfortable and happy. Why risk it all?"

"How did that lead you to Sarah?"

"I was thinking back to our interview together in Ilchester gaol. You made a comment about servants always being around, and I realised there was someone else in the house with access to the jewellery, with access to the belladonna."

"Sarah."

"Yes. A lady's maid, always present but never noticed."

"There is one more thing I do not understand," Lady Waters said. "Why did she not flee after Lord Waters died? Surely she knew there was a risk of being found out."

"I don't know for sure, but I expect she calculated the risk of suspicion was higher if she disappeared. As it was, you had been arrested and the whole of Bath thought you were guilty. In her mind, she was safer playing the maid caught up in the drama that had unfolded."

Lady Waters shuddered. "I keep thinking of what could have happened if you hadn't got to the truth."

"I know. It doesn't bear thinking about."

"What will you do now?" Cassandra asked.

Lady Waters sighed and rested her cup back in the saucer. "I will return to London. I no longer have a home here in Bath, but my husband left me the London townhouse. I will see if I can make that into my refuge, whilst I decide what is next for me."

"Do you think you will marry again?"

"No," Lady Waters said quickly. "Three marriages are quite enough for one woman, and I do not think I could find a better husband than Lord Waters. No, I will think about how best to occupy my time, but I wonder if I might do a little charity work, maybe help some of the orphans of St Giles. How about you? Will you return home?"

"Yes, tomorrow," Jane said. In truth, she was looking forward to returning to Steventon now the case was solved and the right people in custody. She longed for the green fields and the babbling brooks and the fresh country air. She looked forward to taking a stroll through the countryside, sure in the knowledge that at most she might encounter a farmer out with his sheep.

"You will write? And perhaps visit me in London once I am settled?"

"Of course," Jane said. They lived in different worlds, but a bond forged over a matter of life and death was one likely to endure.

"Wonderful," Lady Waters said, picking up her teacup again and beaming over the top of it. "I think we shall be lifelong friends."

EPILOGUE

Jane tucked her feet underneath her and regarded the tiny writing on the piece of paper. She had crossed things out and rewritten so many times that to anyone else it would have looked a mess, but finally she was happy. The drought was over. Since returning to Steventon — following a teary goodbye with their aunt and promises to return soon to visit Dr Black, which Mrs Leigh-Perrot took as very promising in terms of Jane and the doctor's future — she had been consumed by the urge to write, spending every free moment at her desk. Of an evening she would read passages to Cassandra and her parents, and she could see with each change in expression how they became more engaged.

She let her eyes flick over the words, feeling a frisson of excitement. She was always critical, always tweaking this or that, but she secretly felt this book was something special. She loved her heroine, the headstrong Elizabeth, but even more than Elizabeth she loved Jane. Kind, patient, steadfast Jane, so much like her own sister.

Glancing at the bed where Cassandra slept, Jane felt a swell of love for her. She was still in mourning, still melancholy some days, but the worst of the depression had passed. Jane suspected Cassandra would mourn Thomas Fowle for the rest of her life, but at least now she was interacting with the world again.

Carefully she put down the last sheet of paper on the thick pile. She had never told anyone, not even Cassandra, how much the desire to be published consumed her. Her family knew of her ambition, but they did not know its intensity. As she looked at the final words, she gave a nod of satisfaction. She was sure one day she would hold this manuscript in her hands, bound into a book as it was released into the world.

A NOTE TO THE READER

Dear Reader,

Thank you for taking the time to read *A Poisoned Fortune*. If you enjoyed the book, I have a small favour to ask — please pop across to **Amazon** and **Goodreads** and post a review. I also love to connect with readers through my **Facebook** page, on **Twitter**, **Instagram** and through my **website**. I would love to hear from you.

Laura Martin

Sapere Books is an exciting new publisher of brilliant fiction and popular history.

To find out more about our latest releases and our monthly bargain books visit our website:
saperebooks.com

Printed in Great Britain
by Amazon

43930881R00149